Praise for

A Ring

A NEW

★"L'Engle writes eloquently about death and life with provocative passages that linger in the thoughts of the perceptive." —*Booklist*, Starred

"Presents with passion and energy all sorts of theological, scientific, and philosophical ideas to support L'Engle's ultimate theme: that coming to terms with death is an affirmation of wholeness and life."
—*The Horn Book Magazine*

A Ring of
Endless Light

MADELEINE L'ENGLE

For Sandra Jordan

Published by
Dell Laurel-Leaf
an imprint of
Random House Children's Books
a division of Random House, Inc.
1540 Broadway
New York, New York 10036

Excerpts from *Messengers of God: Biblical Portraits and Legends* by Elie Wiesel, translated by Marion Wiesel, copyright © 1976 by Elie Wiesel. Reprinted by permission of Random House, Inc.

Visit us on the Web! www.randomhouse.com/teens
Educators and librarians, for a variety of teaching tools, visit us at www.randomhouse.com/teachers

ISBN: 0-440-97232-9

RL: 5.5

Reprinted by arrangement with Farrar, Straus & Giroux, Inc.

Printed in the United States of America

One previous edition

September 1990

50   49   48   47   46

A Note from the Author

Somebody remarked to me that the books about the Austin family might just as well be about my own family. Indeed, the Austins do a great many things that my family did, including living in a small dairy farm village, having a wild and wonderful year in New York City, enjoying a summer of beauty and dolphins on an island off the New England coast, and even making a trip to Antarctica. But despite all their adventures, the Austins are representative of many families, particularly those in which the parents love each other and are able to share that love with their children, even when the children are being their most impossible. I myself identify with Vicky rather than Mrs. Austin, since I share all of Vicky's insecurities, enthusiasms, and times of sadness and growth.

Vicky's questions and problems are questions and problems that most adolescents have had, whether in the Middle Ages, in distant countries, or right here and now. The big problems of our growing up are not limited by time, culture, or geography. We share our wonder and confusion: Who am I? Why am I here? Does it matter? Ultimately I hope we all answer with Vicky: Yes, it does. We do matter. What we do matters. And that is both a challenge and a joy.

New York
April 1995

1

I saw him for the first time at the funeral.

He stood beside my elder brother, John, and they both had closed, clenched jaws and angry eyes. He was as tall as John, and I could see that he was as full of grief over Commander Rodney's death as the rest of us.

I didn't know who he was, but I liked him.

Because he was standing with John, I assumed that he, too, had a summer job at the Marine Biology Station, which was housed in half of the Coast Guard headquarters.

It was a strange place and a strange time to see somebody and know that I wanted to meet him, to call him by name. But there was something about him that struck me as—to use an old-fashioned word—trustworthy; and that's important in an untrustworthy world where death can strike when you aren't looking.

This wasn't the first time that I'd come close to death, but it was the first time that I'd been involved in this part of it, this strange, terrible saying goodbye to someone you've loved.

I was sixteen (almost), even if not sweet, and I'd had my first proper kiss at fourteen, but I'd never before stood at an open grave, waiting for a pine box to be lowered into it.

The part at the church hadn't been so bad, maybe because it was in a familiar setting, the small white church on Seven Bay Island, the church we've been to every year of our lives when we've gone to visit our grandfather. It was a sad time, the time at the church, yet it was somehow beyond time, on the other side of time.

Commander Rodney had been our friend for ages. He was Mother and Daddy's age. And he'd died of a heart attack after saving the life of some dumb rich kid who'd gone out in his sailboat in complete disregard of storm warnings. The kid, whoever he was, wasn't at the funeral and maybe that was a good thing, because I, for one, held him responsible for Commander Rodney's death. And if I felt that way, what did Mrs. Rodney and their kids think? No matter how often our doctor father said you could never be certain what caused a heart attack, and blaming someone was no help at all, I still felt that the capsized sailboat and the half-drowned kid had a lot to do with it.

My little brother, Rob, stood close by me. Commander Rodney had been his special friend, more Rob's friend even than Mother and Daddy's. Rob wasn't crying; he hadn't cried at all; but his face was white, the way it looks when he's going to get flu.

John was near me on my other side. He'd just finished his first year at M.I.T. and tended to think he was so much bigger than the rest of us he hardly condescended to talk to us. But he reached out and held my hand, firmly, something he hadn't done since we were kids. And on John's other side was this unknown young man with sea-grey eyes. Well. Like John, he probably thought he was much too important to talk to anybody who wasn't in college.

Behind them were the people from the Coast Guard and the Marine Biology Station. One man with thick-lensed spectacles and thinning hair was unabashedly wiping his eyes.

My little sister, Suzy, thirteen, going on thirty, was with our parents, near the Rodneys. Mrs. Rodney had her hand on Daddy's arm, as though she couldn't have stood up otherwise. Leo, the oldest, had his arm around her. His eyes were closed, as though to shut out the people and the coffin and the open hole. There was so much pain in him that I turned away and looked at the group from the Marine Biology Station, and at the young man who had stepped forward so that he was just slightly in front of John, and I could look at him without being obvious. He was tall and thinnish—not skinny—and his hair was what Rob calls hair-colored hair, not quite brown, not quite blond, like mine. His eyes were open, and there was somehow light behind them, the way sometimes the light on the ocean seems to come from beneath the water, rather than just being reflected from above. He was standing in a relaxed manner, but a little muscle in his cheek was twitching just slightly, so he wasn't as easy as he seemed.

Looking at him and wondering about him was a good way to keep my mind off what was happening. Then he stepped back so that he was blocked by John, and I had to come into awareness again.

Grandfather stood at the edge of the open grave, dark earth piled up behind him. When we got to the cemetery there'd been a carpet-like thing of phony

3

green grass over the earth, and Grandfather had said with quiet steel, "Take it away," and two of the Coast Guard men had silently removed it. I wondered fleetingly what Mr. Hanchett, the regular minister, would have done. Ever since Grandfather retired and moved to the Island he's taken the church for one month a year, July, so Mr. Hanchett could go on vacation, and that's why he was burying Commander Rodney. His prayer book was open in his hand, although he wasn't reading it. He looked as finely drawn and as beautiful as an El Greco painting, and it was Grandfather who made me want to weep.

"Wonder who'll be the next to go?" a woman behind us asked in a loud whisper. I shivered, the way you're supposed to if someone walks over the place where you're going to be buried.

Grandfather's voice was low, and yet it could have been heard a mile away, I thought. "You only are immortal, the creator and maker of mankind; and we are mortal, formed of the earth, and to earth we shall return. For so did you ordain when you created me, saying, 'You are dust, and to dust you shall return.' All of us go down to the dust; yet even at the grave we make our song: Alleluia, alleluia, alleluia."

No one could miss the joy in Grandfather's voice as he said those alleluias, and his face was so alive, so alight, that I didn't hear what he was saying next. It was as though I had moved into a dream, and I woke up only when, gently but firmly, he pushed away one of the funeral-type men who was handing him a vial of dirt. It was obvious he was making the funeral people feel frustrated, rejecting their plastic grass and their plastic dirt. He was emphasizing the fact that Commander Rodney's death was real, but this reality was less terrible than plastic pretense.

I looked at the rich, dark brown of the piled earth, and there, hovering over it, was a gorgeous red-and-gold butterfly. Its wings moved delicately and it flew over the coffin and quivered in beauty as it hovered there. Grandfather saw it, too, because he stood still, looking, before he reached down and took a handful of earth and threw it onto the coffin, which had been lowered into the grave. "Earth to earth," he said, "ashes to ashes, dust to dust." The butterfly still hovered. And the words which followed seemed to me to have more to do with the butterfly than with what he had just said. "The Lord bless him and keep him, the Lord make his face to shine upon him and be gracious unto him, the Lord lift up his countenance upon him, and give him peace."

What did those radiant words mean, after the ashes-to-ashes and dust-to-dust stuff? What did it mean to me, and to my family, who were friends of the man who was being committed to the dark earth? What did it mean to his wife, and to his kids?

Slowly, gracefully, the butterfly flew off and was lost in the dappled shadows of the trees.

I looked from the butterfly to Leo Rodney. I've always thought of Leo as a slob and wiped off his kisses (which certainly didn't count as real ones), and I didn't much like him now, but that was his father in that box there, that box that was going to be covered with earth, not plastic, but real earth, which grass could grow in and butterflies fly over. I looked at Leo and his face was all splotchy as though he had cried and cried, but he hadn't cried, and he needed to. I wasn't sure what anybody cried about, not with my grandfather saying those paradoxical, contradictory words.

And my grandfather was dying.

The woman's whisper stuck in my ears: "Wonder who'll be the next to go?"

Grandfather.

Unless some kind of unforeseen accident happened—as it had happened to Commander Rodney—my grandfather was likely to be the next one. He had leukemia.

And he was saying all those words as calmly as though he had all the answers about life and death and God and all the cosmic things. And Grandfather would be the first to say he doesn't.

Leo moved just then, calling my attention to him; and I remembered last year, when he was on a religious kick and was telling us exactly what God is like, Grandfather had said quietly—not rebukingly, just quietly—"As St. Augustine says: *If you think you understand, it isn't God.*"

Looking at Leo, I wished he was still on his religious trip, when he thought he knew all the answers to everything.

John pulled my hand gently.

It was over. We were going to the Rodneys' to help out when the people of Seven Bay Island came to pay their respects. The house was full of casseroles and salads and pies and all the things people had been bringing in; Mrs. Rodney wouldn't have to cook a meal for weeks. It was a good thing they had a big freezer for all those funeral baked meats.

It wasn't too bad at the Rodneys' because I was kept busy serving people, washing dishes, and pouring vast quantities of iced tea. The Coast Guard and Marine Biology people drank the most—I must have filled the grey-eyed young man's glass half a dozen times.

The last time he smiled at me apologetically. "You're John Austin's sister, aren't you?"

"Yes. Vicky."

"I'm Adam Eddington."

So that was his name. A good solid name, Adam Eddington. I liked it.

"It's nice to meet you, Vicky," he said, "even under these circumstances."

"They're not the best." I stood there holding the pitcher of iced tea, which was wet and dripping. "But I don't think I've really taken it in yet. I keep expecting Commander Rodney to come walking in and ask us what we're all doing."

"It's rough. He wasn't that old."

"My father's age." I glimpsed Daddy talking to a cluster of people from the Marine Biology Station. Then I turned back to Adam.

He took a long swallow of tea, and looked at me over the glass. "You know when you cut yourself really badly, it doesn't hurt at all for a while. You don't feel anything. Death—our reaction to death—is sort of like that. You don't feel anything at all. And then later on you begin to hurt." He was speaking with a quiet conviction, as though experience had taught him what he was talking about. I wondered what had happened, who had died, to make him speak like that. He continued, less tensely, "He was a really great guy. He knocked himself out to be nice to me, treating me like an intelligent human being and not a mere flunky. I'll miss him. And I've known him only a few weeks."

I shifted the pitcher from one hand to the other. "I haven't begun to hurt yet, but I guess I will. You've been at the station for a while?"

"I got out of school the end of May, and I was lucky enough to be able to start here the first of June. It's great having John come to work in the lab—I was the only one under forty."

"Are you working with starfish, too?"

"Some. But mostly I have an independent project going, on dolphins."

"I love dolphins! Though I've never met one personally, only at Sea World."

"Would you like to meet one?"

"Would I ever!" I almost dropped the pitcher.

"I think maybe I can arrange that. You strike me as being a dolphiny person."

That might not sound like much of a compliment, but I knew that it was.

"We have one dolphin who's going to pup in a week or ten days. Ever see a dolphin baby?"

"No."

"I'll introduce you to one, then. And—hey, are you good at listening?"

Before I could answer, Dr. Nora Zand, John's immediate boss, dropped a hand on Adam's shoulder and told him it was time to go. And I saw that the crowd was thinning out, and then we were leaving, too.

Leo took my hand. "Vicky, I wish you didn't have to go."

Leo's hand always felt clammy, and now it was cold as well. "I'm sorry." I tried not to pull my hand away. I was filled with pain for Leo, but I'd much rather have had Adam holding my hand. "I think your mother wants to be alone with just you kids for a while."

"Can I come see you tomorrow?"

"Sure."

I managed not to turn away when he kissed me, not a passionate sort of kiss, but I didn't want any kind of kiss from Leo. And yet I ached so for him I found myself giving him a quick hug before we left. When Leo started hurting, he was going to hurt much more than we were, or than Adam Eddington.

We got into the station wagon and drove across the Island and up the hill to Grandfather's, and there, parked in front of the house, was a hearse.

Well, I had hearses on my mind.

It wasn't a hearse; it was an enormous, brand-new, black station wagon. And a tall, pale young man with black hair was lounging elegantly against it.

"Good grief," John exploded. "It's Zachary Gray. Just who we don't need."

Daddy murmured, "His timing has always been unerringly inconvenient."

I hadn't seen Zachary for a year. I'd never expected to see Zachary again. After a summer during which he sort of pursued me, he'd dropped completely out of sight, far off in California, with girls a lot more glamorous than I could ever hope to be. But I didn't think of him as some kind of moral leper, the way the rest of the family did. And it was Zach who'd given me that first real kiss. My cheeks felt hot and my hands felt icy cold.

He waved. "Hi, Austins, long time no see." He grinned at me. "Zach's back."

"Hi," I said stupidly, and hoped my flushed cheeks didn't show.

"Come for a ride?"

Still stupidly, like a ten-year-old kid, I just shook my head.

Daddy said, "Zachary, we've just come from a funeral. We're all tired, and sad, and we need to be alone. Could you come another time?"

"Certainly, sir," Zachary replied swiftly and courteously. "Tomorrow, Vicky-O?"

"Yes—all right." I wasn't sure I liked Zachary's thinking he could drop me for a year and then expect to find me waiting for him as though we'd seen each other the day before. At the same time, something very odd was happening in the pit of my stomach. Zachary was having the old effect.

He took my hand. Unlike Leo's, his was warm and dry. "Sorry, Vic. I see the bad penny's turned up at the wrong moment. I'll give you a ring in the morning." He kept my hand in his, and the look he turned on me was dark and full of pain. Whatever the pain was for, it was as acute as Leo's. "Sorry . . ." he said again, and the flippancy was gone from his voice. "Need you, Vic . . ." He turned his back on us and got into his ostentatious station wagon, the latest, most expensive model of the same kind of station wagon he'd had before. Why did he want a station wagon that looked like a hearse?

And how had he found out we were on the Island?

I went indoors, unhappy and confused. We weren't using the front door, because some swallows had built a nest just above it. We had no idea why, but there were three swallows, not two, fluttering about the nest, and they got very excited if we got too close. The

10

eggs had hatched and occasionally we could see little beaks peeping over the straw, cheeping away for food. So we weren't going to use the front door till they were out of the nest. There was a side door, or we could walk around to the back and go through the screened porch and into the kitchen.

Being confused because of Zachary was nothing new. Unlike Leo, Zachary was completely unpredictable, and his kiss was nothing like Leo's adolescent pawings. Seeing him now, at this moment, and in this place, was so completely unexpected that it was as though two different worlds had bumped into each other, and I was shaking from the collision.

We all went into the big screened porch where Grandfather sleeps when we're at Seven Bay Island so Mother and Daddy can have his big four-poster bed. And suddenly I realized it was hot, early-July hot (and that's why Adam drank all that iced tea), and I'd been feeling cold all day, deep, inside cold.

Mother turned on the big old-fashioned wooden ceiling fan—only it was new-fashioned, because she and Daddy had given it to Grandfather for his last birthday.

Suzy asked, "Okay if I make lemonade?" and, not waiting for an answer, went into the kitchen.

The funeral had been in the late morning, but what with going to the Rodneys' and trying to be useful and available and whatever else one can be at an impossible time to be anything, it was now mid-afternoon. The tide was moving up the beach, and we could hear the soft thrumming of the surf, seeming to say, Relax, relax, let it all go, relax, all is well, all is well . . .

Grandfather sat on the old, sagging couch. Mother and Daddy had urged him not to give up his comfortable bed, but he had just said quietly, "Let's keep it all as normal as possible for as long as possible."

Mother rocked in the old wicker rocker, and she was looking at Grandfather, and I wanted to hug her, to hug Grandfather, to hold them both against the dark. And I could not. Nobody could.

The screen door was propped wide open and Rob sat on the worn porch steps and looked out to sea. Mr. Rochester, our Great Dane, sat on his haunches beside him, and I noticed that Mr. Rochester was getting very grizzled about the muzzle. Mr. Rochester loved us all; we were his family; but Rob was his baby. When Mother used to put Rob outdoors in his carriage or playpen, Mr. Rochester would lie watchfully beside him, and Mother didn't have to worry about anybody coming near. And now Rob was seven and no longer a baby and Mr. Rochester was growing old. A Great Dane's life expectancy isn't more than eleven or so years and that, Daddy reminded us, was something we must accept when we become fond of a dog.

Grandfather's cat, Ned, minced around the corner of the stable and then sat down between Rochester's paws, preening himself. Ned is fifteen, but cats have longer lives than large dogs.

Daddy and John sat in the wicker swing, and the sound of Mother's rocker, of the swing creaking from its hooks in the porch ceiling, and the waves rolling into shore, all merged into a soporific counterpoint.

"Johann Sebastian Bach wrote *The Goldberg Variations* to help some German prince or duke who had insomnia to get to sleep," I remarked.

Instead of jumping on me for showing off, John

asked the ceiling, "I wonder how long Zachary has been at Seven Bay?"

I knew what he was thinking. Ordinarily it would have burned me up and I'd have exploded at my brother, but the same thought had occurred to me, so all I said was, "Don't go leaping to conclusions."

Daddy raised his eyebrows. "What conclusions, Vic?"

"John thinks Zachary was the rich kid Commander Rodney saved from drowning."

Daddy looked from me to John and back again to me. "I don't recall John saying anything of the kind."

"But you do, don't you, John?" I demanded.

John shrugged. "You said it."

Suzy said, "Everybody thought it was queer the Island paper didn't give a name." She stood in the doorway holding a silver pitcher.

Daddy said, "Mrs. Rodney requested the paper to withhold names."

"Jacky thinks the parents paid off the mainland papers," Suzy continued.

I almost started to say, "Jacky and Leo are slobs," and then I remembered that, despite Daddy, I did blame the rich kid for what had happened, and if I were the Rodneys I'd be feeling anger and outrage and probably worse. So all I said was, "We don't know whether or not Zachary just got here this afternoon."

Mother added, "If he knew about it, he'd hardly have turned up here right after the funeral. That the lemonade, Suze?"

And we all looked at the silver pitcher.

Grandfather spoke for the first time. If I noticed a

change in Grandfather this summer, it was that he didn't talk as much as usual. "I haven't seen that pitcher in years, Suze. Where did you find it?"

"Up on the top shelf of the corner cupboard. I just gave it a quick polish. I hope you don't mind?"

"I'm delighted," Grandfather assured her. "Let's use all the pretty things as much as possible this summer. That's what your grandmother always said they were for, to be enjoyed. When I'm alone I'm afraid I tend to be lazy. But when we're together, let's appreciate everything to the hilt."

I don't think Grandfather intended anything he said to have double meanings, but to me, everything did. Let's enjoy it, because tomorrow it may all be cut off.

There are a lot of leukemias in old people which can be arrested, if not completely cured, but Grandfather didn't have one of these. It was a rare kind, and lethal. Daddy was giving him some new medication which might make things easier, but he couldn't stop the disease or even hope for remission. He was completely open with us about this.

John slid to the floor by the low table with the pitcher of lemonade and the tall glasses. "Dad, I know I don't have to declare my major yet, but I'm taking all the pre-med courses I can fit in."

It was a change of subject from Zachary and I was grateful. I even thought John might be doing it on purpose. He may tend to be high and mighty, but he's also nice, much nicer than I am, and since he got home from college we haven't bickered nearly as much as we used to.

"What about space research?" Daddy asked.

"Oh, I'm still into astrophysics. But it would be a

good idea for me to have an M.D. anyhow. Adam and I were talking about it."

"Adam?" Mother asked.

"Adam Eddington. He's working at the Marine Biology Station this summer, too. He's the one who was standing next to me at the cemetery. We're pretty good friends."

"He's cute," Suzy said.

Why did that annoy me? It did.

"The weird thing," John said, "is that he grew up just a few blocks away from our house in New York. We might even have passed each other on the street last year during the Christmas holidays."

"Too bad we're moving back to Thornhill," Suzy said. "The boys around there are all nerds."

"Not true," John said. "Wait and see. You'll find they all grew up as much as you did while we were in New York. Adam knows a heck of a lot more about marine biology than I do, but he's getting a veterinary degree as well as his Ph.D. for his work."

"What's his special field?" Daddy asked.

"This summer he has a project with dolphins, but he's studied a lot about limb regeneration. You'd be fascinated, Suze. Not only starfish, but lizards and tortoises have been able to grow new limbs."

Suzy sparked. She's the beauty of the family, petite and piquante and all the things I'm not. She also has a mind like a scalpel, and she's wanted to be a doctor ever since she could talk, though lately she's been edging more and more toward being a veterinary surgeon. She and John and Daddy got into a scientific discussion that was completely above my head. And nobody said anything more about Zachary.

15

Grandfather's house is, to put it mildly, unusual. It used to be a stable, a real stable for real horses. When Grandfather bought it before he retired, he left up most of the stalls and had bookcases built in them, for all the hundreds and thousands of books he's collected over the years and can't throw away, either because he's going to need to check something in one, or they might be useful for a grandchild or friend or neighbor. Leo, for instance, uses Grandfather's library for most of his school papers.

Grandfather's bedroom is the only real bedroom. Up in the loft there are half a dozen cots, and that's where we sleep. We'd never before spent more than two weeks at a time on the Island, and it's always been special and a holiday and fun to sleep all together in a dormitory.

This time it was different. We were there for a purpose: to be with Grandfather. Mother and Daddy hadn't said anything about time limits, just that we'd stay as long as Grandfather needed us. And yet I knew that Daddy had to be back in Thornhill right after Labor Day. Unlike John and Suzy, I am not scientifically inclined, but what came through to me, and it came through loud and clear, was that our doctor father did not think Grandfather would live through the summer. I could not imagine the world without Grandfather.

At the same time I found myself thinking, totally selfishly, that I wasn't sure I wanted to sleep in a dormitory for more than a couple of weeks. The older I grew, the more I needed times and places of privacy—or *privatecy*, as Rob calls it, which sounds considerably more private than privacy. Privatecy to write in my journal, to write and rewrite, and rewrite again, poems and stories. To try to find out not only who I am but who everybody else is, and what it's all about.

That night after Commander Rodney's funeral, up in my cot in the loft, next to Rob's, I couldn't sleep. Rob was snoring softly; his allergies bother him not only when the pollen count is high in the autumn but whenever he's deeply upset, and I knew that his snoring this night was not because of the pollen count. I thought of going down the loft ladder to ask Daddy for an antihistamine, but Rob was sound asleep and he wasn't wheezing. My urge to go to Daddy was more for myself than for Rob.

I put my hands behind my head and waited for the beam of the lighthouse to swing across the loft, touching each cot with its friendly light. My eyes were so awake they felt gritty. I wasn't quite sure why Commander Rodney's death hit me so hard. He was our good friend, but not so intertwined a part of our lives that things would never be the same again, the way they'd never be the same for Leo. And yet, in a way, when anyone dies, even someone you don't know, someone you read about in a newspaper, life never will be quite the same again.

What was it Grandfather said? If someone kills a butterfly, it could cause an earthquake in a galaxy a trillion light-years away.

From downstairs I heard the sound of Mother's guitar, and I knew that either Grandfather or Daddy had asked her to sing to them, and maybe for the four of us up in the loft. She started with a French song, one of my favorites, "Les filles de Saint-Malo ont les yeux l'couleur de l'eau."

It wasn't *The Goldberg Variations*, but it worked, and I fell asleep.

I woke up in the middle of the night; well, not quite that late, because the full moon was pouring its light through the attic windows and that was what woke me. The loft was filled with a pearly light which almost drowned out the lighthouse beam. The words of the verses Grandfather had painted on the wall were clearly visible:

> *If thou could'st empty all thyself of self,*
> > *Like to a shell dishabited,*
> *Then might He find thee on the ocean shelf,*
> > *And say, "This is not dead,"*
> > *And fill thee with Himself instead.*

> *But thou art all replete with very thou*
> > *And hast such shrewd activity,*
> *That when He comes He says, "This is enow*
> > *Unto itself—'twere better let it be,*
> > *It is so small and full, there is no room for me."*

Sir Thomas Browne wrote those lines at least three centuries ago, but they always made me think of Grandfather, empty of all the horrid things, and filled with gentleness and strength. As for me, I felt replete with very me, full of confusions and questions for which there were no answers.

Suzy cried out in her sleep. John turned over, and the old springs of the cot squeaked as though John had disturbed their rest. Then I looked at the cot on my left and it was empty. I wasn't worried. Mr. Rochester, who slept at the foot of the loft ladder, would have let us know if anything was wrong.

I heard the ladder creak, and Rob clambered up, trying to be quiet.

I sat up and whispered, "Where've you been?"

Rob sat on the edge of his cot. "Talking to Grandfather."

Not Mother and Daddy. Grandfather. "You shouldn't have disturbed him."

"He was awake."

"How'd you know?"

"He was reading."

"What'd you talk to him about?"

"Dying."

Rob was only seven. Still young enough to talk about things you don't talk about, especially to someone who's dying. But why don't you? If I had a fatal disease I'd want people to talk to me about dying, instead of getting embarrassed and pretending I was going to get well.

We weren't pretending that Grandfather was going to get well, but we weren't talking about it, at least John and Suzy and I weren't, not to each other. Perhaps Mother and Daddy were braver. As for Rob—he was Rob.

"Do Mother and Daddy know you're up?"

"They're asleep. Only Grandfather."

"We'd better stop whispering or we'll wake John

and Suzy." As I said that, John bounced, and his springs protested loudly.

Rob gave me a hug and kissed me before getting into his cot. He hadn't done that in quite a while and I'd missed it. Rob's so much younger than the rest of us that I've wanted him to go on being a baby, or at least a little boy, forever. But of course he can't.

I lay down. It wasn't quite warm enough with just a sheet, and a little too warm with the lightweight summer blanket. I pushed it halfway down and tried to relax, listening to the wind in the trees and the surf's slow pounding against the shore.

That, too, was soporific.

During vacations, breakfast is a floating affair. Mother plugs the percolator into a timer before she goes to bed, for those who drink coffee. Otherwise, we're on our own. At Grandfather's, we fix our breakfasts in the kitchen and take them out on the porch, unless the weather is bad.

Our first day on the Island this summer, John gave the big round table a fresh coat of white paint, and this morning it was set with deep blue mats and matching blue seersucker napkins we could just throw in the washing machine. The china was white, with a blue stripe around the edge. Some of it was chipped, so we didn't look like something out of *House Beautiful*, just cheerful and normal.

Mother, Daddy, Grandfather, and John were all there before me. I'd heated up milk in the kitchen, and took a big blue-and-white cup of *café au lait* out to the porch with me.

I said, "Good morning," and sat down between John and Grandfather. The sky was hazy, the kind of soft blue-lavender haze that means a hot day, with clear skies later on, and perhaps a thunderstorm in the late afternoon or evening.

"Any plans for today, Vic?" Mother asked.

"Nothing, except to go down to the beach for a swim."

"Want to take a picnic?" she suggested.

"I don't think so . . ." I stopped myself from looking behind me toward the kitchen phone, or, farther, toward the stall where Grandfather had his desk and his telephone.

But John asked, "Zachary call yet?"

"If the phone's rung this morning, I haven't heard it," I replied stiffly.

Daddy, who'd been reading the paper, missed this, and handed the paper to John, pointing. "This ought to interest your friend Adam."

Suzy came out to the porch, poured herself a glass of juice, waved a general greeting to us all, and leaned against John's chair, reading over his shoulder.

"No, oh, no!" she cried and sat down next to Mother, looking about to burst into tears.

"What?" Mother asked.

Suzy's voice was trembling. "Porpoises, a thousand porpoises beaten to death with clubs."

Mother looked shocked. "Where?"

John looked up from the paper. "Japan."

"But why," Suzy moaned, "why did those fishermen have to kill them?"

"Because they were eating all the fish," John explained, "and the Japanese fishermen depend on the fish for their livelihood."

"But to kill them," Suzy protested, "to club them to

death when they're so friendly and playful and unsuspecting—"

Suzy's relations with animals have always been passionate. But Daddy says she won't be a good doctor or vet until she can control her emotions. Now she was outraged and tears quivered on her long, dark lashes. She brushed them away, shaking her head so that her tousled hair caught the fire of the sun. There's no denying that Suzy's got looks as well as brains. I have brains, I guess, but next to Suzy I don't have looks. However, as Fortescue said, and Mother keeps reminding us, comparisons are odious.

John handed the paper back to Daddy. "Full of comforting little tidbits, isn't it? Porpoises clubbed to death; a bus hit by a train; a lethal explosion at an oil refinery; a—"

"Stop!" I held up my hand. "You sound like Zachary!" And I thought of Adam's summer project, and how he'd probably feel as sick as Suzy about the porpoises.

"It's all there in the paper, Vic," John said quietly. "I thought a year in New York had you over your illusion that we live in a safe and peaceful world."

"But the porpoises!" Again Suzy's purple eyes filled with tears. "Those other things are accidents, but the fishermen clubbed the porpoises to death on purpose."

"As John pointed out," Daddy said, "those fishermen depend on fish for a living."

"It's lousy, Suze," John said. "I agree with you about that. But I can see, too, that the fishermen may have been desperate, with kids to feed and no money coming in. Which do you choose, people or porpoises?"

"Porpoises," Suzy replied without hesitation. "Porpoises don't hurt anybody. They don't murder or have wars. They don't pollute the environment."

"But," John added, "they eat the fish which are a matter of life and death for a fishing village."

"I hate it!" Now Suzy did start to cry.

"Let her weep," Grandfather said softly to Mother. "We've none of us done our grieving about Jack Rodney."

It seemed there was death everywhere. The paper was always full of death, violent death, accidental death, wanton death. I think I felt as bad as Suzy did about the porpoises, as bad as Adam would feel, but my eyes were dry.

John rose. "Time for me to get to work. Dr. Nora Zand's a stickler for people being early. Not just punctual, mind you, but early. Otherwise, she's a super boss and trusts me to do all kinds of things on my own. All right if I bring Adam home for dinner sometime, Mother?"

"Just give me a little warning so I can water the soup."

"Maybe tonight, then, if he's free, okay?"

Mother nodded. "Okay."

"See you a little after five."

John was lucky to have something definite to do for the summer. He finished his first year at M.I.T. with all kinds of honors, which made job hunting easier for him than for people without his kind of record.

I didn't take a job for the summer because Daddy'd asked me not to. The Woods, in the big house down the hill (the people who'd sold Grandfather the stable), wanted me to work for them. Their seven-year-old grandson was spending most of the summer with them, and they wanted me to baby-sit him, and cook lunch, and do odd jobs. We all try to work as much as we can, to help earn money for college, and I thought I was all set. But Daddy took me aside.

"Vic, this is asking a lot of you, but I'd appreciate it if you'd let Suzy take the job at the Woods'."

"Why?" I asked indignantly.

"This is going to be a rough summer for all of us, but particularly for your mother. I'd like you to stick around to help out with anything that's needed—the cooking—though there won't be much of that, because she loves to cook. Basically, to be moral support, and to help with Grandfather."

"Oh." He didn't need to say anything more. "Sure. I'll be glad to."

"And I'll pay you what you'd have got at the Woods'."

"No! I don't want any money, Daddy, honestly. Not for helping Mother or Grandfather. Please."

He looked at me from under his bushy eyebrows, and his brown eyes smiled. "We'll think of something, then. Thanks, Vic."

"Sure."

As it turned out, Suzy didn't want the job with the Woods. She said she'd find something to do around the docks. "Rob's enough of a seven-year-old kid. I couldn't stomach another for a whole summer."

"You're an idiot," I said. "They're offering good money."

"You take the job, then."

I shut up. It wasn't that Daddy'd sworn me to secrecy about staying home, but I knew he didn't want me to talk about it. And Suzy's never liked babysitting. She may want to be a doctor, but her specialty won't be pediatrics.

Three things happened at once. Rob came down for breakfast; the phone rang; and Leo Rodney and his brother, Jacky, came along the path and up to the porch.

"I'll get the phone." Suzy hurried into the kitchen and I let her. It mightn't be Zachary, but if it was, I didn't want to appear too eager.

Leo knocked. "Hi."

"Come in," Grandfather called, and Leo and Jacky pushed the screen door open.

"Where's Suzy?" Jacky asked.

Leo spoke simultaneously, "Come for a walk, Vicky?"

My ears were cocked toward the house. "Suzy's on the phone."

"Vicky," she called, "it's for you."

I called back, "Who is it?" After all, we've been coming to Seven Bay Island all our lives. There were other people it could be besides Zachary.

Suzy slammed onto the porch without answering, so I knew it was.

"Be back," I said to Leo, and went in, nearly falling over Rochester, who was lying in the way as usual. I went through the kitchen and to Grandfather's study. "Hi," I said into the phone.

"Vicky-O."

Nobody but Zachary has ever called me Vicky-O, but automatically I asked, "Who is it?"

"Who do you think it is, idiot?"

"I'm not an idiot, and I'm aware that you're Zachary Gray." It was not the ideal way to begin a conversation.

"Get off your high horse, Vicky. 'Smatter of fact, do you want to come horseback riding this morning?"

To my surprise I heard myself saying, "I can't. I'm going for a walk with Leo." Now why on earth did I say that? When I went to the phone I thought Zachary was going to be my excuse for *not* going for a walk with Leo.

"Who's Leo?"

"He's the oldest son of Commander Rodney—whose funeral we were at yesterday," I replied clumsily.

There was an odd silence at the other end of the line. Then, "How about this afternoon?"

"This afternoon's fine."

"Good. Pick you up about two." He hung up without saying goodbye. Zachary would never identify himself on the phone for me; he was certain I'd recognize his voice. And yet I felt he was far less sure of himself than he wanted me to think he was—or than he wanted himself to think he was.

I went back to the porch. Rob was eating toast and homemade beach-plum jam. Suzy and Jacky had gone off somewhere together. Leo was patiently waiting for me.

"Do you have to go somewhere with someone, Vicky, or can you come for a walk with me?" Leo was anything but sure of himself.

I looked at Mother, who nodded. "I can go for a walk." I tried to sound more enthusiastic than I felt.

We said goodbye and started off. "Where'll we go?" Leo asked.

"To the beach."

Grandfather's stable is up on a bluff, at the highest end of the Island. The quickest way to the beach is down a very steep path cut into the bluff and kept from erosion by logs pounded in horizontally every yard or so. Tough little bushes have grown up on either side, and they can help slow your descent if you get ahead of yourself, or help pull you up on the steep climb home. The beach at the foot of the bluff is a lovely crescent which we call Grandfather's cove. There's a rock there that I like to sit on, particularly when the tide is coming in, and I can watch the little waves coming closer, breaking in pearly patterns of foam.

Now the tide was going out and the rock was high and dry. The sand around it had dried in the morning sun and wind, though if we dug down with our fingers the water would squish against them.

Leo walked slowly along the ocean's edge, letting the waves break over the toes of his sneakers. We both had on jeans and T-shirts, but I was wearing sandals and I took them off so I could wade. It wasn't until his sneakers were thoroughly wet and sandy that Leo bent down to unlace them and pull them off.

We splashed along in silence. We left Grandfather's protected cove, and the waves were rougher and the pull of the undertow stronger. Leo turned inland and I followed him to the bare fallen trunk of a once great elm. All the bark was long gone, and the old wood had washed smooth in the rains and salt winds; it made a comfortable seat. Leo looked at the ocean. "I'm glad it was your grandfather and not Mr. Hanchett at Dad's funeral."

"So'm I. Mr. Hanchett's a dear, but he makes even a wedding sound gloomy."

"What are you going to do after this summer?" Leo asked, as though he were continuing and not changing the conversation.

We had been on the Island barely a week when Commander Rodney died. We were all tired, and we thought we had all summer to catch up with everybody, and our attention was on ourselves and on Grandfather. We hadn't even seen the Rodneys except to wave at in the post office or the market.

Except for Rob. I knew Rob had gone on his own over to the Coast Guard to see the Commander. I wondered what they'd talked about.

"Vicky?" Leo prodded. His face was still splotchy and his fair hair was limp.

"We're going home to Thornhill and the Regional High," I answered. "Daddy's returning to general practice."

"You're not going back to New York, then?"

"New York was never meant to be forever," I replied. "Daddy had a year for the research he never had time to do when he was a busy country doctor. And the doctor who took our house and Daddy's practice was having a sort of sabbatical year from running a big hospital in Chicago, and he has to be back there in September. So we're going home."

"Home." Leo worked at a small sliver of wood on the old trunk. "The Island's always been home to me. How did you like living in New York?"

"I loved it and I hated it. I learned a lot."

"Like what?" Leo stopped pulling at the sliver and looked at me.

I looked out to sea. Near the horizon I saw something dark leap out of the water in a beautiful arc. A porpoise. I shivered. "Oh—how very protected we'd been, living in a tiny village like Thornhill all our lives, with visits to the Island a couple of times a year. I'd been under the illusion that most people are pretty good."

"And now you think most people are pretty bad?"

I shook my head. "But people are a lot more mixed up—more complex—than I thought they were. I thought most adults were like my parents and—yours. But they aren't."

"How come your father's free to spend the summer on the Island?"

"Well—I just told you, the other doctor's going to be in Thornhill till September. And Daddy's working on a book," I said to Leo.

"I thought he was a doctor, not a writer."

"He is. It's not a book-type book, it's scientific. I wouldn't understand a word of it."

"Are you glad to be going back to Thornhill?"

"I don't know," I said. "I just plain don't know."

I certainly wouldn't be the same innocent hick who'd left Thornhill a year ago. And we'd made friends in New York, real friends: I didn't know if we'd ever see them again.

Leo slid from the old dead elm onto the beach. "I was supposed to go to New York next winter. I was accepted at Columbia. I had a good scholarship, too, and I was counting on your being there."

"Well—we lived just a bit below Columbia last year. That's the part of New York we know best. We can tell you lots about it."

"Yeah, but—"

"But?"

"It doesn't look as though I'll be going now. Commanders in the Coast Guard don't leave fortunes to their families."

"Aren't there pensions and stuff?"

"I don't think it's all that much. And I'm the oldest and I'm not sure I ought to go off, leaving Mom and the kids—"

I looked at his round, earnest face. He wasn't trying to play on my sympathies the way some kids might (I'd really become very suspicious about human nature in my old age); he was trying to think things out, and what he ought to do. Only a year ago, Leo knew what God thought, and what he and everybody else ought to do on every occasion, and I liked him much better this way, though life used to be easier for him when he knew all the answers.

I didn't know the answers, either, but I did know one thing, and I said as much to Leo: "Your parents would both want you to get your education, I'm positive of that. You want to go to Columbia, don't you?"

"As much as I've ever wanted anything."

"Okay, then. And we'll give you lots of clues about life in that neighborhood. It's colorful, all right."

"Vicky." He leaned over the grey wood of the elm and reached for my hand. "You really do think it would be all right for me to go off in the autumn? To leave Mom and the kids, with Dad—" He broke off and swallowed hard, so that his Adam's apple bobbed.

"I think your mom and the kids would be furious

with you if you gave up a good scholarship because you thought they couldn't manage without you."

"But I'm the head of the family now . . ." It sounded old-fashioned, and yet I knew he meant it from the deepest recesses of his heart.

"All the more reason you should get a good education." Gently I withdrew my hand from his. "It doesn't have to be settled today. And I really think you ought to talk to your mom."

Leo's mother is short and a bit dumpy—he has more of her genes than his father's—but she radiates good sense. She isn't very exciting, but she's solid; if she says she'll do something, she'll do it. Enough has happened to me in sixteen years that I've begun to stop underrating solidity and overvaluing excitement.

"I always talked to my dad," Leo said, and then clamped his jaws shut so tightly that all the muscles of his face were strained, but that didn't stop the tears overflowing and trickling down his cheeks.

Without realizing what I was doing, I put my arms around him. "Cry, Leo, don't hold it back, you need to cry—" I broke off because I was crying, too, crying for Commander Rodney, for my grandfather, who was dying slowly and gently, for a thousand porpoises who had been clubbed to death . . .

I held Leo and he held me and we rocked back and forth on the old elm trunk, weeping, and the salt wind brushed against the salt of our tears. And I discovered that there is something almost more intimate about crying that way with someone than there is about kissing, and I knew I'd never again be able to think of Leo as nothing but a slob.

Our tears spent themselves. I think he stopped first. He pulled up his T-shirt and used it to mop his eyes. He was all red and mottled from weeping, and I supposed I was, too.

"Let's swim," I suggested.

He looked at me in surprise and I sighed. "Not skinny-dipping. In our underclothes. That's more than a lot of bathing suits." I pulled off my jeans and shirt and draped them over the elm, left my sandals on the sand, and ran across the beach to the water. I splashed through the shallow waves, dove under a big comber coming at me, and swam until I was beyond the surf and could turn over on my back and rest on the undulating swells. Leo joined me; he's a strong, fast swimmer, like any kid who's grown up on the Island.

"Don't go out too far," he warned. "This bay's pretty safe, but the tide's still going out."

I couldn't so much feel it sucking me seaward as notice that I was farther from shore than I had been only a moment before. "Race you in."

The swim back took at least three times as long as going out. I was panting when I flung myself onto the crest of a galloping wave and body-surfed into shore. Leo was a good three lengths ahead of me. As I splashed in to join him, I saw Rob climbing down the cliff and calling to us, so we hurried back to Grandfather's cove and reached him as he jumped onto the beach.

"Mother says Suzy's gone to the Rodneys' with Jacky, so why doesn't Leo stay and have lunch with us?"

This was the kind of casual back-and-forthing we were used to on the Island; only today it seemed different. Suzy's going to the Rodney's was different, even though ordinarily the Commander wouldn't have been home at lunchtime.

"Sure," Leo replied. "I'd love to stay. What time is it? I left my watch down the beach with my clothes."

"Nearly noon." Rob pointed at the sun, which was almost directly overhead.

Leo looked at me. "I didn't think we'd been gone nearly that long."

"We'll just let our underclothes dry," I told Rob. "It won't take more than a few minutes in this sun. Then we'll get our clothes on and come along up to the stable."

"Okay," Rob said. "I'll tell Mother." And he started the hot climb up the cliff.

Leo and I strolled slowly back to the fallen elm, letting the sun and breeze dry us. Leo made a face. "Yuck, my sneakers are all sopping."

"You'll need them for the climb." I pulled my shirt over my head and spoke through the warm cotton.

Leo was strapping on his watch. "Your grandfather—" He stopped, and started trying to shove his sandy feet into his wet sneakers. "I think I know him better than you do."

"You'll get blisters. Go rinse your feet and your sneakers and put them on at the water's edge." I sounded bossy as all get-out, but I did not like, not one little bit, the idea that someone like Leo thought he knew my own grandfather better than I did.

He followed my instructions. When he came back across the sand he said, "In the winters when things get too noisy at home, or I have a problem about something and Dad's too busy and I don't want to bother him"—for a moment the tears filled his eyes again, but this time they didn't overflow—"I bike across the Island to your grandfather's and we have tea together and talk. He's been a very civilizing influence on me. He's a wise man."

"I know he is." I stopped myself from adding, He's my grandfather. I don't know why I was feeling so ungracious toward Leo. Perhaps because our weeping together had been more intimate than I was ready to be.

"I'm sorry he's sick," he said.

"How'd you know?" It wasn't that we were keeping it a secret, as though we were ashamed of it or anything, but we weren't going around talking about it, either. I guess I think death and sex should be allowed privacy.

"He told me."

I wanted to ask, Why? but I didn't.

Leo answered anyhow. "It wasn't long before you came, and I asked him how long you were going to stay, and he answered, Most of the summer. You usually don't stay more than a couple of weeks, so with my big mouth I kept on asking questions, and he told me." And then Leo did something which didn't fit the picture I had of him, even the Leo with whom I'd sobbed out rage and grief. He ran back to the water's edge and shook his fist up at the bland blue sky and the brilliant orb of the sun, too bright to look at, and swore, loudly and steadily. I'd thought, between the kids at school and a year in New York, that I knew all the words, but Leo came out with quite a few that were new to me. He swore with intensity and a strange kind of elegance, and then he dropped his arms and turned his back on the water and the sun and strolled over to me as though he hadn't done anything unusual. We walked without speaking to the foot of the bluff, with the path rising steeply ahead of us.

"Where was your grandfather before he came to the Island, before he retired?"

I looked at him questioningly. After all, he'd said he knew Grandfather better than I do.

He looked down at his wet sneakers. "I never asked him much about himself, because I was so busy thinking about me."

"Aren't we all, most of the time?" My mind flicked briefly to Sir Thomas Browne's words in the loft; surely Leo was no more replete with himself than I was with me, and surely we weren't that much different from anybody else. "About Grandfather—where didn't he go and what didn't he do is more like it. When Mother was my age, he was in Africa."

"Being a missionary?"

"Well—he and our grandmother were living with a very small and ancient tribe, and learning their language and setting down their traditions and their wisdom and their history—which were beginning to get lost as the elders died."

"That's not what most people would consider being a missionary," Leo said. "But then of course your grandfather's not most people. What else?"

"Well, he had a big church in Boston and he was tremendously popular. His sermons got rave reviews in the paper, and our grandmother used to tease him about women swooning over him. And just when the church was overflowing he handed in his resignation, like a bomb, and he and Gram went to a tiny mission church in Alaska. He was sixty, but the only way for him to get to all his congregation was by seaplane or helicopter, so he got a pilot's license, so nobody would go without at least one visit from him every few months." I'd started climbing and stopped to catch my breath. My climbing muscles hadn't been that much used in New York, and the backs of my legs felt the pull. Leo lived on the far, flatter side of the island, and I could hear him puffing behind me.

It had been, I thought, a far more interesting morning than I'd anticipated. I'd learned about the complexity of human beings during the year in New York, but maybe not as much as I'd believed. Leo was certainly much less of a slob than I'd thought.

2

I lost track of time while we were eating lunch, and that may have been just as well, because I wouldn't have known how to get rid of Leo tactfully if I'd realized how late it was getting. Anyhow, he was still there when Zachary arrived in his shiny black station wagon, tooting at the front door.

Because the stable is built on the bluff where it elbows toward the sea, you get a good view of the ocean from both the front and the back of the house, though the kitchen and the porch have the better view. Our grandmother wanted it that way when they were remodeling, because she said she spent most of her time in the kitchen, and if the porch was next to the kitchen it could be used as a dining room for maybe seven months a year. Not that she was a slave to the kitchen like some of the supposedly grandma types on TV commercials for lemonade (artificial) or cake mixes. She was a Boston Bluestocking and a cordon-bleu cook, black hat, and Grandfather used to say that if the church went out of business they could always open a restaurant.

Zachary stood at the front door. He wore jodhpurs and a fawn-colored turtleneck, and he carried a crop with a silver handle which he was switching against his thigh.

"Want to come in for a minute?" I asked, not sure what to do about Leo.

"Why not?"

I led him in by the side door, pointing out the baby swallows. The three parents were swooping around anxiously, and Zachary seemed amused by the strange *ménage à trois*.

"Immoral little buggers, aren't they?" He grinned at me. Once indoors, he looked around, still flicking his crop, glancing into the stalls with all their books; sagging, comfortable chairs; the double stall that was Grandfather's office; and the one next to it, with a long map of the world on the outside wall, which let down to become a table for cold or rainy weather. There was plenty of both on the Island.

"Intriguing," Zachary said. "It looks rather like—"

"It is," I replied. "It was."

"A stable?"

"Yes."

"A big one, then."

"Yeah. It belonged to rich friends of my grandparents, the Woods, who have the big house about half a mile down the road."

"They must have an imaginative architect."

"My grandmother."

"Seriously?"

"She could do almost anything she put her hand to."

"Will I meet her?"

"No. She died a few years after Grandfather retired."

"Oh, I remember," Zachary said. "He's the minister."

He sounded as though he was saying that Grandfather was involved in organized crime. No—as a matter of fact, Zachary probably had considerable respect for organized crime.

Everybody was still sitting around the table.

Zachary said a general hello, politely, and then looked pointedly at Leo. I introduced Zach first to Grandfather, since the meeting the day before hardly constituted an introduction, then to Leo.

You couldn't imagine two people less alike than Zachary and Leo. Zachary was like a negative of Leo, though you couldn't possibly say that Leo was a positive of Zachary. Where Leo's straw-colored hair was bleached by the Island sun and salt, Zachary's was black as midnight. Leo's skin was ruddy-brown and freckled from wind and weather; Zachary's, winter pale. Leo's eyes were hazel and wide apart and guileless; Zachary's were steel-grey, not sea-grey like Adam's, but metallic. Well— Adam's eyes were *grey*, and Zachary's were *gray*, the way his last name is spelled. And the combination of dark and pale—Zachary was just as gorgeous as I had remembered him during those long months in New York when I never heard from him.

Leo said, "I'd better be getting on home. Jacky and I go back to work tomorrow. This is our busiest season."

In answer to Zachary's look I said, "Leo and his brother, Jacky, run charters to the mainland and the other islands, if someone doesn't want to wait for the ferry. They also take people deep-sea fishing."

Leo bowed slightly. "At your service."

"I may take you up on that. Are you expensive?" Zachary asked.

"More than the ferry. We charge the going rate for charters. Monday's our day off. See you, Vicky?"

"Sure," I replied, thinking at him,—Go, Leo, go, before you find out who Zachary is, if he is the rich kid whose boat capsized; and if he is, before he finds out who you are.

He went.

"How about our ride, Vicky-O?" Zachary asked.

I looked at his jodhpurs. "I don't have any riding clothes."

"Jeans are fine. Sandals aren't so good. Got anything else?"

"Sneakers."

Zachary glanced down at his beautiful boots. "Better than sandals."

"I'll go change." And I went off to the loft, leaving Zachary sitting out on the porch, in Leo's chair, accepting a glass of iced tea.

When I returned I heard Mother saying, "Zachary, I'm so sorry."

Sorry about what? That Zachary was in the capsized boat? That he was the one the Commander rescued? If so, better to have it out in the open.

But it wasn't that. It was Zachary's mother. She was dead, killed in an automobile accident in California, only a few miles from home.

"It was her own fault," Zachary was explaining. "She never should have been allowed to drive. She'd been off, buying her spring wardrobe. Pop sent it all back, several thou'worth." He spoke in an even voice.

I wondered if he grieved for her, if her death was what had caused the pain in his eyes the day before, and I wasn't sure. If someone had asked me yesterday morning who I knew best, Zachary or Leo, I'd have answered without thinking: Zachary. If I stopped to think, I knew it was the other way around; and certainly I knew Leo better after this morning than I ever had before.

We'd met Zachary a year ago, during the camping trip we took after we'd rented the house in Thornhill and before moving to the apartment in New York. Zachary and his parents had pulled up to the campsite next to ours in the Great Smoky Mountains National Park in Tennessee, and we watched them set up camp in amazement and amusement. The black station wagon was last year's version of this year's, and I couldn't have told them apart, except that they were both obviously bran-span new. And Zachary had very quickly made it clear that the Grays' things were always new, and whatever was latest. They had every gadget we'd ever heard of, and several we hadn't. Mr. Gray even unrolled a linoleum rug to cover the canvas floor of the tent, and tied an enormous piece of plastic over the top. He had an aura of money; he positively reeked of it. The Woods probably have as much money as the Grays, but they don't reek. Mrs. Gray in this day and age wore corsets—or is it a corset? Whatever, her pouter-pigeon figure was definitely not her own. She looked as though she'd be lots more at home sitting at a bridge table than watching her husband cook steaks over a charcoal fire on a grill that belonged on a patio rather than in a state campground.

And now she was dead. More death. And Zachary didn't look or seem that different. Would the world close around the space that had been Commander Rodney as it appeared to have closed around Mrs. Gray, leaving no mark?

Then I heard Zachary saying, "Do you know anything about the science of cryonics?" He reached for the pitcher to pour himself some more iced tea, but there wasn't much left.

"I hadn't exactly thought of it as a science." There was a chilly edge to my father's voice. Zachary seemed to be having his usual effect on my family. Last summer, when he'd more or less followed us from campground to campground, I'd been flattered and fascinated. I was flattered that Zachary found me worth pursuing across the country, and fascinated by his sophistication. Even now, after a year in New York, I still felt gauche and naïve.

"Oh, come, sir," Zachary was saying to my father. "Quite a few people in the A.M.A. are taking it seriously."

"What's cryonics?" Rob asked.

Whatever it was, I could see that Daddy didn't think much of it.

Zachary was explaining, "We belong to a group in California called the Immortalists. We believe that it isn't necessary for people to die as early as they do, and when we understand more about controlling DNA and RNA it will be possible for people to live for several hundred years without aging—and that time is not so far in the future as you might think."

We were all silent, listening to him. Mother glanced at Daddy, and then took the silver pitcher and headed for the kitchen for more iced tea.

Zachary went on, "Cryonics is the science of freezing a body immediately after death, deep-freezing, so that later on—in five years, or five hundred—when scientists know more about the immortality factor, it will be possible for these people of the future to revive the deep-frozen bodies, to resurrect them."

Grandfather spoke with a small smile, "I think I prefer another kind of resurrection."

Zachary's lips moved in a scornful smile. "Of course, the problem at the moment is cost. Not many people can afford it. We feel lucky that we can."

"You did—you did that to your mother?" Rob sounded horrified. I was, too, come to that. I'd known, vaguely, that this kind of thing was being done in California, but not by or to anybody I knew. I looked at Grandfather.

He gave me his special grandfather-granddaughter smile. "Resurrection has always been costly, though not in terms of money. It took only thirty pieces of silver."

"Oh, that," Zachary said, courteously enough. "We think this is more realistic, sir. While only the rich can afford it now, ultimately it should be available to everybody."

Into my mind's eye flashed an image of the afternoon before, when we were standing by a dark hole in the ground, waiting for Commander Rodney's body to be lowered into it. Somehow that struck me as being more realistic than being deep-frozen. Being deep-frozen went along with plastic grass and plastic earth and trying to pretend that death hadn't really happened.

"Of course," Zachary said, "nowadays a lot of people get cremated, basically because of lack of space in cemeteries."

Rob was looking at him in fascinated horror. "You mean your scientists couldn't do anything with ashes?"

He was sitting next to Grandfather and he reached out to hold his hand.

Now Rob was bathed in Grandfather's luminous smile. "I'm not depending on superscientists, Rob. When one tries to avoid death, it's impossible to affirm life."

I thought of Mrs. Gray, deep-frozen somewhere in California, and Commander Rodney, buried on the Island, covered with good Island soil. And Grandfather—perhaps he and Mother and Daddy had discussed what was going to happen to him, to his body, when he died. But they hadn't talked about it around us. Maybe it wasn't time.

Not yet. Please. Not for a while yet.

Rob was asking Grandfather anxiously, "It doesn't really matter, does it? whether you're frozen or buried or cremated or what, God can manage, can't he?"

"I stake my life on that." Grandfather's smile was only in his eyes, but it was there, warm and confident as though he had laughed out loud.

I'd almost forgotten Mr. Rochester. He was lying in a corner of the porch in the sun; now that he's elderly he likes to let his old joints warm up in the sunlight. He got to his feet slowly, but still supplely, stepped over Ned, and crossed to Rob, sitting protectively beside him, and stared at Zachary with a look so suspicious it almost made me laugh; a laugh right then would have been a good thing. Ned rose, stretched, and swished into the kitchen, tail switching.

Nobody laughed. I said, "If we're going riding, we'd better go."

Mother came back with the iced tea. Grandfather pushed his glass toward her and she filled it.

Daddy asked, "Where are you going to get horses, Zachary? Vicky's not an experienced rider."

"The other side of the Island, sir, at Second Bay Stables."

Daddy nodded. We knew, slightly, the woman who ran Second Bay Stables, the way we know most of the Islanders and the regular summer people.

Zachary promised, "I'll see that Vicky has a gentle horse. We're just going to meander along the bridle paths, nothing dangerous."

"And, Vicky—" Mother called after us. "Don't be late."

I got the message. She didn't finish "—John's bringing a friend home for dinner," because she didn't want me to ask Zachary, too. Mother can manage half a dozen unexpected people for dinner without batting an eyelash. It wasn't that; it was Zachary. John's friend was welcome. Mine wasn't. Which burned me. Nevertheless, at the moment I didn't think I wanted Zachary to come for dinner, either, with his talk about the science of cryonics and deep-freezing his mother. I don't know why that nauseated me so. It wasn't because it was science-fictiony; most science fiction comes true, somehow or other, sooner or later. So it wasn't that it wasn't possible; it was that, as far as I was concerned, it was sick.

"We won't be late," I promised not very graciously, and led Zachary around to the car the back way.

He revved up the engine and started down the zigzaggy road, driving too fast.

"Hey, I don't have a death wish," I protested. "Slow

45

down." He lifted his foot a millimeter off the gas pedal. I swallowed and asked, "When did you get to the Island?"

"On the ferry," he answered. But that wasn't what I'd asked him. I started to repeat the question, *when*, not *how*, and lost courage. I wasn't sure I wanted to know the answer. Instead I asked, "How did you know we were on the Island?"

"Detective work." Gradually his foot was pressing down on the gas pedal. "You're why I came, Vicky-O. There's certainly nothing else here. No golf club, no decent hotel, no night life."

"That's what we like about it. There *is* a speed limit, though."

"Always law-abiding, aren't you?"

"If the law's going to protect me from involuntary suicide or murder, yes." He slowed down to about fifty, which is fast for rough roads with no shoulders and sharp curves. "You still didn't tell me how you found out we were on the Island."

"I tried to get hold of you in New York, and got the address from your old man's hospital."

I was silent. He'd had a whole year to get in touch with me in New York. Why had he waited until now?

"I left Pop on the mainland, where he can play golf all day and drink all night."

I suddenly felt terribly sorry for Zachary's father, who'd spent his life making money, and all the money could do when his wife died was put her in deep-freeze. "Is he all right alone?"

"That's not your problem, Vicky."

He had every right to put me down for asking. I shifted mental gears. "What did you do last year?"

"Graduated from high school—at last. Got bumped

from Choate at Halloween, then went to a punk sweat school for kids who've been bounced out of all the decent places. It was so zuggy I thought I might as well do the work and get it over with if I want to be a lawyer before I'm seventy. If I'm going to live the way I want to, I've got to know law, instead of dishing out all that money to lawyers the way Pop does."

"Where're you going to college?" I was pushing my foot down on an imaginary brake, and I was glad we were nearly to Second Bay.

"I can *drive*, Vicky. U.C.L.A., I suppose. It's close to home."

Why did Zachary, of all people, want to stay close to home?

We drove in silence the last few minutes as we pulled up to the stable. I've ridden a little, enough so that I can post and not fall off if the horse starts to canter. But that's about it. A matronly looking dapple-grey named Daphne, with definite middle-age spread, was chosen for me. I fed her a piece of apple and she nuzzled my palm so gently that I felt pretty relaxed about riding her.

Zachary was on a large bay. He'd asked for a spirited chestnut who was prancing and flinging his head about, but the owner of the stable came up and said it was already taken. I had a feeling she didn't want Zachary riding one of her best and fastest horses. She wore worn riding pants and a plaid shirt and had a determined, wind-burned face, and she wasn't going to take any nonsense.

We started off side by side, on a wide, woodsy bridle path. The trees were their fresh, early-summer green, without the dusty look they get later on. I sniffed the lovely Island smell of green growing things and silver salty breeze. Neither of us spoke, and as the silence stretched out—and it was not a peaceful or companionable silence—I knew that I could not be the one to break it. Zachary hadn't answered my question, and until I knew the answer, nothing could work between us.

Finally he spoke. He turned toward me and his face was white and his eyes dark, and I hadn't noticed before how bruised-looking the shadows under them were. The reflection of the leaves gave a greenish pallor to his skin. "I'm not sure why I needed to see you, Vicky. I'm not good for you."

I looked at him and waited.

"I tried to kill myself."

Again the silence stretched out like an old rubber band.

"Why?" I asked.

"I'm bored with life."

"Bored?"

"Bored. So bored it hurts like a toothache."

"Why?"

"It's a lousy world."

"Would being dead be less lousy?"

"Sure. It would be nothing, nice quiet *nada, nada, nada.*"

"So how come you're still here?"

"Some boy scout Coast Guard foiled me by rescuing me."

His words were like lead in the pit of my stomach. "Commander Rodney."

"That's the name. They took me to the hospital on

the mainland. I'd swallowed a lot of water before he interfered."

Interfered.

I wanted to scream with outrage.

"I know he meant well, Vicky. And I didn't know he'd died until yesterday evening."

"Didn't know—"

"In the hospital I was taken right to ICU and they didn't think I'd live. My lungs were a mess and my heart had been pretty badly strained. At first nobody had time to say anything, they were so busy plugging me into various life-support systems. And I certainly wasn't in any condition to ask questions." He paused, looking at me, but I was staring straight ahead, avoiding his gaze. After a bit he continued. "Then, when I came round in intensive care, mighty displeased to be there, Pop asked that I not be told because he thought it might make me have a relapse—my heart was still fibrillating."

"Would it have made you relapse?"

"I doubt it, though that would have been a consummation devoutly to be wished. And then Pop would have put me in deep-freeze and I could wait quietly to be thawed out in a more enlightened age."

Our horses pushed slowly through the shifting green shadows. A vine brushed across my face and tickled my nose. "Commander Rodney wasn't put into deep-freeze. He was buried. Yesterday. In the ground."

"Stop trying to make me feel guilty, Vicky. I'm not hung up on moralism like you Austins. I didn't know he'd died till after I saw you yesterday and something made me ask a few questions."

Our horses plodded along placidly. Small green

branches brushed against their flanks, scratched my legs through my jeans. The sun filtered sleepily through the leaves. I felt that my mind had turned to dust, to the fallen leaves bruised under the horses' hoofs. "Leo," I said. "The one you met this afternoon at Grandfather's. That's his oldest son."

"So what?" Zachary urged his horse into a trot and Daphne followed.

"Wait a minute. There's something I don't understand. You came to the Island looking for me, and then instead of coming to me you rented a boat and set out to drown yourself."

"There're a lot of things you don't understand." Zachary smoldered his gaze at me. "I came looking for you, and then when I found out where you were, suddenly it didn't seem worth it. It wasn't you. It was everything and nothing. Life. Ma's death. Talking to anybody. Not worth it."

"I'm sorry," I said, wanting to reach out my hand to touch him. "I'm sorry about your mother."

He shrugged. "I miss her in a funny sort of way, but not so's you'd notice it. She gave me anything I wanted, but so does Pop. Nothing's changed that much."

Did he really mean that? "If you've been so sick, should you be horseback riding?"

He glanced at me obliquely. "Why do you suppose we're just ambling along the bridle paths?"

"Up to this minute I thought it's because I'm not an experienced rider."

He reached across and patted my hand. "That's part of it. But also I'm taking care of myself, Vicky-O. I don't want to be back in that stinking hospital again. Give me credit for some sense."

"Capsizing a sailboat wasn't very sensible."

"Shut up! I didn't ask to be rescued, damn him!" He dug his heels into his horse's flanks and they shot off down the path and disappeared around a curve.

My placid dapple-grey broke into a trot and then a gentle rocking canter. I didn't try to push her. I didn't want to catch up with Zachary.

He'd always had a death wish. But I'd thought, when we'd said goodbye a year ago, that he was pretty well over it and ready to get on with the business of living. Now it seemed he was just the same as when we first met. Galloping his horse was proof of that.

Commander Rodney had been committed to life. And he was dead.

The woods thinned. The trees became smaller and scrubbier. Then we moved through some low bushes and the bridle path ended on the beach, the great, gently curving oval of Second Bay. Zachary's horse had stopped its wild gallop and was standing at the water's edge, flanks heaving.

I pulled gently on the reins and Daphne slowed to a walk.

Zachary had accused us of moralism. I'm not positive what moralism is, but I'm sure we're not hung up on it. I think it means that you're certain you know what is right and what is wrong, that you're morally omnipotent. Grandfather, if no one else, taught me long ago what a snare and a delusion thinking you know all the answers to everything can be. Half the time I don't know what's right and what's wrong, and I learned last year that my parents don't, either.

Was Daddy right to pull up all our roots and take us to New York, for instance? I don't know, and I don't think he knows, either. We had a pretty rough time, but on the other hand, we learned a lot of things we'd never have learned in Thornhill. And are Daddy and Mother right in leaving New York and going back to Thornhill? The big New York hospital offered Daddy a grant for another year. Was he right to turn it down? Maybe time will tell, but right now we certainly don't know.

No, I don't think we're hung up on moralism, not nearly as hung up as Zachary on his death wish and cryonics and outsmarting the world. And yet when he cried out, "Damn him!" I knew it was not Commander Rodney he was damning but himself.

I think I was even sorrier for Zachary than I was for Leo, and that was peculiar indeed. In a strange way Zachary and Leo were bonded together by Commander Rodney's death, and I wondered what Leo would feel or do when he found out who Zachary was. I wasn't predicting. If you'd asked me yesterday, I'd have thought Zachary was quite likely to stand at the ocean's edge and curse the universe, not Leo. But at this moment Zachary was simply sitting slumped on the big bay.

Daphne and I drew up alongside them, facing the ocean and the long stretch of water out into eternity.

Still hunched over, Zachary turned toward me. "This Leo."

"Yes—"

"When you introduced us, he didn't react or anything. He didn't seem to know who I am."

I thought for a moment about Mrs. Rodney and how, if she knew the name of the kid in the capsized boat, she'd quite likely have kept it to herself. "I guess he didn't." What was important to Mrs. Rodney was that her husband was dead; that was what mattered, not Zachary.

"Is he going to come between us?" Zachary asked.

"What's to come between?"

"Come on, Vicky-O. You know you and I have something very special going."

"Why did it take you a year to bother to get in touch with me, then?"

"I told you. I spent last year at this prison of a cram school so I could go to college next year. I put everything else out of my life."

"I'm not sure I want to pick up where we left off." I kept my voice level and steady. "I've changed a lot since last summer."

"Have you?" He straightened up and smiled at me, slowly, intimately. "Seem the same lovely Vicky-O to me."

I nudged Daphne's flanks and she started ambling along the beach. Zachary followed. "I've done a lot of growing up. I'm not just the hick kid from Thornhill any more. I've had nearly a year in New York."

"Fancy that." His tone was lightly mocking. "And after this summer?"

"Back to Thornhill."

"Your old man couldn't make it in New York?"

I didn't even bristle. I just said calmly, "It's not a question of making it or not making it. He wanted a year of doing research, but he's a people person and he wants to get back to being a people doctor."

"Okay. Gotcha." He smiled at me and this time it was a real smile. "But this summer you're going to spend on this one-horse island?"

"I see two horses right now."

"You know what I mean."

"Yes. We're going to spend the summer here." I didn't explain. I'm pretty confused on the subject of death myself, but Zachary, I was sure, was even more confused. "I haven't ridden in a while, Zach, and I want to be able to sit down tomorrow. Let's go back."

"Wait." When Zachary wanted to, he could move like greased lightning. His hand flashed out and took hold of Daphne's bridle. "What are you going to do about Leo?"

"Do? Nothing."

"Do you see a lot of him?"

"The Island's pretty small. We all bump into each other."

"That's not what I'm talking about."

I let Daphne shuffle along in the soft sand. Leo and I didn't date, or go together. I've never really properly dated or gone with anyone, which has bothered me, because most kids my age have. As for Leo, this morning on the beach had changed things between us. "I see Leo."

"Are you going to tell him about me?"

"I don't know."

He wheeled his horse so that he was looking straight at me. "Vicky, I need you. I knew I needed you when I came to this godforsaken spot looking for you. And then—things—just got the better of me and I wanted out. And now I don't. I want back in. But I need help."

"I'm not a psychiatrist." I started walking Daphne back toward the stables.

"I've been seeing a shrink. That's not what I need. I

need you. I think I need you in the setting of your whole peculiar family."

"We're not peculiar."

"Oh, yes, you are. Don't you realize that in my world my parents were peculiar because they'd never been divorced? Basically because it would have been too much trouble. But you live in a world where not only are your parents not divorced, they appear to love each other."

"They do."

"And you do things like going to church and saying grace and zuggy stuff like that. I don't know anybody else in the world who does that. And the weird thing is that in spite of it all you're real." He gave me his fullest Hamlet look, and reached out and gently touched the back of my hand with his forefinger, a tender caress which sent ripples all through me. "And you—you're such a mixture of being much older than you are and much, much younger."

"Well—how long are you going to be on the Island?" I asked weakly.

"As long as I can stand that fourth-rate hotel."

"We like the Inn."

"Sorry. As long as you'll put up with me is a better answer. And truer."

I felt like asking, along with Pontius Pilate, What is truth? But I just posted gently as the horses trotted along the bridle path.

When we got back to Grandfather's, I didn't ask Zachary in. I thanked him for the ride and held out my hand.

He gave me a funny look, but there was pleading in his eyes that really got to me. "Vicky, you don't know—"

"What?"

"You're sanity in an insane world. You're reason where there isn't any reason. Reason to live. I need—" He stopped. And I waited. He looked at me intensely. "Oh, Vicky-O. I'm so damn confused."

Zachary. Confused. Vicky's the one to be confused.

"Vicky," he said in a very low voice. "My old lady—" He stopped and swallowed. "I need you. You don't know how much I need you." He turned and walked quickly away.

Was he overdoing it? I didn't think so. His voice had none of its usual flip sophistication. And there was a naked vulnerability about him he had never been willing to reveal before.

I went into the stable and hallooed. I needed some nice, stable (no pun intended) conversation. Not about death. Or guilt. Or moralism. Or porpoises being clubbed or people being frozen. Something homely, like how you tell your spaghetti's done by throwing a strand against the wall; if it sticks, it's done.

Grandfather called from the porch. He was lying on the couch, a book in his hand, and I could see that it was poetry. He told me that Mother and Daddy had gone into town, marketing, and Rob was with them. Suzy was still somewhere with Jacky Rodney, and John, of course, was at work. I could smell the comforting aroma of simmering spaghetti sauce, and I wanted as much comfort as I could get.

I sat on the floor by the couch and echoed Zachary. "Grandfather, I'm horribly confused."

He looked at me questioningly.

"You met Zachary."

His eyes probed mine. "Handsome indeed, and troubled."

"He is, oh, Grandfather, he is, and it's way over my head."

"I think your parents would like you to steer clear of him."

"I'm nearly sixteen. Is it right for me to steer clear of someone who needs me?"

"I'd have to know more about it." He reached out with his long fingers and ruffled my hair, which I'd had cut short for summer.

For a few minutes I sat and enjoyed the feel of his fingers in my hair, and the soft breezes from the ocean and the ceiling fan. Then I sighed. "Grandfather, it was Zachary who was in that capsized sailboat, Zachary who was rescued by Commander Rodney."

He was silent for a minute, as though thinking. Then: "It did seem odd that he should have appeared right after the funeral."

"He didn't know."

"Didn't know what?"

"He nearly died, and what with one thing and another, he didn't know about Commander Rodney till yesterday—after he'd seen us. He said something made him ask questions. And so he found out."

"And he's upset and guilty?"

"I'm not sure. He says he isn't. But what Zachary says and what he means aren't always the same."

"But you've been blaming him, haven't you? Not perhaps Zachary, but someone you didn't know."

"Scapegoating, you mean?"

"That's the easy way out, isn't it?"

"Yeah, easier to blame some rich dumb kid than God."

"God can handle your anger, Vicky."

"Maybe I didn't want to face my own anger. And then that someone turned out to be someone I know."

"How well do you know him, Vicky?"

"I don't think anyone knows Zachary well. Not even Zachary. You never know what he's going to say or do. And, Grandfather—just to make it more complicated, he wasn't just some dumb kid who didn't know how to handle a sailboat. The boat's capsizing wasn't an accident. He wanted to drown. He wanted to die."

"Do you know why?"

"He has a heart condition, and I think it's made him sort of flirt with death. But he keeps talking about being a lawyer so he can take care of himself and not let other people get the better of him."

The ceiling fan whirred softly. "Do you think he really wanted to die?"

I thought about this for quite a while before answering. "It's funny—even when he courts death, I don't think he really believes in it. But maybe I'm wrong, because I just don't understand anybody wanting to die, at least not somebody young, with everything going for him the way Zachary has. But you heard him this morning, all that cryonics junk and Immortalists."

"I heard."

"But that kind of stuff isn't what immortality is about, is it?"

"Not to me." The smile lines about his eyes deepened. "To live forever in this body would take away much of the joy of living, even if one didn't age but stayed young and vigorous."

I didn't understand, but I had a hunch he was right. "Why?"

"If we knew each morning that there was going to be another morning, and on and on and on, we'd tend not to notice the sunrise, or hear the birds, or the waves rolling into shore. We'd tend not to treasure our time with the people we love. Simply the awareness that our mortal lives had a beginning and will have an end enhances the quality of our living. Perhaps it's even more intense when we know that the termination of the body is near, but it shouldn't be."

I wanted to reach over to him and hold him and say It is, oh, it is, but I couldn't.

Again his eyes smiled at me. "I like the old adage that we should live each day as though we were going to live forever, and as though we were going to die tomorrow." He ruffled my hair again. "This cryonics business strikes me as fear of death rather than joy in life."

"That's it! Zachary doesn't have much joy. But neither do—did—his parents. All that money—and they've used it to spoil him rotten, not to love him."

"Poor little rich boy, eh?"

"Sort of. Yes." I looked up at the white painted boards of the porch ceiling, and the light was moving on it in lovely waving patterns from the reflection of the sun on the water; and the ceiling fan stirred the patterns so that it was like a kaleidoscope made of ocean and air and sun. And the beauty moved through me like the wind. And I thought again of Zachary, and the dark behind his eyes that kept him from seeing this kind of joy. "And, Grandfather, what makes it all the more complicated is Leo."

"How so?"

"When I introduced them this afternoon, Leo didn't react at all, so I guess he doesn't know the name of the kid his father rescued. I guess that was how Mrs. Rodney wanted it. And I guess she never thought they'd meet."

He nodded. "Nancy Rodney is more than the salt of the earth. She's the leaven in the bread. And the light that's too often under a bushel."

"But, Grandfather, if Zachary stays around, they're going to be seeing each other, it's inevitable."

"Is he staying around?"

"He wants to."

"Because of you?"

"That's what he said."

"That's a pretty heavy burden, Vicky."

"Do you think I'm strong enough to carry it?"

"I think we're given strength for what we have to carry. What I question is whether or not this burden is meant for you."

"He needs me, Grandfather."

"You, Vicky Austin, specifically?"

"Well—yes. I think so." I did not like the way Grandfather's eyes were stern as they looked at me.

He said, "There's a sermon of John Donne's I have often had cause to remember during my lifetime. He says, *Other men's crosses are not my crosses.* We all have our own cross to carry, and one is all most of us are able to bear. How much do you owe him, Vicky?"

I replied slowly. "I don't think of it in terms of owing, like paying a debt. The thing is—he needs me."

Grandfather looked away from me and out to sea, and when he spoke, it was as though he spoke to himself. "The obligations of normal human kindness—*chesed*, as the Hebrew has it—that we all owe. But there's a kind of vanity in thinking you can nurse the world. There's a kind of vanity in goodness."

I could hardly believe my ears. "But aren't we supposed to be good?"

"I'm not sure." Grandfather's voice was heavy. "I do know that we're not good, and there's a lot of truth to the saying that the road to hell is paved with good intentions."

I said, slowly, "I can't make Zachary leave the Island if he wants to stay. Zachary's used to getting his own way. But when everybody finds out it was he who took the sailboat out—well, you already know the family thinks he's poison—" I stopped as I heard the car drive up, and Mother and Daddy and Rob came along the path, loaded with bags of groceries.

"Your daughter," Daddy said accusingly to Grandfather as he came up the steps and pushed through the screen door, nearly dropping two enormous bags, "told me all she needed was more spaghetti for tonight."

"Oh, I said I might need to pick up one or two other things," Mother explained airily. "We got some beautiful cheese to have before dinner. And some Parmesan, which Rob has promised to grate for us. It does have a much more delicate flavor than when it comes out of a jar."

"Nevertheless," Daddy said, "there are three more bags of 'one or two other things' out in the car." We heard him go into the kitchen and dump his load on

61

the kitchen table. Then he headed for the car again, and I could hear Mother putting things away and Rob chattering to her.

"How many people does my daughter think she's cooking for?" Grandfather asked the porch ceiling.

It still and always startled me when Grandfather referred to Mother as his daughter, though of course she is. But Suzy and I are the daughters, and Mother is the mother. Confusing enough when there are three generations together. How much more confusing it would be for Zachary and his Immortalists if there could be ten or fifteen generations of one family all alive at the same time.

The smell of spaghetti sauce wafted out to the porch as Mother took the lid off the pot.

Grandfather sniffed appreciatively. "How about cooking up a poem for me, Vic?"

I pushed closer to him and leaned against his knee. "I'll try. I just wish I could get Zach off my mind."

Daddy came in with the rest of the groceries. "I've got some reading and note-taking to get done before dinner. I've got to get on a better work schedule. I'll tell Mother to shout for you if she needs you, Vic."

"Sure," I called after him as he went into the kitchen.

Grandfather looked down at me. He touched the back of his hand lightly against my cheek and tears rushed to my eyes and I blinked them back. "You've had a lot thrown at you in a few short weeks."

To hold back my tears, I asked, "Like what?"

Grandfather held up one finger. "Leaving New York. Leaving a way of life you'd learned to enjoy. Leaving a school where you were challenged and stimulated.

62

Leaving your friends. To leave a friend is like a death and calls for grieving. And then, instead of settling down again in your own home in Thornhill, you came to me." He held up a second finger. "And you came because I'm dying."

"But we wanted to come!" I cried. "We want to be with you for as long as—as long as possible."

"Until I die," he corrected quietly. "It's still something thrown at you that you didn't anticipate." He held up a third finger. "Jack Rodney's death. That's a rough one for us all." A fourth finger. "And Leo. You spent a good part of the morning ministering to Leo."

"But I didn't—"

"You listened to him, didn't you?" I nodded. "That's ministering, and it takes enormous energy. And this afternoon you had Zachary." The fifth finger. "That's a lot to have thrown at you all at once. No wonder you're confused."

"Confused and confounded." But he had made me feel better. I looked at the book lying open in his lap. "What're you reading?"

"Poetry. I felt rather tired this afternoon and not in the mood to concentrate for long spaces of time. So I went back to one of my old favorites." He picked up the book. "Henry Vaughan. Seventeenth century."

"That's your special century, isn't it?"

"One of them. Listen to this; I think you'll like it:

"*I saw Eternity the other night,*
Like a great ring of pure and endless light,
All calm, as it was bright,
And round beneath it, Time, in hours, days, years,
Driven by the spheres,

Like a vast shadow moved, in which the world
    And all her train were hurled."

He paused and looked up at me, and when I didn't
say anything, because I was thinking about the words
of the poem, and what they meant in connection with
Leo, with Zachary, he flipped the pages and read:

"There is in God, some say,
A deep but dazzling darkness: as men here
Say it is late and dusky, because they
    See not all clear.
O for that Night, where I in him
    Might live invisible and dim!"

I didn't hear the last lines because my mind stopped
with *A deep but dazzling darkness.* And then it picked
up the first poem he'd read, with eternity being *a great
ring of pure and endless light.*

Grandfather looked at me.

"He's terrific, this Vaughan guy," I said.

"There's no one like the sixteenth- and seventeenth-
century writers for use of language." He closed the
book gently. "How is your writing going, Vicky?"

"Well, my English teacher last year really encour-
aged me."

"I liked the poems you gave me for Christmas."

"Not like Henry Vaughan."

Grandfather laughed and absently patted the book as
though it were an old friend. "I doubt if Henry Vaughan
was writing finished verse when he was your age. This
should be a good summer for poetry for you, Vic. A poet

friend of mine told me that his poems know far more than he does, and if he listens to them, they teach him."

I knew what he meant and I didn't know what he meant. The only way to find out was to try to write more poetry; I already knew that if I listen to the ocean long and quietly enough, the rhythm of the waves will move into the rhythm of verse and words will come.

Rob came out to the porch and I slipped away, figuring that the next half hour or so would be the only time this day I'd have to myself. Mother said everything was under control for dinner, so I climbed the ladder to the loft and turned on the big built-in ceiling fan, which was all that made the loft bearable in mid-summer. Then I opened the wooden shutters we closed in the morning to keep out the sun; they also kept out the breeze. The sun was well on the other side of the house now, so between the fan stirring the air and the ocean breeze coming in the windows I could sit on the edge of my cot and be moderately comfortable.

We each had a wooden box under our bed for our special junk, and I pulled mine out and picked up one of my notebooks. Some of the words Grandfather had read me were weaving around in my head.

I thought I'd try a fugue-type poem, since Mother has made us fond of fugues with their haunting, recurring themes. I started with a ballade, but it didn't work, so I fished around in my box for my journal. I didn't know why, but I found it difficult to write about the morning with Leo. There was something so intensely private about our crying together that it seemed a violation even to write it out in my journal, which is a dumping place for me, and definitely not for publication. But I knew that it was important, so I simply set it down. And I wrote about the afternoon with Zachary, again just setting down the bald facts. It was, I felt, a very dull entry.

It was the same thing when I tried to write about Adam. What was there to say about Adam? Not much. That he was working at the Marine Biology Station with John and that they were good friends and he was coming for dinner. That I'd met him at Commander Rodney's funeral. That he'd said I was a dolphiny person.

I wrote it all down, but I didn't say what any of it *meant*, and I felt frustrated, so I turned back to poetry, this time a rondel, and at last words started to flow.

A great ring of pure & endless light
Dazzles the darkness in my heart
And breaks apart the dusky clouds of night.
The end of all is hinted in the start.

When we are born we bear the seeds of blight;
Around us life & death are torn apart,
Yet a great ring of pure & endless light
Dazzles the darkness in my heart.

It lights the world to my delight.
Infinity is present in each part.
A loving smile contains all art.
The motes of starlight spark & dart.
A grain of sand holds power & might.
Infinity is present in each part,

And a great ring of pure & endless light
Dazzles the darkness in my heart.

It wasn't great poetry, but it was better than the nonwriting I was doing in my journal. And I thought Grandfather might like it, so I made a fair copy for him.

I felt warm and sleepy, and stretched out on my cot for a nap.

3

John and Adam got home about five-thirty and immediately changed to trunks to go swimming. Adam's
trunks were zebra-striped and showed off his tan. And
his lean, long body. He had strong shoulders and arms
and narrow hips and looked like a statue of a Greek
charioteer I'd seen in an art book.

I made the salad while Rob grated the cheese and
Suzy set the table, and when John and Adam got back
we all sat around on the porch for Cokes or whatever
anybody wanted to drink, and Mother put a plate out
with the cheese she'd bought. We didn't feel hurried,
and it must have been well after seven, when most of
the Islanders were long through dinner, and we were
still sitting around with our drinks, that John called out,
"Leo's coming along on his bike. Were you expecting
him, Vicky?"

Suzy said, "I didn't set a place for him."

"I wasn't expecting him."

We all watched as Leo jumped off his bike and
came panting up to the screened porch. All I could
think of was that something else awful must have happened, and then I realized that if it were an emergency
Leo would have phoned, instead of biking all the way.

"Come in, Leo," Mother called. "Welcome."

Leo came up the porch steps, saying, "Hi," and looked at the round table set for dinner. "You're just about to eat and I'm interrupting."

"We're in no rush," Mother assured him. "If you haven't had dinner, why don't you join us?"

"We've just finished," Leo panted. "While we were eating—that's what I wanted to talk about, and I wanted to talk to you all, so I thought I'd bike over."

"Sit down," Daddy ordered. "You must have biked at top speed. You're all out of breath."

Leo pulled out a handkerchief and mopped his face, which was red from exertion.

"Hey, Leo," John said, "you remember Adam Eddington. We're working at the lab together."

They said "Hi" to each other and Leo put his damp handkerchief away.

"What happened at dinner?" I was sitting on the wicker swing, and he came and sat beside me.

"Your friend Zachary Gray came to call on us."

"What?" John's voice was loud.

"The fink—" Suzy started.

"No," Leo broke in. "He came to apologize. He found out about Dad only late yesterday. It must have been a terribly hard thing for him to do, to come to us that way."

"Only found out yesterday," John expostulated. "What're you talking about? What'd he come apologize about?"

I hadn't told anybody except Grandfather about Zachary; for one thing, there hadn't been time; so now I said, "Okay, John was right. It was Zachary in the sailboat, but he nearly died. And when he was in intensive care in the hospital they didn't tell him about Commander Rodney—I mean, when you're in intensive care all that happens is you get intensively cared for—" I stopped to catch my breath.

"So, then what?" Suzy demanded.

"When he got out of intensive care, Mr. Gray didn't want him told because he thought it might make him relapse . . ."

I thought I heard Suzy mutter to John, "Zachary wouldn't relapse. He wouldn't give a hoot."

I didn't want to fight in front of Adam and Leo, so I said, "He's a lot more upset about his mother than he lets on."

"So who told him about Commander Rodney?" John asked.

"And when?" Suzy added.

I hated all this. "He said that after he saw us yesterday afternoon something made him wonder and ask some questions, and that's how he found out."

Suzy started to speak, but Daddy shushed her. "I see."

Nobody asked why Zachary was so dumb with a sailboat, and Grandfather didn't say anything. Neither did I. Enough was enough.

Leo put his hand down on the canvas cushion of the swing, so that our fingers touched. He had obviously sensed Suzy's and John's antagonism toward Zachary. "Hey, Zachary was extremely nice, he really was. I mean, it can't have been easy to come to us, after—after everything. He told us that he knew there wasn't anything he could do for us, but he knew that Dad had saved his life, and he would try to make it worth saving. Mom liked him." After a second, he added, "So did I."

I looked at Grandfather, but he was looking out at

the sky, rosy with afterglow. Did Zachary really mean that? Or was he just trying to ingratiate himself with the Rodneys? But Zachary had never been one to bother ingratiating himself with anyone. And just as he pretended to be less touched by his mother's death than he really was, so maybe he was more upset by the Commander's death than he'd led me to believe.

Leo said to Daddy, "He also said that you'd tried to talk sense into him last summer, to make him take care of his health, and he hadn't always kept his word to you, but now he's really going to try."

I'd changed a lot during the past year. Why shouldn't Zachary have changed and grown up, too? I could tell by John's skeptical raising of his eyebrows that he didn't believe all that Zachary had told the Rodneys. I did.

Mother said, lightening the charged atmosphere, "Suzy, be an angel and put in the spaghetti and give it a good stir and then set the timer. Oh—and put the big colander in the sink so it'll be there for me when the buzzer goes off." Leo stood up. "Don't take off, Leo. That wasn't a hint for you to go. Stay as long as you like."

Suzy went into the kitchen and Leo sat beside me again. "I also wanted you to know, Vicky, that before Zachary came, I talked to Mom about going to Columbia next year, and you were right, she's determined for me to go."

"Hey, Leo," John said, "both Adam's parents teach at Columbia, and that's where he grew up, just a few blocks from where we lived last year. Talk about coincidence."

"Grandfather says there's no such thing as coincidence," I said, and looked at him.

Grandfather's lips quirked into a small smile. "The pattern is closely woven."

Adam, who had been silent all through the discussion about Zachary, spoke up. "You really think there's a pattern, sir?"

"It seems evident to me."

"What does that do to free will?" John asked.

"Not a thing. Any one of us can cause changes in the pattern by our responses of love or acceptance or resentment." He held a thin hand out toward Leo. "You're finding that out, aren't you? And your mother. Her response is always on the side of life. She's going back to nursing, isn't she?"

"How'd you know!" Leo exclaimed.

"I know Nancy Rodney."

"You're right about her going back to nursing." Leo still looked at Grandfather bemusedly. "She's going to the mainland to the hospital for a refresher course, and the visiting nurse on the Island's retiring in January, and Mom thinks she can get the post."

"Splendid," Daddy applauded. "I've a feeling your mother's an admirable nurse. She has a very special way of inspiring confidence."

"My mom's quite something," Leo agreed. "And during the time she has to be on the mainland, Jacky and I can take her over in the morning and bring her home at night. It'll all be in the day's work for us. At first when Mom talked about working again I was dead against it, but she made me see that it will be much better for her than sitting around doing nothing, and as you said, Dr. Austin, she's a good nurse and she knows it, and she said she'd been thinking about it anyhow, now that we're old enough so that we don't need her at home all the time." He stood up again. "I really do have to go. I told Mom and the kids I wouldn't stay long. Thanks for being here when I need you."

Suzy came back out. "What's your rush?"

"Jack and I have to be up and out before dawn. We have a fishing party from the Inn. My mom's going to go back into nursing, Suzy."

"Super! I set the timer, Mother. Ten minutes."

"Vicky—" Leo reached for my hand, then didn't take it. "I've got a full rest of the week, but maybe we could do something on Monday? Take a picnic or go to a movie or something?"

"Sure," I said. "Give me a ring."

"I will. But not with a diamond in it. Not yet." And he rushed off.

"Gross," was Suzy's comment.

"Didn't think Leo had it in him," was John's.

"Seems like an okay guy," was Adam's. "Must be a really rough time for him right now."

—He's growing up, I thought.—Does it take something terrible to make someone like Leo grow up?

Suzy plunked herself on the floor by Mother's chair. "May I have a sip of your drink?" She sipped and handed the glass back. "And what do you think about Zachary going to the Rodneys'? I don't believe it."

"Don't believe he went?" I asked.

"Or don't believe what he said?" John asked.

"Both. I mean, if I'd been responsible for someone's death I wouldn't go rushing to the family."

"He didn't exactly rush," I defended, "and I think he really meant what he said. Give him a chance, for a change."

"Why should I?" Suzy demanded. "He's the pits. And I don't want to see him, that's all. If it weren't for Zachary, Commander Rodney would be alive."

Before Daddy could speak, to my surprise Adam cut in. "Wait a minute. You can't pile a load of guilt on someone like that."

Suzy looked her stubbornest. "It was his fault, wasn't it?"

"Suzy," Daddy remonstrated, "we've been through this too many times already. I thought you'd taken in some of the things I said."

"I still blame him." She scowled. "And so did Vicky, until it turned out to be her precious Zachary."

Before I could think of a response, Adam said, "I don't mean to butt in, but I have to. You can't hindsight that way. When something happens, it happens, and you have to accept it and go on from there. I know that. I know it from personal experience." He spoke with quiet intensity.

"But if the boat hadn't capsized—"

"The heart attack could have happened while he was weeding the garden," Daddy said. "Adam is right."

I could see that Suzy was dying to ask Adam what his personal experience had been, and I knew that John, if not Mother and Daddy, would jump on her if she did. I guess she knew that, too, because she turned away without saying anything more.

Grandfather pulled himself up from the couch, sliding Ned from his lap. "Excuse me a minute. I won't be long." He walked toward the kitchen, Ned following and rubbing against his legs. Mother's always been worried about Ned tripping him, but Grandfather says that he and Ned know each other's ways. "You all right, Father?" Mother's voice was calm, but there was anxiety under it. And I noticed that Grandfather was walking more slowly than he used to.

"Just want to get something," he called back.

"He wants to read us something from a book, I'll bet," I explained to Adam. "Whenever we have an argument about anything, Grandfather has something in a book that settles it, or at least makes us ask some new questions. And in spite of all his books, he knows exactly in which stall and on what shelf every single one is, and what's in it."

"What'll it be this time?" Mother asked.

"Shakespeare," Suzy said.

"Einstein," John said.

"Could be the Bible," Daddy added.

Grandfather came out with a paperback book. "It's by Elie Wiesel." He riffled through the pages. "It's not quite as pertinent as I thought, but it will do. *Adam thus bequeathed us his death, not his sin . . . We do not inherit the sins of our fathers, even though we may be made to endure their punishment. Guilt cannot be transmitted. We are linked to Adam only by his memory, which becomes our own, and by his death, which foreshadows our own. Not by his sin."* . . .

"Hey, I like that; that's interesting." Adam's face lit up. "What's the book, sir?" he asked.

"*Messengers of God*, about some of the Old Testament characters, not only your—" He frowned slightly. "You're Adam's namesake. What's he to you? What's the opposite

75

of namesake?" He rubbed the heel of his hand across his forehead. "I can't think, I can't think—"

I saw Mother looking at him worriedly. "It'll probably come to you at two in the morning, Father."

He nodded. "It's a fascinating book, though there are some sections I'd love to argue with him, especially when he writes about what Christians think, which by and large is far from what I think." He turned a few pages. "Here's something else in the Adam chapter that I like. Listen well, young Adam. *He had the courage to get up and begin anew . . . As long as he lived . . . victory belonged not to death, but to him . . . It is not given to man to begin; that privilege is God's alone. But it is given to man to begin again—and he does so every time he chooses to defy death and side with the living."*

A shadow seemed to move across Adam's face. Then: "I learned that the hard way, but I learned it. Hey, may I borrow that book?"

"How'd you—" Suzy started.

John shut her up by cutting across her words. "When I'm through with it."

Unrepressed, Suzy said, "And all this stuff about man being privileged to start again is very sexist. What about women?"

Mother laughed. "Correct me if I'm wrong, Father, but doesn't the Bible say, *So God created man in his own image, in the image of God created he him; male and female?*"

"That's right," Grandfather corroborated.

"So we females are half of mankind, Suzy, and don't let inverse sexism cheat you of your fair share."

"Oh—okay." She did not sound convinced.

"So," I ventured, "maybe Zachary can begin again?"

"I doubt it," John muttered.

"Give him a chance, John," Mother said.

"Nancy Rodney's doing that, isn't she?" Grandfather said. "If she can give him a chance, I think the rest of us can, too."

I looked at him gratefully. "She's giving Zachary a chance, and she's beginning again herself, in going back to nursing. It ought to be going forward to nursing, oughtn't it?"

Grandfather had been turning the pages. "One more thing. This is for young Leo." He looked about, as though surprised at not finding Leo, then turned back to the book. "*Suffering, in Jewish tradition, confers no privileges. It all depends on what one makes of that suffering. It is possible to suffer and despair an entire lifetime and still not give up the art of laughter.*" . . .

Adam was looking at Grandfather, his lips slightly parted. He seemed to be taking what Grandfather read very personally, and I was as curious as Suzy.

"Wiesel knew what he was talking about," Grandfather said. "He survived the hell of Nazi concentration camps and the loss of almost everyone he loved, and yet he somehow or other kept the gift of laughter."

"Oh, wow," Suzy said. "Jacky's going to do okay. We had a good time today in spite of—of everything. And we laughed some, too."

"Leo and I—" I started, and didn't have to finish, because Suzy said, "I thought you didn't like Leo."

"I didn't. Until today. He's not nearly as much of a slob as I thought. We had a good time. We really did. But we didn't do much laughing."

"Tears need to come first," Grandfather said softly, just

to me. How did he know? He went on, speaking to everybody, "Who was it who said, *It was by the force of gravity that Satan fell?*" Again he pushed the palm of his hand against his forehead. "I'm losing my memory . . ."

John spoke lightly. "Join the club."

Grandfather dropped his hand to his knee. "Gravity and levity—wherever there's laughter, there is heaven. Real laughter, that is, not scornful or cynical laughter." He handed John the book. "Here. But I want it back when you're through."

"I'm very reliable about returning books. And I'll vouch for Adam. That is, I'll see to it that he gives it back when he's through."

"I'm pretty reliable about books, too," Adam assured him.

"Look!" Suzy pointed, and there was Rob, curled up beside Rochester in the corner, sound asleep.

Daddy laughed. "We can hardly blame him. That was pretty heavy conversation for a seven-year-old."

"Or a thirteen-year-old," Suzy commented.

"You held your own." Adam smiled at her.

Maybe it was a pretty heavy conversation for a lot of people, but it didn't seem to bother Adam, and that made my heart lift.

The buzzer in the kitchen rang, loud and shrill.

"Come help me, Vicky," Mother said, and we went into the kitchen.

When we gathered around the table, with the candles lit under the hurricane globes, we all held hands and sang grace. I wondered how Adam would feel, but I looked down at the table and not across at him. And then I heard his voice, and he was singing with John, in a good, strong baritone.

I wondered if we were really as peculiar a family as Zachary thought. On the other hand, I didn't think Zachary and his family were that average, either. Our family is our family and I've always taken us completely for granted, and I was glad Adam seemed to take us for granted, too, us kids, and our parents, and our grandfather, who talked about gravity and levity and heaven and all the things Zachary said nobody talked about.

I looked up and Adam was eating and Suzy was asking him something about his family.

He reached for the Parmesan and spooned it liberally onto his spaghetti. "I'm an only, and since both my parents are academics, I've lived pretty exclusively in an adult world. I think I missed out on a lot." And he smiled on us all.

"What are you working on this summer?" Daddy asked Adam.

"Oh, I do have a project going, and like John, I'm a general bottle washer. This is my summer for no excitement whatsoever. And I hope those aren't famous last words."

"I hope not, too," Mother said. "We've all had enough excitement to last us a long time."

John explained, "Adam's much more than a bottle washer; that's me. He's into other bottles, the bottlenosed dolphin."

"I thought you were working on starfish," Daddy said. "Didn't you work with Dr. O'Keefe last summer?"

"Yes, sir. But this summer I've asked if I can do a special project."

Suzy asked, "Are the dolphins in pens?"

"For a while. Jeb—Dr. Nutteley, my boss—never keeps them penned for more than six months. Then he lets them back out to sea."

"You mean so they won't be corrupted?"

"This is Suzy's year to be down on humanity," John said.

"If humanity can club a thousand innocent porpoises to death, do you wonder I'm down on it?" Suzy demanded.

I saw Adam wince and knew he felt as terrible about the porpoises as Suzy did.

"Nature isn't all that pure and noble," John told her.

"Isn't it?"

"Nature is red in tooth and claw."

"Who says?"

"Alfred Lord Tennyson. And it's true."

"That still doesn't excuse clubbing porpoises and being greedy about oil, and wars and murder and polution and everything people do."

Adam looked at her thoughtfully. "There've been, and still are, some pretty good people, Suzy."

"A few."

"It's those few who make it all worthwhile. Like my boss this summer, for instance. The Marine Biology Station is loosely connected to the Coast Guard, but Jeb Nutteley isn't having anything to do with experiments which would manipulate dolphins, or use them in ways that are contrary to their nature."

"Like what?" Suzy demanded.

Adam paused, as though deciding what to say. "Well—not by the Coast Guard but other agencies, there've been experiments in training dolphins to detect submarines, which maybe is all right. But there've also been experiments in training dolphins to carry a bomb to an enemy submarine, to blow it up, a kamikaze act."

Suzy let out a yelp of outrage.

"It's vile," Adam agreed. "And Dr. Nutteley won't have anything to do with that kind of thing. Experiments in using dolphins to save life is something else again. If a dolphin can lead us to a ship in distress, or a lifeboat with people in it who need to be rescued, that's okay."

"What about dolphin shows," Mother asked, "where they jump through hoops and play baseball and do tricks?"

"It's not as bad as clubbing them," Suzy said. "But isn't it sort of ig—ig—"

"Ignominious?" John suggested.

"Yeah. Humiliating."

"I'm not sure," Adam replied. "I've given it a good bit of thought—or at least Jeb Nutteley has, though we don't teach the dolphins any tricks. We're just trying to learn how to communicate with them. But do you think it's ignominious or humiliating for a ballet dancer to dance in public? Or an actor to perform? Or for a musician to give a concert? The dolphins do seem to enjoy being performers; according to Jeb, they really get a lot of fun out of it. Hey, if anybody urged me I'd have another helping of spaghetti. And some of that super salad."

I was glad I'd made the salad.

Mother filled his plate with spaghetti and sauce and passed him the salad, but Suzy wasn't about to be deflected. "Adam, could I come over and see the dolphins?"

Adam hesitated.

And Rob was asking, "Me, too?"

Adam twirled spaghetti skillfully around the tines of his fork. "Maybe I'd better ask you one at a time. One of our dolphins is about to pup and Jeb doesn't encourage mobs of visitors."

"Then could I come? Please?" Suzy looked all golden and fringed gentian eyes, and at thirteen she was (as Zachary had once pointed out) way ahead of me.

So I wasn't prepared to have Adam say, calmly and firmly, "I think next week, Suzy. I'd already planned to ask Vicky to come over tomorrow." He looked across the table at me. "Okay?"

"Sure. Yes. I'd love to. I'm not a scientist like Suzy and John—but I'd absolutely love to."

Grandfather smiled on me. "You can write a new poem for me. I very much like the one you wrote this afternoon, Victoria."

Grandfather never calls me Victoria. Victoria is Mother, and I'm Vicky, so there won't be any confusion. I looked at Mother and Mother was looking at Grandfather. And Grandfather's hand had gone up to his forehead again.

But Adam asked with interest, "So you're a poet?"

"Not yet. Maybe one day. I sometimes write verses."

"You know what, that doesn't surprise me. When we get to know each other a little better, I'll ask to see some of your poems, okay?"

Poems are private, and I appreciated his wanting to wait. That was nice, really nice.

Daddy pushed back a little from the table. "If we all pitch in and do the dishes, we'll have time for some singing. Go get your guitar, Victoria, and the kids and I'll take the dishes out to the kitchen."

It didn't take us all that long. Grandfather doesn't have a dishwasher, but the men brought everything out to the kitchen and I washed and John dried and Suzy and Daddy put things away and Rob and Adam wiped off the table and the counter.

And then we were back on the porch, to catch whatever ocean breeze came across the water on this hot night. Rob's hair was damp with heat.

"If it's like this at the ocean, what do you suppose it's like in the city?" Daddy asked the world at large. "Guitar tuned, Victoria?"

"Adequately." Mother twiddled the little knob for one of the strings. "There. That's better. What'll we start with?"

"You start," Daddy said. "How about *Come unto these yellow sands*?"

When Mother had finished, nobody said anything. I was sitting on the floor by Grandfather's couch, leaning back against it. Daddy and Rob were on the swing. John and Adam had their chairs tilted back, leaning against the porch rail. Suzy sat on the floor near Mother. The fan whirred slowly above us, stirring the sluggish air. A moth beat its pale wings against the screen. There was no need for words.

Mother plucked a few chords, then sang another song from one of Shakespeare's plays, *When that I was and a little tiny boy*. She'd sung us those songs as lullabies, and we all loved them. They made me feel safe and comforted and secure.

When she put down her guitar this time, Adam said, "Mrs. Austin, that's tremendous! You could have been a professional!"

"She was," Suzy told him proudly. "She sang in a night club."

"Very briefly." Mother smiled. "I met your father and that was the end of my career."

"But it didn't *have* to be." Suzy was vehement. "You could have gone on if you'd wanted to. Daddy didn't make you stop."

"Of course he didn't, Suzy. I stopped singing in public because I made other choices. And"—as though to answer Suzy's unspoken but almost audible arguments—"they were my own choices. Society didn't force them on me; neither did your father. It's inverse sexism again not to allow me the freedom to make the choice I did."

Daddy laughed. "Victoria, I do love you when you get up on the soapbox."

"And other times, too, I hope." Mother laughed back.

Suzy continued her own train of thought. "Mrs. Rodney's going back to nursing."

Mrs. Rodney was going back to nursing largely because her husband was dead and she needed the money. But Leo had said she'd been thinking about it anyhow . . .

Mother said calmly, "I've sometimes wondered what I'll do when you kids are all out of the nest. But it won't be to go back to singing. I can put over a song, but I don't have a real voice. We'll just have to wait and see." She looked at Rob, leaning sleepily against Daddy. "I still have a few years before I have to worry. Okay, now, let's all sing together." Her fingers moved over the guitar strings again, the merry strains of *The Arkansas Traveler.*

So we all joined in.

And while we sang I remembered that Adam was going to introduce me to his dolphins the next day.

And I wondered where Zachary was and what he was doing.

4

In the morning I biked over to the station with John, my bathing suit rolled in a towel and stuffed in my wicker bike basket, because Adam had said something about maybe going for a swim.

For the first time I found myself wishing I'd paid more attention to science in school and less to composition and music and things like that. I didn't know anything at all about dolphins, not even the difference between a dolphin and a porpoise, though I thought that porpoise was a generic name which included several kinds of dolphins. At breakfast I'd thought of asking and then decided against it. Anything I was going to learn about cetaceans (as John called them) was going to have to come from Adam. My excitement about going on a date with Adam was very different from the way I felt when I went out with Zachary. With Zachary I was excited and nervous and somehow playing a role, almost like when we used to go up to the attic in Thornhill to the costume trunks and put on plays. With Zachary I wore at least an imaginary costume, because I was trying to live up to his expectations of me, and maybe that was why I felt uncomfortable with him at the same time that I was thrilled. And going out with Adam was even more different than going out with Leo. Leo was turning out to be human, but I didn't think doing something with Leo was going on a date.

Adam was different from anybody I'd ever known. He wasn't spectacularly gorgeous, like Zachary, but he had a kind of light within that drew me to him like a moth to a candle. At the funeral his light was doused, and I felt a deep hurt within him, beyond the hurt caused by Commander Rodney's death. And then, when he talked about dolphins, he was alight and alive and I wanted to know why. And I didn't think this was going to be easy, because there was something—reticent, I guess is what I mean—about him.

He was living in a kind of barracks, a long, grey building up on stilts, which would make it cool in summer and cold in winter. He was sitting on the steps, waiting for us. He had on cut-off blue jeans, and his legs were long and tan. Old sneakers, with the ties broken and knotted. A faded blue T-shirt. He smiled, and the light came on inside him.

He jumped down the steps and came over to show me where to park my bike in the long rack in front of the lab, which was a building like the one he lived in. Inside the lab was a smell of ocean and fish and Bunsen burners. There were lots of tanks with various species of fish, and what seemed as many starfish as Grandfather has books. Most of them were growing arms: fascinating.

John went off to the other end of the lab to check on a tank of lizards. I could see his boss, Dr. Nora Zand, talking to him in an excited way, and John was peering into the tank. Adam and I stood by a big tank in which there were a dozen or more starfish, each with an arm partly regenerated.

"Wouldn't it be terrific," I suggested, "if people could do that? Then surgeons wouldn't have to pull out their knives so quickly."

"It's not outside the realm of possibility." Adam was looking into the tank, studying the starfish. "Human beings and starfish are both chordates and come from the same phylum."

I wasn't sure what that meant. "You mean they're sort of our distant ancestors, way back on the family tree?"

"Yah." Adam moved on to the next tank, and I followed. At the end of the lab, John was sitting on a high stool, writing on a clipboard. Dr. Zand had gone. Adam bent over the tank. "So what we learn about starfish and how they regenerate could someday apply to human beings. You're quite right, it would revolutionize medicine."

"Isn't it more what things ought to be, rather than knives and stuff?"

"Probably."

"How much do we know about it?"

"The central nerve disc is vital. We've been able to make some isolated arms regenerate by implanting them with part of the central nerve disc, which seems to provide the electric energy for regeneration. But we haven't made that much progress. Starfish have fascinated people for centuries. The first formal paper on regeneration was written by an Italian, Lazzaro Spallanzani, way back in 1768. We know a little more than he did, but not as much as you might expect."

I stared down at a starfish with all five arms, the fifth not quite complete, still in the process of growing itself back. "We've been spending more time on machines and bombs and industry than we have on things like starfish, haven't we? Has anybody tried anything with people? I mean, do we have an equivalent of the central nerve disc?"

He gave me an oblique look. "We don't know all that much about it yet. Electrical charges have been used in stimulating broken bones to heal. But in the wrong hands it could be disastrous, producing malignancies and all kinds of horrors. Come along and I'll show you the dolphin pens. Got your bathing suit?"

I indicated the rolled-up towel.

We paused as we passed John, who pointed at a lizard in the tank; regeneration was just barely visible in a severed foreleg.

"Terrif," Adam said. "We're off to Una and Nini. See you later."

I assumed Una and Nini had to be dolphins. We left the lab building and walked downhill toward the water. One of the loveliest things about Seven Bay Island is that each of the seven bays has several coves, some quite large and open, some small and protected, like Grandfather's cove. The path down to the beach from the lab hairpinned and zigzagged instead of descending precipitously like the one to Grandfather's cove, so it was easier walking. Even so, the sun beat down on us and I could feel sweat trickling down the small of my back. We headed for a long and narrow cove in which several pens had been built. We paused at the first pen, where two pale-grey dolphins were leaping up into the air, shedding sparkles of water, while a middle-aged man with a balding head tossed them fish from a bucket. I thought he was the man who had cried at Commander Rodney's funeral. His baldness was sort of like a monk's tonsure, a dark fringe all around his head, with a pink circle of skin at the crown. He had brown spaniel eyes and I liked him.

He saw us, gave me a quick look, and called out, "Hey, kids, want to take over?"

"Sure, Jeb. This is John Austin's sister Vicky with me today. Vicky, this is Dr. Nutteley, my boss."

We shook hands, and his eyes met mine in a brief smile, and then Dr. Nutteley took off at a jog trot for the next pen.

Adam reached into the bucket and took out a silver wriggling fish and tossed it high into the air. "Get it, Una!" One of the dolphins leapt completely out of the water and caught the fish in mid-air. Adam threw another fish across the pen. "Get it, Nini!" The other dolphin dove down and in less time than I would have thought possible, even knowing how swift dolphins are supposed to be, she surfaced with the fish in her mouth.

"You've probably heard," Adam said, "that according to the laws of aerodynamics it's impossible for a bumblebee to fly."

I nodded. "But it flies. I like that."

"Okay, and according to the laws of hydronomics, it's impossible for a dolphin to swim as swiftly as it does. Nobody's figured out why the bumblebee can fly, but we think that with dolphins it's something to do with their delicate skin, which ripples with the movement of the water, and also sheds, far more swiftly than we human beings shed our skin. Una and Nini, I think I told you last night, are bottle-noses. The absolutely fascinating thing"—as he was talking, his light was really turned on, bright as the sun—"is that dolphins were once land animals, mammals like other land creatures."

"Aren't they still mammals?" I watched, fascinated, as Una and Nini bobbed up and down in front of us, half their sleek bodies out of water, as they chirruped at us for more fish.

"Yah, they're mammals. They aren't fish. They're small whales who left the land somewhere in prehistory, and returned to the sea. Here, Vicky, you toss them a fish."

I didn't want him to think I was chicken. Those fish wriggling in that bucket of water were still alive. I'd never been fishing, and never had I touched a live fish. I was afraid they'd be slippery, afraid they'd slide out of my fingers before I could throw them. To mask my fear, as much from myself as from Adam, I said, "Didn't someone call the sea the primordial womb from which all life came?" And while I was speaking I reached into the bucket and grabbed a fish and threw it. "Get it, Una!" And another. "Get it, Nini!"

I don't think Adam realized how nervous I was. He said, "All life started in those early oceans as far as we know, and then when weather and land masses more or less stabilized, some of the ocean creatures ventured ashore and became land creatures." He reached into the bucket and pulled out a small fish, but he didn't throw it. Instead, he leaned so far over I thought he might lose his balance and fall in. "Nini!" he called. Then he held the tail of the fish in his teeth, and Nini jumped up and took it from his mouth, delicately, gently.

Delicate and gentle or not, I hoped he wouldn't ask me to do that.

"Dolphins don't chew their food," he said. "They swallow the fish whole."

91

I had seen Nini's open mouth. "They appear to have very formidable teeth."

"They use their teeth to grasp the fish. They don't have fingers, after all." He tossed a fish to Una. "As far as I know, whales and others of their kind, like these dolphins, are the only land creatures who left the land and returned to the sea."

"Mermaids," I said, without stopping to think how unscientific I was going to sound.

But, instead of putting me down, Adam said, "Some people think mermaids came from porpoises, and their singing sounds like dolphins chirruping. Dolphins have always fascinated human beings. It's amazing, for instance, how so much that Aristotle wrote about dolphins is true. How could he have known all that he knew, way back then?" He tossed the dolphins a few more fish, looked into the nearly empty bucket, and turned to me. "Give Una and Nini the rest of the fish."

I didn't exactly like it, but I did it, and without flinching, because I *did* like Una and Nini. In a funny way, they reminded me of Rochester, not in looks, of course, but in essence.

When the fish were gone, we moved on to the next pen, where Dr. Nutteley was studying three dolphins.

"Next week Ynid"—Adam pointed to one of them—"is going to give birth. The other two you might call her midwives. Dolphins can't deliver alone. They're communal creatures."

"Like us."

"In that way."

I looked at him, and his eyes had that deep inward look. "You mean," I ventured, "we hear about man's in-

92

humanity to man, but never dolphin's inhumanity to dolphin?"

He nodded, without speaking.

"What about John's *Nature is red in tooth and claw*?"

"It doesn't seem to apply to dolphins."

"They do eat live fish," I pointed out regretfully.

"Yah, but I can't see that it's any worse than if they were dead and cooked. One way or another, they're eaten. And there's no getting around the fact that all life lives at the expense of other life." He stared at the three dolphins for a long moment. "Porpoises are warm-blooded, like us, not cold-blooded, like fish. And if you look carefully at their flippers you can see that they're really made-over paws; they're not fish's fins. They have the bone structure of forelimbs." He moved along, waving goodbye to Dr. Nutteley, and I followed, clutching my towel, which had got quite damp from splashes while we were feeding Una and Nini. I didn't know where he was taking me now, but I didn't ask; I just followed.

"What really gets me"—he paused on the sandy path which led in a rambly way across the dunes—"is that when the dolphin returned to the sea, he had to give up what once may well have been hands." He held his hands toward me and I looked at him as he stood at the crest of a dune, silhouetted against the incredible blue brightness of sky, so it was difficult to see his expression. "The hand with its opposable thumb—can you imagine what it would be like not to be able to pick anything up, not to be able to hold anything and look at it?"

I, too, held out my hand, putting thumb and forefinger together. "Yesterday when I was swimming with

Leo we saw a dolphin leaping, and it looked so free and—and joyous. Do you suppose way back millions of years ago the dolphin had to *choose* to give up its hands in order to have that kind of freedom?"

"I don't know." Adam started toward the ocean, so that the dolphin pens were hidden by an arm of dune. We were in a larger cove, a wide, gentle curve of sand. "I don't even know if I think it would be worth it, at that price." He stretched out his fingers again. "Without writing, writing down words on stone or papyrus or parchment or paper or microfilm so they can be kept, we wouldn't have any history. And without history there isn't any future."

"Word of mouth?" I suggested. "Oral tradition?"

"It gets changed, like in the whispering game we played at kids' birthday parties."

"Someone whispers a sentence, and you pass it along, and in the end it comes out all garbled?"

He looked at me over his shoulder. "Yah, that's what happens to oral tradition unless someone comes along and sets it down."

"Oh, wow," I exclaimed. "I guess that's why Grandfather thought it was so important to write down the stories and traditions of the tribe he was living with. I never thought about it that way before."

"I didn't either, not till I began my project this summer. We take an awful lot for granted. Without hands, we wouldn't have any painting, or sculpture, or poetry."

I thought of Grandfather reading to me the day before: *I saw Eternity the other night like a great ring of pure and endless light.* And then I thought of the dolphins returning to the sea, and losing fingers and thumb and the ability to grasp, and Una and Nini and their loving smiles, and they seemed to me to be bathed in a deep but dazzling darkness.

Adam stood at the water's edge. "We wouldn't have any music, any symphonies or operas or even the songs we sang last night to your mother's guitar." We left the shallow cove and turned into a deeper half-moon of beach. "Jeb is making tape after tape of Una and Nini, to see whether or not their Donald Duck gabblings and their underwater whistlings are part of a real language, with a complex vocabulary, or whether it's all—I mean, do they think, or is it all instinct, the way it is with ants?"

I looked across the blinding glare of ocean disappearing into the horizon. "Ants never seem to me to be particularly happy."

"Yah, you have a point there. Dolphins undeniably have a great sense of fun. And humor is a sign of intelligence. You're quite a girl, Vicky. Before I—" He stopped and looked at me, probingly, and I waited for him to say something, and when he did, it wasn't at all what I had expected. "This Leo: are you his girlfriend?"

Why did Zachary and now Adam care about Leo and me? Me, Leo's girlfriend? Day before yesterday, I'd have been outraged.

"Are you?" Adam prodded.

"He's my friend," I said carefully. "But not my boyfriend. I don't know him that well."

"Don't you? Last night he surely looked at you the way someone looks at his girlfriend."

"Adam, I never even really talked to Leo till yesterday. We see the Rodneys when we come to visit Grandfather, the way we see lots of other people on the Island. Leo and I never had a conversation till he talked about his father dying, when we walked on the beach yesterday. I think maybe we can really be friends. But I'm not anybody's girlfriend."

"And what about Zachary?" Adam bent down and started unlacing his sneakers. His hair fell across his eyes.

"Zachary—I guess what I think I have to do with Zachary is give him a chance, the way we said last night." About Zachary, I wasn't ready to say anything more than that.

Adam looked up at me and grinned as he unlaced his other sneaker. "Friends. Friends are what make the world go round for me." He stood up, tying his already knotted laces together and hanging his sneakers about his neck. "John says you're a pretty good swimmer."

"I won't win any races, but I'm good at long distance. I mean, I can swim on and on forever as long as there isn't any rush."

"Long distance is what I want from you, not speed. When I asked you to come to the lab this morning, I wasn't sure how much I was—but now I think you—" And then he stopped.

He stopped for so long, and stood there on the beach, sneakers dangling about his neck, hands dropped by his sides, not moving, that finally I spoke to break the silence. "Another thing about dolphins not having hands—they can't take a gun or a harpoon and kill."

"Yah." A brief silence. "And here's another mystery: the dolphin's brain is forty percent larger than ours and just as complex."

I figured we were going to go swimming, so I

kicked off my sandals. "How much of the brain does the dolphin use? We use only a tiny portion of ours."

"Vicky."

I waited.

"Would you like to meet a dolphin?"

"You mean like Una and Nini?"

"I mean out at sea. Like the one you saw yesterday."

"Well—sure."

"You wouldn't be afraid?" He was looking at me, hard.

"I don't know." I couldn't pretend with him. "I don't think so—but—well, meeting a dolphin except in a pen never occurred to me."

"Will you swim out with me and try? If you're afraid, you can swim back. And he may not come, anyhow. I mean, this is something entirely new in my experiment with Basil."

"Basil?"

Suddenly his voice was brisk and business-like. He pointed to a large rock behind us, bigger than my rock in Grandfather's cove. "Basil's the dolphin who's my chief project this summer. There's your dressing room. Go behind the rock and put on your bathing suit. Then swim out and join me, but stay a few yards behind. I'm going to call Basil. He's a little bigger than Una and Nini, but don't let that worry you." He started to run toward the surf, then turned and called back, "The tide's coming in now and, anyhow, this is the safest bay on the Island." Then he splashed into the water.

It didn't take me long to change. I stood for a moment behind the shelter of the rock, feeling the fierce strength of the sun, and at the same time feeling cold because of what Adam had told me we were going to do. To calm myself I turned around slowly, looking, smelling, hearing. There was no steep cliff behind this cove, but a series of white rolling dunes, shadowed by pale beach grasses and the dark green of sea grapes. Above me sea gulls were whirling and mewling against the blue. The wind moved in the grasses and echoed the sound of waves moving gently into shore. I could see Adam swimming out, but there was no dark body leaping joyfully on the horizon, such as I had seen the day before with Leo. Adam had said it—Basil—might not come.

Did I want it to?

I walked slowly toward the water's edge. Adam's shorts and shirt and sneakers lay in a little clump on the sand. I moved past them and splashed through the shallow waves.

It was one thing to toss fish to Una and Nini, smiling at me from their pen—and I hadn't been exactly comfortable about that—and another to meet a dolphin face to face in the open sea.

I dove through an approaching wave and started to swim. I had managed to pick up a fish from the bucket in my bare hands and toss it to a dolphin. I could manage to look at a dolphin in the ocean just as well as I could look at Una and Nini in the pen, couldn't I? Adam had said to stay several yards behind him. I needn't get close.

I swam. As I neared Adam I could hear him making funny blowing sounds, something like air going slowly out of a balloon, and it was something like the sound I'd heard from Una and Nini. He was treading water, and I began to tread water, too, staying well behind him. He kept on making balloon sounds, and then he began a strange whistle. There was something magnetic about it. His face had its illuminated look, and I was so busy paying attention to him that I was taken completely by surprise when a great grey body rose in a swift arc just a few yards behind him, showing the pale pink of its belly, and disappeared into the sea. Then it surfaced, and there was a dolphin half out of the water, beaming at Adam, who swam swiftly toward it. The creature exuded friendliness. But I stayed where I was, a good distance away, treading water, while my heart thumped with excitement and fear. What would I do if that great animal stopped smiling and came at me?

Basil, I reassured myself. Adam said his name was Basil, and just the fact that he had a name made him less frightening. He was swimming around Adam in swift circles, and the long, sleek body seemed to be quivering with delight, much as Mr. Rochester's entire bulk trembles with joy when we come home after leaving him alone for an hour or so. My heart was still banging, but I was less afraid.

Adam put his arm around Basil with the same affectionate fearlessness with which Rob put his arm around the big Great Dane, and Basil rubbed close against Adam. I would like to have somebody, animal or human, feel about me like that. Not in the least subservient, but total.

For a few moments Adam and Basil swam together. Then the dolphin leapt above the surface, throwing spume in every direction so that I got showered, dove down and surfaced again, not far from me. I trod water furiously. I had not expected Basil to come so close. I had thought that I would be an observer only.

"He's curious about you," Adam said in a calm, quiet voice. "Don't be afraid of him, Vicky. He won't hurt you."

—How do you know? I wanted to ask. —He's still a wild creature. Suppose I frighten *him*? Suppose I don't have the right smell?

"Don't be afraid," Adam said again. "Touch him. Gently but firmly. Dolphins have extremely delicate skin, but once he realizes you won't hurt him, he'll make friends."

I wasn't going to say so to Adam, but I wasn't about to make the first move.

Basil nosed tentatively toward me, smiling benignly. Do dolphins ever frown? Very gently, he butted against me.

And suddenly I was not afraid. As clearly as though the dolphin had spoken to me, I understood that he wanted me to pet him. And I was, as clearly as I can express something that is really unexpressible, out on the other side of fear. I reached out and touched the top of his head, gently patting, then stroking. As I stroked, the eyes, one on each side of his beaming mouth, closed. He wriggled closer to me, and I kept on stroking.

Adam dove down, almost like a dolphin, and came up on the other side of Basil and me, shaking water from his head and wearing an expression of delight, and, I thought, of surprise. "He likes you. I thought he might."

I nearly asked, 'What would you have done if he

hadn't?' But Basil gave a wriggle that seemed to say, *Go on stroking me*, so I decided to save all questions till later.

"Tell me what he feels like to you," Adam urged.

How can anybody describe the feel of a dolphin? "Something strange, alien," I murmured, "like touching a creature from a different planet—and yet completely familiar, too, as though I've always known what a dolphin feels like. Do you suppose there are planets which are all water, and no land, and only dolphins and fish and no people?"

"Very likely." Adam was leaning back in the water, comfortably, almost as though he were sitting in a rocking chair. "Go on. What else does he feel like?"

I kept on stroking. "Like—like a balloon, but a balloon filled with something much heavier than air."

"What else? Anything familiar?"

"Like—like a wet inner tube, the kind kids use when they're learning to swim. And—and—what he feels most like is polished pewter, only pewter is rigid. Like *resilient* pewter."

"Terrif!" Adam applauded. "Resilient pewter. I like that. Jeb will appreciate that." And he added, "When I tell him."

The dolphin rolled over.

"He likes to have his chest scratched."

But I already knew why Basil had rolled over. I didn't know how I knew, but I knew. And I was no longer in the least afraid. I scratched under Basil's great jaw, and then a little farther down toward his chest, scratched gently, and something a little gritty, like dolphin dandruff—no, that's not right; dolphin pollen—came off on my fingers, but when I raised my hand out of the water there was nothing there, and no odor, either.

Basil bumped me, the way Ned butts his hard little head against you when he wants you to go on scratching, so I began again, asking, "What keeps coming off on my fingernails?"

"His skin. As I said, dolphins continually shed skin, and that's likely another reason they can swim faster than we think they ought to be able to, because they don't have the skin resistance to water that we do."

Again I lifted my hand from the water, but I couldn't see anything, and this time when I stopped scratching, Basil dove down, his great fluke flicking so that again I was drenched in spray, and appeared far beyond us, leaping up in a great and glorious arc before diving down again.

"He's gone to join his pod," Adam said.

"Pod?" I was still treading water and feeling more exhilarated than I have ever felt in my life.

"His—community, you might call it. Hey, Vicky, you were terrific. You were so terrific I can hardly believe it. You exceeded my wildest expectations. Let's swim in. I want to talk." And he turned and headed for shore.

Leo was a strong swimmer, but Adam's crawl was tidier. There was almost no splash as he cleaved through the water nearly as cleanly as Basil. I followed, not trying to keep up, but doing the Australian crawl because I like the respite of the scissors kick. And I was happy. Sometimes when you're happy you don't realize it till later. But swimming into shore after my meeting with Basil, I was shiningly aware that I was happy.

Adam was doing cartwheels along the edge of the

water. My cartwheels are floppy and inelegant, but his were perfect, as tidy as his swimming, and full of *joie de vivre*. When I splashed out of the water, he landed on his feet, beaming.

He led the way to a low dune in the shelter of a scrubby kind of tree. He spread his towel out in the shade, and we sat. He looked at me with his probing look. "Maybe I was taking a risk in having you meet Basil. I didn't tell Jeb I was going to do it, because I was positive he'd have told me not to. A dolphin in a pen is one thing; a dolphin in the wild is another. But I trust Basil. I thought he might ignore you completely, but I knew he wouldn't hurt you. And I did ask John."

"Has John met Basil?"

"Yes. But Basil's never stayed with John as long as he did with you—and the very first time, too. He wouldn't come near John the first few times. Are you sure you've never met a dolphin before?"

"Sure I'm sure. We saw the dolphin show at Sea World, and we went to the petting tank, but it was so crowded we couldn't get near."

"John thought you might be afraid."

"I was. Terrified. At first."

"But you didn't show it, not for a minute."

"Well—in a funny way Basil reminded me both of Mr. Rochester and Ned."

"So at least you've always been used to animals?"

"Sure. But none of them's ever talked to me the way Basil did." As soon as I said that, I realized how peculiar it sounded.

Adam pounced on it. "What do you mean?"

I shrugged. There was no way I could explain. "I just—it was just—I knew he was my friend. I knew—

I knew how he wanted me to scratch him. It was as though—oh, Adam, I don't know!" I felt totally frustrated that I couldn't put any of what I had felt into reasonable words.

"Have you read much about dolphins?"

"No."

"Has John talked to you much about them?"

"No. John's thing has always been space and astrophysics. And this summer he's talked about starfish some, but he always gets back to cosmology and dimensionless numbers and mass energy and stuff that's way over my head."

"How about your hearing?"

"My hearing? It's okay."

"I mean, did you *hear* Basil when you were petting him?"

I thought for a moment. "I don't remember. It was more like knowing what he wanted than hearing it. Though he was sort of chirruping, wasn't he?"

Adam had a twig and was drawing triangles in the sand. "When dolphins talk with each other, a great many of their sounds are supersonic, way beyond human range."

"Like birds?"

"Somewhat. And when Una and Nini are trying to communicate with Jeb they lower their sounds to within human range. Which shows consideration as well as intelligence. I was wondering about your hearing range."

"I can't hear birds any better than anybody else, so I guess it's just normal."

Adam broke his twig into small pieces. "If I'd been an objective observer this morning, I'd have said that you'd probably been in close contact with dolphins for years. I might even think you were lying to me, if it wasn't for John."

"Why would I lie?"

"You wouldn't," he assured me. "Let's dress and I'll take you along to the cafeteria. The food's horrendous, but you can't do much to ruin a hot dog." He ran swiftly to the hard sand near the water, stood on his head, balanced himself, and began waving his legs in great semaphore Vs.

He gave a little flip and landed on his feet. "Hey, Vicky—you can mention it to John, but I'd rather you didn't to anybody else."

I wanted to tell the entire world about my encounter with Basil.

But Adam said, "I'm going to tell Jeb, even if he yells at me after the fact. Basil is my special project for this summer, and Jeb's pretty well given me free rein. I report to him, but he doesn't make suggestions. He leaves it all to me." He grinned. "That's how I justified not telling him I was going to take you to meet Basil. So, for my project's sake, I really have to limit Basil to you and John."

I thought about Suzy, and her passion for animals, and what it would mean to her to stroke a dolphin. And at the same instant I felt a surge of jealousy when I thought Basil might prefer Suzy to me.

"You're thinking about your sister, aren't you?" Adam asked.

I looked at him in surprise. "How'd you know?"

"Last night she was pretty obvious about wanting to come over to the lab. After Ynid's had her baby I'll bring Suzy over to see all the dolphins in the pens."

"And Rob."

"Sure. Rob, too."

"I was feeling mean about Suzy," I said. "I didn't really want to have to share Basil with her. Suzy's—"

"Suzy's what?"

"I don't think I'm an idiot or a freak or anything, but Suzy did better in the Austin gene pool than I did."

"You're out of your mind," Adam said. "Suzy's got plenty going for her, you're right, but it's all out there, on the surface. I prefer to dig for gold. Let's go eat. The thing is, Victoria Austin, that I had a hunch you could help me with my dolphin project, and my hunch was more than right." He turned another cartwheel. "I'm glad you and Basil got along."

"So'm I."

The cafeteria was as bad as Adam said.

He looked at me and made a ferocious grimace. "Did I tell you they couldn't do much to ruin a hot dog? Wrong again. This is pure plastic."

He was right. "Is this where you eat all the time?"

"Where else? John and I don't get paid enough even to eat at a hamburger joint. Food is part of our pay check."

"But John comes home for dinner. Is it this bad in the evening?"

Adam smeared mustard and catsup on his hot dog. "I'm not writing home about the cuisine."

I looked around at the white-coated people sitting at the tables. Some were reading, some talking intently. Nobody seemed to be paying much attention to the food. I didn't see John. "Adam, how did you get to know Basil? I mean, he didn't just swim up to you and introduce himself, did he?"

"Getting to know Basil—or at least *a* bottle-nosed dolphin—was part of my project. Commander Rodney gave me the use of one of the small Coast Guard launches, and I'd go out to sea and then cut the motor and float there. Quite often I'd see dolphins playing at a distance, but they didn't come near me and I was about to give up and think I'd wasted all that time and energy for nothing. And then one afternoon Basil's pod came over to investigate."

I leaned on my elbows. "What'd you do?"

"Nothing much. I talked to them. And then— maybe you'll think it's wacky—but I sang to them."

"What'd you sing?"

"Oh, anything that came into my mind. Folk songs and rock and country—and then I talked to them again, and they made noises at me and then they all dove down and that was that."

It was easy for me to imagine Adam singing to a pod of dolphins in the same nice strong baritone I'd heard him use the night before. I liked the image. "And then what?"

"Then I came on back to the lab. And went out again the next day. No luck. They came again the third day, and then they began coming regularly. As soon as I'd cut the engine, they'd come over to me. And then I began to reach out to pet them, and, as you saw, Basil likes to have his chest scratched. One afternoon I was scratching him and—well, I'm sure he did it on purpose. I had to lean further and further out to reach him and suddenly I fell in."

"Were you scared?"

"It was so sudden I didn't have time to be scared. The others didn't come near me, only Basil. And that's how it began."

I shivered with pleasure.

A hand came down on my shoulder and I turned around and there was John, looking relieved. "You're okay."

"Sure. Oh, John, it was—I can't tell you how exciting it was."

"Okay," John said. "I'm glad it was exciting. But I've felt anxious ever since I told Adam he could take you out to meet Basil."

"Basil didn't hurt *you*, did he?" I demanded.

"No, but—"

"Cut it, you two," Adam said. "Vicky made a big hit with Basil. Are you sure you didn't tell her anything about him, John?"

John and I both started to protest, indignantly.

Adam apologized, "Sorry, sorry. Vicky just acted as though she'd been palling around with dolphins all her life."

John pulled out a chair. "Are you through, or shall I join you?"

"We're going to have ice cream. So join us. But don't have a hot dog."

"What else?"

"Ham and cheese?"

"They leave the plastic wrapping on both the ham and the cheese. Maybe I'll have a BLT."

"You won't find much B and the T won't be ripe and the L will be wilted."

"You can't win." John went off to get in line. Adam took our tray.

I felt relaxed and happy and definitely older than not-quite-sixteen. I liked this world in which John and Adam were living. I liked the fact that Adam was pleased and surprised at Basil's reaction to me.

Adam and John came back. Adam said, "Dr. Nutteley approved of Vicky."

"But he didn't say anything—"

"If he hadn't approved, he'd have said something. He sizes people up in less than a second. And you're part of my experiment, Vicky. John doesn't have the time to give—Dr. Nora's a hard taskmaster—and anyhow, you and Basil quite obviously tune in to each other. Can you come again?"

"I'd love to come again. As long as Mother doesn't need me to help with Grandfather."

"Dad told me he'd asked you not to take a job this summer so you can help out at home. But he didn't mean you couldn't ever get away."

"I can't think of anything I'd like better than being part of Adam's experiment."

"You're a good kid, Vic." John isn't one for giving compliments and I could feel myself flushing. "It's easiest for me, with my job keeping me busy and out of the house all day. I think Suzy's an idiot for not taking the job at the Woods', which would have paid her better than anything else she can get, but she'll get something, probably helping Jacky Rodney service the launch and being general girl Friday."

"Well, Suzy loves boats and machines and things like that."

"Sure," John said, "and it will give her a legitimate reason to make herself scarce around home."

I put down my ice-cream spoon. I'm the one John usually criticizes, not Suzy.

As though reading my mind, he said, "I'm not criticizing Suze. She has a healthy sense of self-preservation. And that's okay. If Nora wants me to stay late and do some extra work, I don't protest that I ought to get home to help out. So what I'm getting at is that it's you and Mother who have to be available for Grandfather."

"And Rob," I added.

"Sure. And Rob. But Rob has his own special way of handling the—oh, I guess you might call them major life problems."

"And I don't?"

"You're pretty vulnerable, Sis."

Adam said, "But that's one of the nicest things about her. It means she's very much alive."

I smiled him my thanks.

John nodded. "I'm pretty miffed that Basil took to Vicky faster than he did to me. But, Vic—you're the one Mother's going to need to lean on. Did you see the look in her eyes last night when Grandfather forgot, and called you Victoria?"

Adam spoke gently. "He's had his threescore years and ten and quite a bit more, Vicky. It's never easy, but it's comprehensible when someone has had a full life, like your grandfather."

I said slowly, "I don't want to be like those Immortalists in California, wanting to live forever, and going in for cryonics . . ."

"What's that?" Adam asked.

I looked at John and he told him, and I loved John because he didn't use it as an excuse to demolish Zachary. He ended, "I think it's easier to understand

Commander Rodney, buried here on the Island, than Mrs. Gray, frozen in California."

"When Grandfather—" I started, and could not go on.

"What Grandfather wants, and what Mother wants for him"—John's voice was level—"is to have it all as simple as possible. A plain pine box, and he'll be at the church, not in a funeral parlor, and be buried next to our grandmother. He says they'll be good for the land. That's a lot better than freezing him, trying to hold on to something which isn't there."

"You mean you agree with Zachary, and when you die it's *nada, nada, nada*?"

"No, Vicky, I didn't say that at all. But whatever it is, it won't be anything we can understand or talk about in the language of laboratory proof." He took his tray and stood up. "I've got to get back to work. Nora's waiting. Adam?"

"I'll walk Vicky out to her bike. Then I'm going to go report to Jeb."

John left from one door of the cafeteria, Adam and I from the other. We walked without talking till we came to the bike stand.

Then he said, "It's been a good morning for me, Vicky."

I was still feeling choky. "For me, too."

Adam gave me his probing look, the look I was beginning to think of as his scientist-looking-through-a-microscope look. "Have you cried about your grandfather?"

"I'm not sure." I didn't feel free to tell him about crying with Leo. But surely my tears had been as much for Grandfather as for Commander Rodney.

Adam took both my hands in his, a firm, warm grasp. "It's hard to let go anything we love. We live in a world which teaches us to clutch. But when we clutch we're left with a fistful of ashes."

I wanted to clutch Adam's hands, but I didn't. I withdrew mine, slowly. "I guess I have a lot to learn about that."

"At the end of the summer, when I go back to California, I'll have to say goodbye to Basil. That's not going to be easy. Maybe Basil will be able to teach us both something about letting go."

I thought of the great, smiling mouth, and the lovely feeling of resilient pewter as I scratched Basil's chest. "If anybody can teach us, Basil can."

5

I biked along slowly, partly because it was uphill almost all the way to the stable, and partly because I wanted to hold on to the morning, not the troubling conversation in the cafeteria, but feeding Una and Nini, and seeing Ynid, who was going to have a baby.

And meeting Basil.

Meeting Basil was so special that it colored the entire day.

And somehow meeting Basil made a difference to how I felt about Adam. The strange thing was that, while I felt excited about Basil, I felt comfortable with Adam, comfortable in a strengthening way, a way that made me feel that growing up and becoming an adult was not so terrible, even though we grow up and sooner or later we die; sooner, like Commander Rodney, or at the traditional threescore and ten like Grandfather.

I put my bike in the shed and went around to the front of the house to check on the swallows. All I could see was a grey fluff of feathers up above the nest. The babies were taking their afternoon nap. I trotted around the table and went in through the screened porch. Ned and Rochester were lying curled up together, but I didn't see anybody else. Grandfather was not in his usual place on the couch.

"Hello!" I called.

Nobody answered.

I looked in all the stalls and in the kitchen and nobody was there. Grandfather was not in the stall which was his study, where I'd hoped he might be. Not anywhere.

"Hey, where is everybody?" I shouted.

No answer. Rochester stalked arthritically in from the porch and whined at the foot of the ladder, so I climbed up to the loft and Rob was lying face down on his cot. If he'd been asleep I'd certainly made enough noise to wake him.

"Rob."

He didn't move.

I hurried across the loft and sat down on the cot beside him. "Rob, what's the matter?"

He rolled over and his face was all blotchy from crying.

"Rob, what is it?"

"It's Grandfather—" he started, and couldn't go on because he was choked up with sobs.

My heart seemed to stop. "He isn't—"

"He had a nosebleed," Rob managed to say. "Oh, Vicky, he bled and bled and Daddy couldn't stop it for the longest while and Mother—" He fished under his pillow and took out a wad of wet tissues.

"What about Mother?"

"She sat by Grandfather and held his hand and she—she didn't look like Mother at all."

"But where is she? Where are Grandfather and Daddy?"

"Daddy called the Coast Guard and they're taking Grandfather to the hospital on the mainland for a blood transfusion. Daddy said they should be back by late afternoon."

"With Grandfather?"

"Yes. Daddy promised him he wouldn't leave him in the hospital."

I looked at Rob's tear-streaked face and the strange darkness in his eyes, and I wondered fleetingly if all this was too much for Rob, if not the rest of us.

He blew his nose, and then wiped his cheeks with the palms of his hands, leaving grubby streaks. "Where's Elephant's Child?"

Elephant's Child is the much-loved remains of the stuffed elephant which had always been Rob's special thing. But he hadn't bothered about Elephant's Child for ages. Now he stretched across the cot on his stomach, leaning over and peering under and wriggling until he pulled Elephant's Child, worse for wear, from under the bed, and wound the music box, which amazingly still worked, and Brahm's *Lullaby* tinkled across the loft.

"Mother asked me to stay home so I could tell you about it."

"Where's Suzy?"

"Off somewhere with Jacky Rodney. She's going to work for him."

So John, as usual, was right.

"Suzy's not old enough to have a pilot's license." I don't know why I sounded so cross.

"Neither is Jacky. Leo has the license."

"She'll just get in the way."

Rob looked at me questioningly, then said. "Suzy can be mighty handy."

I sighed. "I know. How'd it happen, Rob, how did it start?"

"We were all sitting out on the porch, and Mother was just about to bring out lunch, and suddenly blood began to pour down Grandfather's face . . ." His lips started trembling.

"Sorry, Rob," I said swiftly. "If Daddy's not making him stay in the hospital, it can't be too bad. Hey, I had a great time with Adam this morning. I even fed two of the dolphins, Una and Nini." I wanted to tell him about Basil, to give him a present to take his mind off Grandfather, but I knew Adam was right and Basil shouldn't be talked about.

I told Rob about Una and Nini, and how Adam held a fish in his mouth and Nini took it as delicately as Suzy eating strawberries and cream. And I told him that Ynid was going to have a baby soon and that there were two dolphins with her to be midwives. And after a while I realized that Rob was curled up on his cot, sound asleep.

I slipped quietly down the ladder and went into the kitchen to get things started for supper. I set the table and made the salad dressing and cut up celery and scallions and green peppers, washed the lettuce, and then fixed the tomatoes and put them in a small bowl to be added later. I looked in the refrigerator to see if I could figure out what Mother had planned for supper. There were peas, so I shelled them. I saw some hamburger and a basket of mushrooms, so I figured at least I could make Poor Man's Beef Stroganoff, which I set about doing.

I am really not usually that great around the

kitchen. Far too often Mother has to prod me—and the rest of us—to get our chores done. Now I was keeping busy to help myself as much as Mother. But I could not turn off my mind; Rob's description of Grandfather bleeding had been all too graphic. So I let my mind drift to Basil and Adam.

Dolphins are communal creatures, Adam had told me. They cannot give birth alone; they need midwives, need friends. What about dying? What does a pod of dolphins do when one of them has been hurt—maybe by a harpoon—or is old? How do they help, birthing or dying, without hands? Do they surround the one who is dying and hold him by their presence? Do they have any conscious thoughts about life and death? Can they ask questions? Or do you give up questions when you give up hands?

I jerked as Rochester barked, his welcoming, friendly, happy bark. So it must be all right.

I was somehow hesitant to go out to the porch. But I went. Grandfather was sitting on the lumpy couch, looking a little pale, but calm and serene. Mother, I thought, looked paler than Grandfather.

Daddy sniffed. "I smell something delectable."

"I just threw some things together . . ."

Mother gave me a quick hug. "Vicky, you're an angel."

"How's—how's everything?"

"I'm fine," Grandfather said. "All that new young blood and I'm ready to go try climbing one of those mountains I never had time for while I was in Africa and Asia."

Daddy sat down on the couch beside him. "The mountain climbing mightn't be too bad, but I wouldn't advise jet travel just yet."

"I wasn't thinking of flying over," Grandfather said. "I thought I'd swim. Where's everybody?"

"Rob's asleep. John and Suzy aren't home yet. They're late. Oh—I vaguely think I heard John say something about Dr. Zand wanting him to do something after five . . ."

Mother went out to the kitchen, not with her usual brisk pace, but sort of wandering. I sat in the swing. Rochester hunched down beside Grandfather and Daddy, and put his head on Grandfather's knee. Ned sprang up into his lap and started purring. It was somehow as comforting as Basil's smile. And I wanted to tell Grandfather and Daddy about Basil. Instead, I pushed the wooden floor of the porch with my toe so that the swing creaked back and forth.

"Father," Daddy said, "I am going to rent a hospital bed for you." Grandfather started to protest, but Daddy went on, "It will be more comfortable. This old couch is a mess."

Grandfather's hand stroked Ned and the purr came louder. "During my lifetime I've learned a good bit about dying. In Alaska, for instance, an old man or woman would prepare to die, and would call the family for instructions and farewells. And when they had done what they wanted to do, wound up their affairs as we might say, they died. It was a conscious decision, a letting go which involved an understanding of the body that we've lost. And I thought then and I think now that it's far better than our way of treating death. But what I didn't realize when I was watching someone's sons and daughters standing around the deathbed, sometimes stolid, sometimes weeping, always moving deeply into acceptance of grief and separation, was that I do not have the strength of my Eskimo friends. It hurts me too much to see you being hurt."

Daddy took his hand. "It's a part of it, Father, you know that."

Grandfather looked at me. "I know. But the look in my daughter's eyes this afternoon . . ."

Grandfather was looking at me but he was seeing Mother.

"Perhaps I'd be better off in the hospital. Perhaps you shouldn't have brought me home . . . I thought I could die with you around me, and I did not realize how much it would hurt you and that I cannot stand that hurt."

"Perhaps," Daddy suggested, "you ought not to deprive us of that hurt?"

I knelt by Grandfather, and Rochester leaned against me, almost knocking me over. "I think the Eskimos are right, Grandfather, and I know you're just as strong as anybody else in the world."

He looked at me and blinked, as though clearing his vision. "Vicky?"

"Yes, Grandfather. We don't want you off in the hospital where you're a number and a case history. We want you to be strong enough to let us be with you." I bit my lip because tears were beginning to well up in my eyes.

The screen door slammed and Suzy banged in. "Hi, sorry to be late."

I scrambled to my feet.

"Jacky's really giving me a lot of responsibility," she announced triumphantly.

"That's great," I said without enthusiasm.

"Suzy." Daddy stood up. "Come in the kitchen with me for a minute."

Grandfather continued to stroke Ned. Rochester

yawned and flopped at his feet. "I frightened Rob," Grandfather said.

"Rob's been frightened before. He had all kinds of scary things happen in New York, I mean really scary."

"Victoria," Grandfather started, then stopped. "No, it's Vicky, isn't it? You look very much the way your mother did at your age."

"Grandfather, you told us once that if we aren't capable of being hurt we aren't capable of feeling joy."

"Yes . . . yes . . ."

"You were with Gram when she died."

He continued to pat my hand absent-mindedly. "That is different. Caro and I were one. This—"

"It's a different kind of oneness. It's a deep but dazzling darkness."

Now he took my hand in his. "Poetry does illuminate, doesn't it? Bless you for understanding that, and for remembering."

Daddy returned then.

Grandfather said, "About that hospital bed. I think I would like to have it in my study, where I'm surrounded by the books that have been my friends throughout my life."

"I think we can manage that, Father."

"And where I can have some privatecy. This porch is rather like a railroad station—in the days when there used to be railroad stations. I will need some time to be alone, to meditate."

When the screen door banged again, I jumped. So did Grandfather, who had closed his eyes. It was John, and Mother and Suzy came out of the kitchen, and at the same moment the phone rang and Suzy rushed to answer it. I haven't raced her for the phone in ages.

She called back out, "It's that nerd Zachary."

"I'll take it in Grandfather's study," I said. "Hang up in the kitchen."

"Well," said Zachary, "why haven't you called me?"

I wasn't in the mood for this. "Why would I call you?"

"Because I left three messages for you to call me, one with your father, one with your mother, and the last time with your little brother."

"I guess they forgot, because—"

He cut me off. "Forgot, nothing. I'm persona non gratis in their eyes."

"Grata," I corrected automatically.

"I told you my cram school was lousy. Didn't make us take Latin, most of us would have flunked it. Anyhow, your parents forgot accidentally on purpose."

"Zachary. My grandfather has leukemia and he had a hemorrhage today. Daddy had to call the Coast Guard and get him to the hospital on the mainland for a transfusion. They had other things on their minds than phone messages."

"Oh. Doesn't this two-bit island even have a hospital?"

"There's a fund drive on for a cottage hospital. We should have it by next summer, but that doesn't help us this year."

"So your grandfather's on the mainland?"

"No, Mother and Daddy brought him home. He's much better."

"Good, then. Listen, I've hired your pal Leo for Saturday afternoon and evening. I want to take you to

121

the mainland for a swim at the country club, and then dinner, and there's a concert you might like to hear, a pianist. Okay?"

"It sounds fine. I'll have to check with my parents."

Zachary sighed exaggeratedly. "So check."

"I'll call you back tomorrow."

"When?"

"Right after breakfast."

"Okay." He hung up without saying goodbye, typical Zachary fashion.

I went back to the porch and Rob had come down and was sleepily rubbing his eyes. Daddy had fixed drinks, and John handed me a Coke with a good big wedge of lemon, the way I like it.

"Thanks to Vicky," Mother said, "dinner's all ready. I've just put some rice on to go under the stroganoff. It'll take a few minutes, so let's relax while we wait."

And for a brief moment the world seemed stable again.

In the morning after breakfast I was puttering around the kitchen helping clean up, when Daddy came in and put a call through for a hospital bed, and then a call to Mr. Hanchett, on the mainland, saying that Grandfather would not be able to take the church services for the rest of the month. I was glad I wasn't around when he told Grandfather; Daddy's voice had that just-too-level quality it has when he's doing something he has to do and doesn't want to do.

Mother came in as he hung up. But she'd heard.

Her voice, too, was unnaturally level. "We're really unusually lucky." She put her hand on Daddy's arm in an affectionate gesture. "It seems almost providential that you'd already planned to take this summer to write that book."

"I haven't done much so far," Daddy said. "I'm going to have to set up a regular routine of work. If I don't get it done before I resume private practice—"

"—it'll never be done," Mother finished. She looked around the kitchen, as though seeing it for the first time. "There are so many people who live in cramped quarters, and when something like this happens, they don't have the choice we do, to keep Father at home, to be with him. They have to resort to a nursing home; they don't have any alternative . . ."

Daddy put his arm around her. "Perhaps it's easier when there is no alternative."

"No, no," Mother murmured. "I'm always boring the kids by telling them that something easy isn't worth anything. And it seems somehow as if this—this is meant. You'll never have another summer like this when you're able to work anywhere you want. How's that article going?"

"The article's finished, at any rate," Daddy said. "I sent it off to the *New England Medical Journal* this morning." He looked at me. "I've got more than enough work to keep me busy this summer. Vicky, I've appreciated that you were willing to give up a good job."

After the complimentary way in which Daddy spoke, I didn't say that it burned me that Suzy'd been allowed to turn down the same good job and do what she wanted to do.

Daddy continued, "Even though you're going to be

more, rather than less, needed as the summer goes on, you don't have to be a slave here twenty-four hours a day."

"She certainly doesn't," Mother agreed.

"I wish you had some kind of a project, Vicky."

"Well, I sort of do."

"What?"

"Adam has a dolphin project going, and I'm helping him."

"You don't have any background in marine biology or any other kind of biology," Daddy said.

"Adam's filling me in on what I need." I stopped then, because I could see that Daddy thought my helping Adam was just about as made-up a job as Suzy's helping Jacky. Only he thought that Suzy had more qualifications for helping Jacky than I did for helping Adam. And without telling about Basil there was no way I could explain anything.

And as for people living in cramped quarters, Mother and Daddy had Grandfather's bedroom, but we kids were all together up in the loft.

"Don't scowl," Mother said. "You're getting lines in your forehead."

"I'm not scowling."

"Vicky, this summer's not easy on any of us . . ." Mother turned away.

"Who's complaining?" I couldn't keep the brittleness out of my voice. I sounded grimly ungracious. So I added, "We all want to be with him. You know that." And then, "I'll go make your bed. I'll get Rob to help me."

We had to take Grandfather's desk out of his study stall to make way for the hospital bed. Daddy put the desk in the stall with the science books and announced that it was going to be his office from now on, and if we wanted any of the books we'd better take them now, because when he was in his office he was going to be writing and he was not to be disturbed.

The hospital bed was electric, with buttons which raised and lowered it, up and down, head and feet, and when it was flat down with one of those Indian bedspreads on it, it looked like an ordinary bed, but even an ordinary bed had no place in Grandfather's study. Daddy found a sturdy table to put by the bed to hold the phone, and a reading lamp, and Grandfather's Bible, and whatever other books he might want to have right by him.

Later that day the phone men came to put the phone on a jack, so that it could be unplugged if Grandfather wanted to nap. Or, as he said, to meditate.

And in the afternoon Mrs. Rodney came by.

Since the house was empty, Grandfather was in his usual place on the lumpy couch on the porch, "where I can see the ocean and sky."

Mother and I were in the kitchen, preparing the vegetables for a pot roast. We weren't talking, but it was an all-right silence. I didn't know what she was thinking, but her face didn't have the white, pulled-tight look it had when she and Daddy brought Grandfather home after the blood transfusion. I was working on a poem in my head, hurrying to get the carrots scraped so I could go up to the loft and set it down.

We heard a knock on the door, and Mother said, "Go see who it is, Vicky, and check that the swallows aren't upset."

I slipped out through the porch, shutting the door

quietly behind me, because Grandfather had his eyes closed. When I got around to the front of the house, Mrs. Rodney was backing away.

"Those swallows were dive-dombing me. And their nest is much too shallow. They'll be lucky if those fledglings learn to fly before they fall out. Are your parents at home?"

"Yes. Daddy's writing, and Mother's in the kitchen."

"I'd like to see them for just a few minutes. I take it you're not using the front door for the duration?" She looked at the three parent swallows anxiously fluttering about the nest.

"That's right." We went in through the side door, the one that leads into the stall where Daddy was working. He looked up, frowning, then smiled as he saw Mrs. Rodney. I knew he hated being interrupted, but I also had a hunch that Mrs. Rodney had something important to say, so I left her there and went to the kitchen to get Mother.

When we got back to Daddy's stall, Mrs. Rodney was saying, "And since my refresher course at the hospital doesn't begin till September I'm free as a lark this summer, and I'd like to be Mr. Eaton's nurse."

"That's very kind of you," Daddy said. "At the moment he doesn't need much in the way of nursing."

"But he's going to."

"I can—" Mother started.

Mrs. Rodney broke in. "Please let me. It will make me feel needed. I love your father, and I *am* trained to do things like giving a bed bath without jolting or hurting."

Daddy nodded, twirling the felt pen he'd been writing with. "Victoria, I think your father would rather not have you see his weakness. Nancy, it's very generous of you, and we're most grateful."

Mrs. Rodney said, "And this is friendship on my part, not business. I want that understood."

Daddy said, "We'll see about that when the time comes."

"Suzy told us about the transfusion. It helped?"

"Greatly."

"If you think he should have them on a regular basis, I think we could manage them here, rather than putting him to the fatigue and stress of going to the hospital."

Now Mother spoke. "Oh, good. The hospital was— efficient, for the most part, and altogether horrible."

"Most city hospitals are," Mrs. Rodney said briskly, "especially the emergency rooms. Many people get frustrated with the long waits in the clinics, and so they come to the emergency rooms. The result is that there's no way everybody can be treated promptly."

Mother said, "If my husband hadn't been a physician, and able to cut through red tape, we might still be there. And I waited in the emergency room—it seemed hours."

"City emergency rooms can be pretty awful," Mrs. Rodney said. "It's a pity we won't have our cottage hospital on the Island till next summer. But Dr. Austin can arrange for the blood, and Leo can bring it from the mainland. The kids and I'll all donate some blood. You'll let me know whenever I'm needed?"

Mother put her hands swiftly to her face, covering her eyes, then dropped them. "Nancy, to say thank you is simply inadequate—"

"It's little enough. My nursing is the one gift I have to offer a family that's very dear to me. By the way,

Vicky, that black-haired young Lothario is planning quite a day for you on Saturday."

I'd phoned Zachary to tell him it was all right, but now I wasn't sure I wanted to leave, even for a few hours. "Zachary likes to do things elegantly."

"Poor young man," Mrs. Rodney said. "It took courage for him to come talk to me the way he did. I hope he makes something of himself."

"I hope so, too," Daddy said, but he didn't sound optimistic.

"If Vicky gives him a helping hand, that'll do a lot for him. You've been very good to Leo, Vicky. Thank you."

"Leo's—quite a guy," I fumbled.

"He's got a lot of growing up to do. Well, folks, I've got to get along home. Thanks."

"Thank you, Nancy," Daddy said, and got up from the desk to see her out. "After those fledglings are out of the nest, this door becomes *verboten*."

When we lived in Thornhill, bedtime used to be one of the best parts of the day. Mother always read to us, and we sang, and said prayers, and sometimes Mother would get her guitar and sit on the stairs where we could all hear her equally well, and sing.

In New York it changed, not because it was New York and a very different world but, as Mother said, in the nature of things and our growing up. John was away at college, and anyhow for the past couple of years he'd stopped being part of the good-night ritual because of homework. And I had enough homework to occupy me till bedtime, and I stayed up an hour later than Suzy and a couple of hours later than Rob, and my bedtime routine had become little more than saying good night to Mother and Daddy.

So that evening after dinner I was pleased to have Daddy say, "How about some reading aloud in the evenings?"

"I'd like that," Grandfather said.

"What kind of a book?" John asked.

"I hadn't really thought that far," Daddy said. "Your mother reads aloud beautifully and I'd be happy to hear almost anything."

"How about the phone book?" John suggested.

"How about *Twelfth Night* or *The Tempest*?" Grandfather put in. "We run quite an age gamut and they'd be as good for Rob as for me."

"*Twelfth Night*," Mother said. "It's not quite as much of a fairy tale as *The Tempest*, but it's got some lovely stuff in it."

"And all those songs, too," Daddy said. "If you'll tell me where it is, Father, I'll get it."

Instead of getting up, Grandfather nodded. "In the art and drama stall, there's a big set of Shakespeare. You can't miss it."

"One act a night," Mother announced as Daddy handed her the book. "Unless we set a definite limit at once, you won't be able to stop me."

Twelfth Night begins with music, so she started with a song, and then began: *If music be the food of love, play on*.

I lay on the worn porch floor, my eyes closed, listening. Suddenly I realized that Mother does read beautifully. In Thornhill she was simply Mother, reading to us, the way anybody's mother might read. Now I knew that not many people could put the richness and life into the words that she did, and that bringing words and music to life was her very special talent.

When she finished, she closed the book with a

bang. Nobody spoke for a moment. Then she said, "Bedtime."

Daddy sighed, a long, contented sigh. "Thank you, Victoria. This is going to be a good pattern for our evenings." He looked at Grandfather. "Come along, Father, I'll give you a hand." And I remembered that Grandfather would be sleeping in the hospital bed in his study instead of out on the porch.

6

Those swallows were on my mind. That nest was entirely too shallow.

When I brought it up at breakfast Saturday morning, Suzy and Rob were all for getting some hay and building it up so that the fledglings wouldn't fall out, but it was Suzy herself who said, "No. We can't."

"Why not?" Rob demanded.

"If there's the slightest smell of human hands on the straw the swallows will just abandon the nest. They won't feed the fledglings."

"Why?"

"They don't trust human beings. And small wonder."

"But what'll we do to keep the fledglings from falling out and killing themselves?" Rob's face was puckered with anxiety.

Grandfather had come out for breakfast, to sit in the morning sun. "Last year they fell out," he said quietly.

"And died?" Suzy's voice rose.

"Yes. Swallows tend to be careless about their nests."

"Let's put a nice cushion of hay or something soft *under* the nest," I suggested. "We can put it on the stone step, and then if they fall, it will be soft and maybe won't hurt them."

"It'll still smell of human hands," Suzy objected.

"Maybe not if it's been there for a few days. Anyhow, it's worth a try."

"Can't hurt," John said. "We've got some hay at the station. I'll bring some home tonight."

"But that may be too late." Suzy frowned anxiously.

"We'll just have to risk it," John said.

"Couldn't Vicky bike over and get it this morning?"

"Why can't you bike over and get it yourself?"

Both John and I thought Suzy's work was made-up work, and that she'd turned down a real job to do something she liked better. Maybe that was so, but I also knew that her work was real to Suzy. And I had brought up the subject of the baby swallows and the nest myself. "I don't mind biking over. I've got a couple of things I need to do after breakfast, but then I'll go."

"Oh, thanks, Vicky, thanks," Suzy breathed.

"I'll leave it for you, right by the entrance to the main lab," John said. "I'm not sure where I'll be this morning, but you'll find a nice pile of hay waiting for you—and for the swallows."

After breakfast I helped Mother with the dishes, and to make up the big four-poster bed for her and Daddy—it takes about a quarter of the time with two people. And we made up the hospital bed in Grandfather's study.

"Need me for anything else?" I asked.

"No, Vicky. Thanks."

"Well—if you don't need me, I'll go get the hay."

It was still hot. The sun beat down on me as I biked along. For us, in our part of the world, the sun means life. But in some very hot countries it means death, and with the sweat running down my legs, and my mouth parched and dry, I began to understand why. I should have worn a sun hat or something.

I was wondering if I'd feel cooler if I wore long white robes and had my head covered, like an Arab, and I almost fell off my bike when I saw Adam in the doorway to the lab, his arms full of hay.

"Where on earth were you?" he demanded.

"On earth. But I was thinking of being an Arab. It's hot."

Adam didn't need explanations. "We should all be wearing burnooses. Here's your hay. John told me you'd be coming by. I'll help you get it in your bike basket so it won't fly all over the road."

"Thanks. How's Basil?"

Adam's light came on, full. "Sends you his love. How about Wednesday, Vicky? Can you come over with John?"

"Wednesday's perfect." Monday, I remembered, would have to be saved for Leo. "And how's Ynid?"

"Nearly to term. As a matter of fact, Jeb thinks it may be Wednesday. You'll go out of your mind with delight at the sight of a baby dolphin. Okay, I think you ought to get the hay home safely, though I take a dim view of its ultimate usefulness."

"It's worth a try."

"Sure, anything on the side of life's worth a try. I'll see you soon."

"Good. Thanks. Thanks a lot, Adam."

"Sure." And he ran back into the dimness of the lab.

I went for a swim when I got home, to cool off, but climbing back up to the stable made me just as hot as ever. We had cucumber sandwiches for lunch, which is about

133

as cool as anything you can have to eat, and then I took a long, cold shower and dressed to wait for Zachary.

I heard the familiar honk, and he came around to the screen porch. He had on black jeans and a white turtleneck and he looked spectacular. I wore a pale-blue sundress and Mother had lent me a misty white shawl. It was almost the first time I'd had on a dress since we'd been at the Island. Well, the other time had been at Commander Rodney's funeral.

"Those idiot swallows are cheeping away," Zachary said. "I see you're hoping to keep them from suicide. Or matricide. Anyhow, that nest's too shallow. Ready, Vicky-O?"

"Ready."

Leo was waiting for us at the dock. So was Suzy. I saw her eyeing me critically, and waited for her to make some kind of snide remark, but all she said was, "I polished all the brass on the launch. Appreciate it."

"Looks gorgeous."

"Like yourself," Leo said.

Zachary looked at me with the same appraising eye as Suzy. "She'll do, by Jove, she'll do. That dress brings out the color of your eyes, and you're getting to have a splendid bod."

Leo scowled, and I could tell he didn't like the way Zachary was looking at me as though he were undressing me. Leo stepped in front of Zachary and held out his hand to help me jump into the launch. Zachary followed, close on our heels, jostling Leo and immediately apologizing. Jacky came out of the boathouse and he and Suzy waved as we took off.

"It's a perfect day," Leo said. "Water's as smooth as glass. It was rough early this morning when I took a couple out fishing. Vicky, you're saving Monday for me, aren't you?"

Zachary smiled his most charming smile, first at me, then at Leo. "It's a good thing you have only one day off a week, pal. I can see you'd want to monopolize Vicky-O otherwise." He put his hand on mine.

I was not used to having people complete for me. It felt pleasant, if slightly confusing.

It's about half an hour by launch to the mainland—more than twice as quick as the ferry. Zachary and Leo did most of the talking. Zachary was trying really hard to be friends, and Leo, being Leo, responded without hesitation. There they were, night and day. Everything that Zachary said and did was calculated, not necessarily in a bad way, but Zachary planned things, like an artist, for effect. And Leo responded like a puppy who's been thrown a stick to retrieve. And I thought, too, that Leo was trying to go more than halfway, to encourage Zachary to begin again, to remove that burden of guilt which Zachary didn't seem to feel but which would have weighed Leo down. It was easy to know what Leo was feeling; there it was, right on the surface. What Zachary was feeling lay deep within, and he didn't often open his doors to friend or stranger. Zachary was a private person but he had a polished façade. Adam, I thought, was equally private, but there was no façade.

I leaned back against the seat of the launch and let the spray fly by me and the rays of the sun caress me. It was cool on the water and the wind blew my hair and dried the salt spray. It made me feel tingly with life.

The dock on the mainland was far busier and more bustling than on the Island. Zachary told Leo we'd be back at eleven o'clock that evening, or shortly there-after, and then he took my elbow and steered me along the dock, past coils of rope, past clusters of people, workmen in rough clothes, summer people in shorts or suburban-type dresses, to a small red convertible with the top down.

"Thought you might like this for a change." He patted it in a proprietary way, as though it were a prize horse.

It was a change from the hearse, all right. "It's yours?"

"No car rental's apt to have an Alfa Romeo, at least not around here. Talked Pop into it, as a reward for graduating from high school after all these years. Hop in." He opened the door. "We'll drive right to the country club."

"I thought the country club was supposed to be wildly exclusive."

"So 'tis. But money and connections can do wonders. We have a special membership for as long as we're here. There's an Olympic-size pool, and some pretty fair tennis courts, and Pop says the golf course is one of the better ones. He's off with some cronies he's picked up, making business deals. Won't bother us."

The drive to the club was along the shore for a few miles. Then we turned inland in the direction of the city, and drove past the hospital, a large, cold cube, and I thought of Grandfather being rushed there, and Mother sitting in the emergency room and being horrified.

Zachary's glance followed mine. "It's a reasonably good hospital as big hospitals go nowadays," he said, "though once I got out of intensive care and into a private room I could have died and no one would have noticed; there was only one nurse and a couple of aides for the whole floor. Stay out of it, Vicky-O."

A small chill moved up my spine. "I intend to."

We left the ugliness of the hospital behind us and drove up through green hills. Zachary handled the Alfa Romeo more gently than the hearse, and I didn't have to keep pushing my feet against imaginary brakes. The club was at the crest of a hill, a rambly white building. There were lots of expensive-looking cars parked around, and people with expensive-looking tans against white linen tennis skirts or shorts. Zachary took me into a wide entrance hall, carpeted in pale gold. At a leather-topped desk I was given a day visitor's card by an elegant-looking lady with elaborately dressed lavender hair. A maid in a grey uniform and white apron told me that she'd take me to my dressing room, and I could join my friend at the pool. My dressing room, to which I was given my own key, was a largish square divided into a shower and a place to dress. There was a wide seat across the back, with fluffy white towels in a neat pile. A terry robe hung on a hook. In the shower there was a brand-new cake of soap, a shower cap, and a pair of Japanese thongs.

I changed to my bathing suit, which was just a plain old bathing suit, nothing new or elegant suitable to my surroundings. Well, I'd just pretend it was reverse chic.

I looked at myself in the mirror and I was not displeased at what I saw, which, as far as mirror gazing is concerned, is a fairly new state of affairs. I'm long, but no longer all angles of sharp knees and elbows. And my reverse-chic bathing suit was black and the sun had brought out the lights in my hair and I had just the right beginnings of a tan—not too much. Good.

I went out to the pool.

Swimming is something I can do. Between trips to the Island and swimming in the ocean, and our regular summer swimming in the spring-fed Beagle Pond in Thornhill, I'm at home in the water—not as at home as Basil, but home enough so that I don't feel self-deprecating or self-conscious. I balanced on my toes on the diving board and plunged in.

Zachary was lounging on an inflated rubber raft. He looked pale in his bathing trunks, and not in his element. Not in the least like Adam. He was dabbling his fingers in the water and I swam up to him. "Coming in?"

"Not yet. I'm feeling anti-water at the moment."

"Why?" I asked stupidly.

"I looked to water to bring me beautiful oblivion, and instead I got a bellyful and strained my heart again. So no swimming or tennis or anything strenuous for a while. I meant it when I told your Mrs. Rodney I was going to take care of myself."

"I'm glad." Zachary, as ever, was unpredictable.

"So you swim, Vicky-O, and I'll admire you. So will everybody else."

I turned and swam underwater the length of the pool and then pulled myself up, gasping for air, and walked along the slick wet border of the pool, back to Zachary.

He had left the rubber raft and was sitting at a round table with a flowered umbrella to keep off the heat of the sun. There were a number of these umbrellaed tables scattered about, and people of all ages were sitting at them, from Suzy's age up, all the way up. Lots of bright clothes and beach hats and bags stuffed with knitting and needlepoint. It was a world of people who didn't have anything to do except whatever they felt like doing. A new world in which I wasn't sure I felt comfortable. I'd felt much more at home and much more myself in John and Adam's lab.

Zachary waved at a few people but didn't introduce me to anybody. He beckoned to a white-coated man, saying, "Want something to drink, Vicky?"

I was thirsty. "Sure."

"How about a rum and Coke?"

When I'd first met Zachary I'd lied about my age. Now I didn't feel the need to. I didn't even feel the need to remind him that I'm not quite sixteen. "What I'd really like is some lemonade, real lemonade with freshly squeezed lemons and not too much sugar."

He cocked one silky black brow at me, then turned to the waiter. "We'll have two real lemonades. Anything to eat, Vicky? We'll be going in to dinner early because of the concert."

"Just the lemonade."

The sun was hot, even in the shade under the umbrella. The canvas seemed to intensify the rays. I could feel myself flushing with heat; Zachary, on the contrary, just got whiter, so that his black brows and lashes were startling against his pallor. The waiter brought the lemonade and I sipped it slowly, letting the lovely sour tangy coolness slide down my throat. It was so hot that it was too much effort to talk, and I was surprised at myself for not feeling that I had to make the effort. I just sat there and sipped lemonade and watched people clustered about the tables and getting in and out of the pool. And because I didn't feel that I had to struggle for things to say, I was more comfortable with Zachary than I'd ever been before.

Time slipped by, as lazy as a bee that came and

buzzed about our table and fell into the dregs of Zachary's lemonade. I had another swim to cool off, and then went back to the dressing room to shower and dress. The soap smelled of sandalwood, and there was powder that smelled equally exotic. I took my time and felt luxurious.

Zachary was waiting for me in a large room off the dining room, elegant and air-conditioned, with sofas and chairs and low tables set about in groups. There were flowers on all the tables, and a great bouquet in a silver bowl on the marble mantel, reflected back by a great, gilt-framed mirror. The floor was carpeted in something subtly flowery and soft to walk on, and the long French windows had equally subtle flowery curtains. It was, I realized, beautiful as well as expensive taste. The coolness felt marvelous after the heat outdoors.

I've never thought of myself as being deprived. On the other hand, I've never been around people who don't have to think about where the next dollar's going to come from. And even if we had that kind of money, Mother and Daddy are both too busy for country clubs and the kind of living Zachary took for granted.

He was waiting for me at a small table near one of the windows, where we could look out across the gardens to the golf course. Sprinklers were sending out little fountains of water over the already velvety green lawn.

"Our table's reserved for six o'clock." Zachary looked at his watch. "What'll it be, Vicky?"

"What'll what be?" Why did I always have to seem stupid in front of Zachary?

"What do you want to drink before dinner? I'm on a moderate kick so I'll just have a glass of dry sherry."

"I'm on an even more moderate kick. I'll have a Coke with lemon."

His eyebrows drew together for a moment, then relaxed. "Added to which you're underage and law-abiding. For your reassurance, I'm twenty, and in this state allowed to have alcohol." He beckoned to a waiter and gave our order. A smiling waitress came over, bearing a silver tray with hors d'oeuvres.

"The canapés are so-so. Try the caviar. It's beluga; you can't go too far wrong with that," Zachary advised.

Behind the waitress with the silver tray came a man pushing a steam table with a copper rolltop. He swung it open and there were dishes of all kinds of hot hors d'oeuvres.

"I like the chicken liver and water chestnuts rolled in bacon." Zachary pointed.

In a short time I had a little plate loaded with tidbits, and when I had finished my Coke, which I drank too quickly because such elegance made me nervous, it was immediately and silently replaced. Then we were summoned into the dining room, which was as large and elegant as the huge salon. There were crystal chandeliers, which Zachary said were Waterford, and candles in silver holders, and flowers, and round, white-napped tables. My chair was drawn out for me and I sat down, rather clumsily, and helped the waiter hitch me in. I'm not accustomed to this kind of service, though I think I could quite easily get used to it, given the opportunity.

The menu was enormous, a leather folder with pages of appetizers and fish and entrees and salads and desserts. There weren't any prices.

"Have whatever your little heart desires." Zachary smiled his very nicest smile. "Once in a while you deserve to be treated like the princess you are. How about lobster?"

Lobster is something we can have quite often on the Island, buying the lobster right off the fishing boats as they come into shore in the late afternoon. "I think I'd like something really exotic."

"How about pheasant under a glass bell?"

I looked under the poultry section of the menu, and there it was. "Why is it put under a glass bell?"

"Got me. But they make it with an excellent sauce here. I advise it."

"Fine—except—is pheasant an endangered species?"

Zachary groaned. "Maybe in the wild. These are grown on a pheasant farm, especially for the purpose of being put under glass bells. Relax and enjoy."

"Okay. Pheasant under a glass bell."—Because, I reminded myself,—as Adam said, all life does live at the expense of other life.

"What's on your mind?"

I wasn't about to tell him it was Adam. I looked at the menu. "For dessert I'm wavering between Baked Alaska and crepes suzette."

The pheasant actually came under a glass bell, though I couldn't figure out what use it served except maybe to keep the pheasant warm. Zachary talked about going to law school and how it would help him to be in control of his life and not taken advantage of by the rest of the world, which seemed in his mind to consist largely of other lawyers, out to get people.

For dessert we had peach Melba because it was quicker than baked Alaska or crepes suzette and our time was getting short and I certainly didn't want Zachary to speed in that open, unprotected car.

And then we were in the little red Alfa Romeo on our way to the concert. We drove past the airport, and one of the huge jets came in for a landing, so low over us that I ducked.

Zachary patted me. "Take it easy, Vicky-O. That plane's a lot higher over us than it seems. This is a really nice little international airport—not big enough for Concordes, of course, but it can handle pretty much anything else."

"I've never been on a plane," I said.

Zachary turned and looked at me in astonishment. "*What!*"

"Look at the road, not at me. I want to get to that concert, please. I said I've never been up in a plane."

"What a little country mouse you are, despite your year in New York. Next week, would you like to go up?"

Ever stupid, I asked, "In a plane?"

"What else? I can't preempt a jet for you, but there are plenty of little charter flights, the equivalent of your pal Leo's boat. We can fly over the Island and buzz your family and then come back and have dinner at the club. Would you like that?"

I gazed at another plane over our heads, its underbelly looking like a strange air fish. "Oh, Zachary, I'd adore it, but I'll—"

"I know. You'll have to ask your parents. But you can reassure them that I won't be doing the flying—at least not till I get a pilot's license. I've started flying lessons so I won't go out of my mind with boredom. Art—he's my teacher—has his own little charter plane, and he'll fly us."

"Oh, Zach—it sounds marvelous."

"Pop says that if I get through my first year of college

without any problems—and he really means without *any* problems—he'll buy me my own plane. I love flying, and Art says I'm a natural. It's much better than driving a car. So it's worth avoiding problems to have my own plane. So, how's about we go flying on Saturday, next week? There's a dinner dance at the club."

"Saturday'll be fine."

The concert was held at an estate which had become some kind of foundation for the arts. There were chairs scattered about a vast green lawn, shining with golden light from the setting sun. Japanese lanterns were hung from the trees, great oaks and maples, and even some elms, and there aren't many of the old elms left; these must have had a lot of attention.

The house was whitely visible between the trees, a great stone building with many gables and chimneys and wings. Between the house and the chairs was a platform holding a grand piano.

The seats were arranged in clumps, and our tickets took us to the clump just to the left of the piano, where we'd have a perfect view of the keyboard; Zachary was really doing me proud. I looked at the program and it was everything I like—Bach's Fifth French Suite and a Mozart sonata and some Poulenc and Ginastera—a nice mix. There was a little breeze and I put Mother's lacy shawl over my shoulders and watched while some girls in long swirly dresses came out with tapers and lit the lanterns. Zachary slipped one arm across my shoulders.

I should have felt comfortable enough to lean against it and I was furious at myself for automatically stiffening.

"Relax, Vicky-O." His long fingers moved gently across the hair at the nape of my neck.

I tried to sound sophisticated and experienced. "Okay, but I want to listen to the music."

At that moment there was a burst of applause and a woman climbed the steps to the platform, bowed to the audience, and sat down at the piano. She was small and slight, with dark hair piled high on her head, showing a beautiful neck.

When she raised her hands over the keyboard I had a sense of total authority, and also a sense of terrific love, as though the piano were not an inanimate object but a dearly beloved person. And when she started to play, it was as though she and the piano were playing together.

Music has always been part of my life, taken for granted like the air I breathe. At home, Mother has the record player going most of the time; she says she'd never do any housework without the help of music: for cleaning she puts on something loud, like a Brahms or Beethoven symphony, which can be heard over the vacuum cleaner. For cooking, which she enjoys, it's more likely to be Bach or Scarlatti or Mozart, or chamber music of some kind. So, sitting there in the gathering twilight, I was lifted up on the music, soaring with almost the same freedom and joy as Basil leaping into the sky.

The notes of the Bach hit against the air as clear as stars on a cold night. The audience shifted and stirred and then, caught in the music, stilled and listened. The wind blew softly and the heat of the day fled away. The lanterns moved in the breeze and the shadows rippled to the music like dancers. The long, lingering mid-July day slowly faded to streaks of rose and mauve, forecasting another clear, hot day. And then the color was gone and the stars began to come out, seeming to tangle with the Japanese lanterns. It was magic. I put my head down on Zachary's shoulder and closed my eyes and let the music wash over me like the ocean.

When the concert was over, the applause was long and sustained.

"We've got to go, Vicky." Zachary patted my arm gently. "It's nearly eleven now, and Leo'll be waiting."

Reluctantly I rose, leaving the music. "Oh, Zachary, that was superb."

"Vigneras's got a good reputation," he said shortly. "Come on, Vic."

"It's so beautiful it's hard to leave."

"Glad you liked it. That kind of music doesn't do much for me."

I turned to him, amazed. "Then why did we come?"

He bent toward me and with one finger drew the lines of my eyebrows, and a slow shiver of pleasure went through me. "I knew it was your kind of thing." And, as I continued to look surprised, he added, "If I remember correctly from last summer, don't you have an aunt in California who's a concert pianist?"

For Zachary to remember, for Zachary to care . . . "Thanks—thanks, Zachary, thanks."

We were walking toward the parking lot. "Don't you know I'd do a lot to make you happy, Vicky-O?"

"Thanks," was all I could repeat, inadequately. For Zachary to spend an entire evening doing something he didn't like was not what I would have expected of him. But then, I should have learned not to have preconceptions.

Not only had I never been up in a plane, I'd never

ridden in an open car before today. After the heat of the day it was so cool that I had to put Mother's shawl up over my head, and Zachary spread a rug over my knees.

"It's too pretty to put the hood up."

It was. The sky was purply black, with the galaxies clustered above us and a lopsided moon just rising. If music means a lot to me, so do stars, and I missed them desperately in the city, where the street lights and neon signs take away from the stars so that only the most brilliant ones are visible. If I'm confused, or upset, or angry, if I can go out and look at the stars I'll almost always get back a sense of proportion. It's not that they make me feel insignificant, it's the very opposite, they make me feel that everything matters, be it ever so small, and that there's meaning to life even when it seems most meaningless.

Zachary must have felt the beauty, too, because he didn't press his foot down on the gas pedal. "I don't want this evening to end," he said as we approached the dock.

Leo was there, sitting on a keg, opposite an old-salt-type man with a long beard and a woolen cap. They had a chessboard between them, also on a keg, and were playing by the light of a street lamp. We stood and watched until the old sailor checkmated Leo, who groaned and hit his hand against his forehead. "I'll get you one of these days, Cor, so help me." And the old man cackled with pleasure and began putting the chessmen away, touching each one lovingly, and I saw that they were hand-carved, and figured that probably he'd carved them himself.

Leo insisted on helping me into the launch. The

ocean was swelling gently and I relaxed into the rocking boat like a baby in a cradle. Leo was concentrating on piloting us back to Seven Bay Island, and Zachary sat silhouetted against the night sky, looking like an enchanted prince out of a fairy tale.

At the Island dock Zachary's hearse was waiting darkly. We said good night to Leo, and then drove the winding way up to the stable. We went around to the porch and just before we got to the screen door Zachary stopped and kissed me.

Well, I'd expected him to. I wanted him to and I didn't want him to. He'd kissed me before and I'd liked it. I'd liked it very much. I still liked it. I liked it in a lovely warm tingle all through my body.

After a moment Zachary drew back and made a funny, groaning sound. "I won't push you too quickly, hon." He kissed me again, gently. "Don't you know you're all that's between me and chaos?" And then he broke away and said. "I'll be calling you," and ran around the stable and I could hear the door to the station wagon close with a slam.

It's amazing how quickly you can get into a routine. And how quickly you can get used to things you never thought you could possibly get used to, like Grandfather more and more often calling me Victoria and confusing me with Mother when she was my age, and wondering where Caro was. Caro. Our grandmother, Caroline. I didn't like it. I hated it. But I got used to it, and I stopped trying to make him know who I was, and let him see me as whoever he wanted me to be.

The best parts of the routine were breakfasts on the

porch; Grandfather usually got up for these and his mind was clearest in the early morning. And then there was the reading aloud at night, which usually ended with all of us singing. And it was good knowing that Adam would likely be with us for dinner several times a week, because John was rescuing him from the cafeteria.

Zachary dropped by to ask Mother and Daddy about taking me flying. After he'd left, Suzy said, "Why does Zachary keep on saying *zuggy*?"

I hadn't even noticed. "Oh, it's just his word."

"Some word," she said.

"What's wrong with it? He says all the other words simply reveal a paucity of vocabulary and a lack of imagination and he's tired of them."

Suzy said, "I wish he'd use his imagination then; he was saying *zuggy* last summer. Has he graduated from high school yet?"

"Yes," I said stiffly.

"I don't get what you see in that moron."

"You're just jealous," I replied automatically, and then thought that maybe she really was. Jacky Rodney was the one who looked like his father, not Leo, so it was okay for Leo to like me. But Suzy was not used to having people prefer me over her.

We dropped the subject.

After breakfast I read to Grandfather. A lot of what I read was over my head, because, somewhat unexpectedly, he asked me to read the works of scientists, mostly cellular biologists or astrophysicists.

"Grandfather, I didn't know you were interested in science."

"I'm interested in everything," he said gently, "but I

want the scientists right now because they are the modern mystics, much more than the theologians." So we read about mitochondria, and we read about black holes, those weird phenomena which follow the death of a giant star. I found myself nearly as fascinated as Grandfather obviously was. When a giant star dies, there's what one article called a "castastrophic gravitational collapse." The extraordinary thing is that the star collapses so totally that it actually collapses itself out of existence and becomes what mathematicians call a "singularity." How can you take an enormous mass and shrink it down to nothing? But this nothing isn't really nothing. Its gravity is so great that nothing can escape it, and if you went through a black hole you might find yourself in a completely different time, or even a different universe. And this isn't science fiction. I began to see what Grandfather meant about the scientists being mystics.

Grandfather's span of concentration was about an hour, but it was very dense stuff we were reading, and my own span of concentration wouldn't have been much longer.

Sometimes at dinner I discussed our reading with John. "You've got a lot more sense of science than I thought you had," he said.

"Science is a lot more like poetry than I thought it was," I replied.

Rob, who had been listening, said, "Maybe when you die, it's like going through a black hole."

Suzy opened her mouth, but Daddy stopped her, saying quietly, "We won't any of us know till it happens."

And John said, "You know what, I'd like a good thick milk shake right now, after those skim-milk and water ones we get at work. I'll make one for dessert if everybody'd like."

Grandfather had another nosebleed, but not a bad one. Daddy got it stopped quite quickly. But he decided that Grandfather should have weekly transfusions, and that Mrs. Rodney could give them, as she suggested, right at home, without having to put Grandfather through the hard trip to the mainland hospital.

This was Monday and I didn't know about it till it was all over because Monday was my day with Leo.

It was a quiet day. We didn't get cosmic about anything. We swam, and had a picnic, and walked along the beach and swam again, and had another picnic and went to the movies. Nothing exciting, and yet there was a warm, summery beauty about it. I didn't have to worry about what Leo was going to do or say next. We talked about Columbia and New York. And I told him about reading to Grandfather, and black holes, and he asked, "How does anybody's individual death fit into that enormous picture?" His eyes were bleak and I thought of Commander Rodney, and the empty space in the world his death had made.

"If a star's dying matters, so does a person's."

"To you and me. But to the universe?"

"I don't think size matters. Every death is a singularity," I said slowly. "Think of all the tiny organisms living within us. I somehow think every mitochondrion and farandola has to be just as important as a giant star."

"Well—" Leo sounded both hopeful and doubtful, and characteristically changed the subject. "I was going to major in something practical, like accounting, but I don't think I could spend my life behind a desk. I think I have to do something that will keep me by the sea."

"Marine biology, like Adam?"

"Something to do with ships, I think."

"Building them?"

"Designing, maybe. But mostly sailing them."

And then he kissed me.

I knew he was going to.

I sort of patted him like a brother and turned away.

"Why, Vicky?"

"Why what?"

"Why won't you let me kiss you?"

Zachary's kiss touched every part of my body. It made me quavery with excitement. Leo's kiss didn't do any of that. It didn't do anything. And yet I found myself liking Leo more and more. "I don't think we're ready for kissing yet."

"I am."

"I'm not."

"Okay." He drew away. "But I don't disgust you or anything?"

Not any more. "No, Leo. I like you. You're my friend."

He looked out over the ocean, but the sky was cloudy. There weren't any stars, and the air was almost chilly. "I guess I'll have to settle for that. For now."

Wednesday was still cloudy, though warm.

I thought Adam seemed a little preoccupied when I met him at the lab, but he said quickly, "Let's go see Basil, first thing."

152

I changed to my bathing suit behind the big rock, and we swam out, past the breakers, swam for a good ten minutes, steadily. This time Adam didn't have to call for more than a few seconds before Basil came leaping to greet us. And this time my heart was beating with anticipation and excitement, not fear.

Adam put his arms about Basil's great silvery bulk. Then Basil leapt up into the air, dislodging Adam, and dove down and surfaced by me, butting at me.

"He wants to play. He's apt to be a bit rough," Adam warned, "but he won't hurt you."

I knew he wouldn't. I began to scratch Basil's chest. He closed his eyes with pleasure. Then he went under the water and came up again, between my legs, lifting me, so that I was sitting astride him. He was slippery and I almost slid off him, but he wriggled his body in such a way that I stayed on while he swam in a slow circle around Adam. Then he went underwater again, leaving me, and I watched, treading water, as he turned toward Adam, his great body wriggling playfully. Adam seized the dorsal fin, and Basil leapt up into the air, with Adam holding on and shouting. Down Basil dove, not too deep, just deep enough so that Adam was gasping for air when they surfaced. Fascinated, I watched them play. I couldn't possibly have held on as Adam did, and the game was evidently to see how quickly Basil could dislodge him. Finally the dolphin dove down and Adam surfaced while Basil flashed up into the sunlight, giving every evidence of laughing because he'd won the game. In a funny way he reminded me of the old sailor beating Leo at chess.

Then he dove again, and I was looking for him in the direction of the horizon, when suddenly he popped up out of the water behind me, making a loud noise which startled me so that I went under and choked on a mouthful of salt water. Basil was as pleased as a child coming out from behind a tree and shouting "Boo!" He butted at me and asked me to play.

I grasped the dorsal fin in both hands the way Adam had done, and held on for dear life. Basil swam swiftly toward the horizon, towing me with him, then turned with such speed that he almost, but not quite, dislodged me, and returned to where Adam was waiting for us. Then Basil submerged and did his Boo! trick for Adam, and I knew as clearly as though Basil had spoken to me that he was trying to make us laugh because something was wrong.

What could be wrong?

Basil butted very gently at Adam, who reached out for the dolphin and leaned his cheek against the great grey flank.

Somehow or other Basil knew that something was wrong, knew without words far more about whatever was troubling Adam than I knew.

Adam leaned against the dolphin, his eyes closed, the lines from nose to mouth etched with pain. He leaned there till Basil submerged, and reappeared far from us, leaping against the horizon. And then another dolphin was leaping with Basil, in unison, the two together in perfect rhythm, like ballet dancers.

Adam turned to me in surprise. "That's another of the pod."

He stopped, watching in awe as the two dolphins came toward us in flashing curves, rising from the sea, gleaming through the air and seeming to brighten the cloudy sky, then diving down again, until they surfaced just in front of us, standing on their great flukes, their bodies almost entirely out of the water, smiling benignly down at us. Then they flopped down, splashing us so mightily that once again I swallowed a mouthful of sea water and choked, sputtering, which they seemed to find extremely funny. And it was as though I heard Basil telling me: *A good laugh heals a lot of hurts*. And I thought of Grandfather's gravity and levity.

Then the two of them swam, one on each side of Adam, as though holding him against whatever it was that was hurting him. It couldn't have been for more than a few seconds, though it seemed longer, like time out of time. Then they left us and were gone like a flash, to reappear near the horizon and vanish from our sight.

"How did Basil know?" Adam asked the vast, cloudy sky.

"That something's wrong?"

"You know, too?"

"Only that something's upsetting you."

"Have I been that obvious?"

"No. I don't think so."

"Then how—"

I trod water, looking down at the surface of the sea and away from Adam. "It sounds nuts, but I think I knew because Basil knew. Adam, what's wrong?"

"Ynid's baby is not going to live."

"Oh—Adam. Why not?"

"Jeb says the heart's not right. That's why I didn't take you to the dolphin pens. Jeb wants to be alone with Ynid and the baby and the midwives."

"Oh, Adam, Adam, I'm so sorry. Can't anything be done?"

"Jeb says not. The heart isn't pumping enough blood and the baby's dying for lack of oxygen."

"Couldn't he operate?"

"No. He says the heart's too badly damaged."

I felt as though a wave had broken over me.

"Let's go in," Adam said. "Maybe Jeb might need me. If he does—"

"I'll evaporate. Don't worry."

We swam in and dressed without waiting to dry; it would have taken too long, anyhow. The cloudy sky held the dampness of the day down on us, as though we were in an inverted bowl. We walked through air so saturated with moisture you could almost have put out your hand and squeezed it. We walked without speaking until we came to Ynid's pen. There were no cartwheels today. Adam walked as though gravity pulled him down.

Dr. Nutteley was standing, slumped, looking down into the pen, and if he saw us he gave no indication of it.

Walking softly, not to disturb him, we approached the pen.

Ynid was swimming in slow circles, carrying a tiny, motionless dolphin on her back. The two midwives swam beside her, pressing close against her as the two dolphins had swum with Adam.

I did not need to be told that Ynid's baby was dead. Or that Ynid, swimming with the perfect little dead body on her back, was hoping against hope that the stilled heart would start to beat again.

And then she must have had a stab of hopelessness, the realization that her baby was dead, because suddenly she streaked ahead of the two midwives and began beating her body wildly against the side of the tank.

"No, Ynid!" It was Jeb who, with a great cry,

156

plunged into the water and swam to the distraught dolphin, trying to put his arms about her without dislodging the dead baby, trying to keep her from beating herself against the side of the pen, in complete disregard of his own safety, putting himself between Ynid and the side of the pen. He was calling out to her and tears were streaming down his face.

And Ynid, perhaps because she would not hurt Jeb, stopped her wild beating. It seemed that Jeb was shedding for her the tears that she could not shed, a wild sobbing such as I had never heard from a grown man.

I slipped away and got my bike from the rack and went back to the stable.

John brought Adam home for dinner.

It had rained in the afternoon, but by late afternoon the rain had stopped completely. The wind was moving from the southeast to the northwest, and the heaviness was gone from the air. As the breeze lifted, the weight that had been tightly clamped about my heart loosened just slightly.

Grandfather didn't come out for dinner. I took him his tray, and he was propped up in the hospital bed, his Bible by him, but he wasn't reading. I thought he probably knew most of it by heart.

He jerked slightly as I knocked and came in.

"Here's your dinner, Grandfather. I'm sorry if I woke you."

"You didn't wake me. I was meditating."

Mrs. Rodney had brought over a hospital table, which I swung over the bed for the tray. "What were you meditating about?" I asked, unfolding his napkin for him.

"You don't meditate *about*." His nicest smile twinkled at me. "You just meditate. It is, you might say, practice in dying, but it's a practice to be begun as early in life as possible."

"Sort of losing yourself?" I asked.

"It's much more finding than losing."

I wanted to stay and talk, because his mind seemed completely clear, but I knew I had to get back to the dining table.

"Vicky," Grandfather said as I turned to go, "I'll come out to the porch for the reading."

Mother'd finished *Twelfth Night* and we'd started on *Joseph Andrews,* a really funny book by Henry Fielding, who also wrote *Tom Jones*, but *Joseph Andrews* is lots shorter and, according to Grandfather, funnier, and wouldn't take us all summer.

After Mother'd read, we sang, and then she sent Rob up to bed, and Daddy went with Grandfather to help him get ready for the night. Suzy scrambled up from the floor, yawning.

I still felt that the day was somehow unfinished.

Adam looked across the porch at me. "Want to go for a walk?"

For answer I nodded and stood up.

Mother looked at her watch. "Don't be too long."

Adam also checked his watch. "We won't be. But Vicky and I have things we need to talk about."

He had talked about Ynid and the dead baby at dinner, and Suzy had demanded to know if the baby would have died if it had been born at sea rather than in captivity. And Adam had replied that there was no way of knowing, but that congenital birth defects did occasionally happen in the wild. He had not said anything about Jeb and his bitter grief.

"Better put on a sweater, Vicky," he advised.

After the heat of the past days it was hard to believe that I'd need a sweater, but I went up to the loft, where Rob was sound asleep and Suzy was getting ready for bed, and grabbed a bulky fisherman's sweater that would have fitted any of us, and pulled it over my head. It was still warm in the loft so I opened the windows wide before going down the ladder.

Mr. Rochester was waiting, his thin tail whipping back and forth in anticipation, so we took him with us. The steep path directly down to Grandfather's cove is too difficult for Rochester, in his arthritic old age, so we walked along the road toward the lighthouse, and then turned oceanward.

Not looking at me, Adam said, "I didn't stay this morning, either. Jeb didn't need me. He didn't need anyone except Ynid. I'm not sure he even knew we were there. Not that he'd have minded. He's probably one of the most free and open people I've ever known."

I thought of Jeb wiping his eyes at Commander Rodney's funeral when almost everybody else was being stoic. Then I asked, "Is Ynid all right?"

"She's going to be. She let Jeb take the baby. And she's stopped trying to beat herself to death against the side of the pen. She wouldn't eat, but that's to be expected for a day or so."

"And Jeb?" We had reached the beach, a cove or so up from Grandfather's, past the dead elm, and were walking close to the water's edge, Rochester prancing along ahead, looking for the moment like a young dog.

"Jeb lost his wife and baby in a car accident."

"When?"

"A couple of years ago. But he still isn't over it. He was driving, and that has to make it all the harder, though it wasn't his fault. The car had defective brakes." We walked a little farther, both looking down at the faint whiteness of the lacy edge of the wavelets as they lapped against the night beach. Then Adam said, "In the end I think Ynid comforted Jeb as much as the other way round, and maybe that was the best thing he could give to Ynid, his own pain."

Adam turned in from the sea and headed for a low dune which leaned against the cliff. He brushed away the damp sand on the surface, till he had cleared enough space for the two of us and Rochester to sit on warm, dry sand. The sky was covered with clouds which were moving in the wind. The cloud cover was still so thick that the only hint of starlight was a faintly luminous quality to the night, and a delicate tracery of light as the waves moved and turned. The breeze was cool and I was grateful for the warmth of the big, bulky sweater.

Mr. Rochester sat on his haunches beside me, peered intently into my face, and gave me a gentle kiss on the nose. Then he flopped down and put his heavy head on my knees. Adam sat on my other side, picking up sand and letting it trickle slowly through his fingers.

"Like an hourglass," I said.

"What?"

I indicated the softly falling sand. Sand sifting down through the hourglass of life, time irrevocably passing, passing swiftly, too swiftly . . .

"Vicky—"

I turned toward him.

He was looking at the sand slipping through his fingers, not at me. It was as though he were somehow thinking my thoughts. "You're upset because Ynid lost her baby."

"Of course. Probably not as upset as you are, but sure, of course I'm upset."

"You're more upset than just *of course*. Why?"

"It's just—it's just—there's death everywhere—Commander Rodney—and watching Grandfather, and now Ynid's baby for no reason—it's just everywhere."

"Always has been. It's part of the price of being born."

"It just seems that lately . . ." My voice trembled and I leaned forward and carefully scratched Rochester behind the ears.

"Is the price too high?" Adam asked.

I shrugged, in the way that Mother hates.

"Are you afraid?" he asked softly.

Yes. I didn't say it aloud. I didn't need to.

"Of what, Vicky?" He picked up another handful of sand, and started trickling it through his fingers. "Dying?" His voice wasn't loud, but the word seemed to explode into the night.

Mr. Rochester shifted position and I continued absent-mindedly to scratch behind his ears, his short fur rough under my fingers. "Not so much of dying, if—I'm afraid of annihilation. Of not being."

Adam let all the sand fall. "I guess we all are, if it comes to that."

"Is that what you think it comes to? That Commander Rodney was just snuffed out? And Ynid's baby? And that Grandfather will be? And all of us?"

There was a long silence against which the waves moving into shore and the light wind in the grasses and Rochester's breathing sounded in counterpoint.

At last Adam spoke. "I'm not a churchgoer, Vicky. I hadn't darkened the doors of a church since I sang in choir at school till—till Commander Rodney's funeral. So maybe what I think is kind of heretical."

"What *do* you think?" I desperately wanted to know. Maybe because of Basil, I trusted Adam. The breeze lifted and blew across us, pushing my hair back from my forehead. I must have shivered, because Adam put one arm lightly across my shoulders.

"When are you most completely you, Vicky?"

It wasn't at all what I had expected him to say. I was looking for answers, not more questions.

"When?" he repeated.

Maybe because I was feeling extraordinarily tired I was thinking in scenes, rather than logical sequences, and across my mind's eye flashed a picture of the loft, with the old camp cots, and the windows overlooking the ocean, and the lighthouse at night with its friendly beam, and on the far wall the lines of the poem Grandfather had painted there, *If thou could'st empty all thyself of self . . .*

I was *not* really myself when I was all replete with very me. So when was I?

"When you first took me to meet Basil," I said slowly, "and when I was petting him and scratching his chest . . ."

"Who were you thinking about?"

"Basil."

"Were you thinking about *you*?"

"No."

162

"But you were really being you?"

"Yes."

"So that's contradiction, isn't it? You weren't thinking about yourself at all. You were completely thrown *out* of yourself in concentration on Basil. And yet you were really being really you."

I leaned my head against Adam's shoulder. "Much more than when I'm all replete with very me."

His right hand drew my head more comfortably against his shoulder. "So, when we're thinking consciously about ourselves, we're less ourselves than when we're not being self-centered."

"I suppose . . ."

"Okay, here's another analogy. Where are you when you write poetry?"

"This summer I'm usually up in the loft."

"You know that's not what I mean. When you're actually writing a poem, when you're in the middle of it, where are you?"

"I'm not sure. I'm more in the poem than I am in me. I'm using my mind, really using it, and yet I'm not directing the poem or telling it where to go. It's telling me."

His strong fingers moved gently across my hair. "That's the way it is with science, too. All the great scientists, like Newton, like Einstein, repeat the same thing—that the discoveries don't come when you're consciously looking for them. They come when for some reason you've let go conscious control. They come in a sudden flash, and you can receive that flash, or you can refuse to. But if you're willing to receive it, then for that instantaneous moment of time you're really you, but you're not conscious in the same way you have to be later on when you look at what you saw in the flash, and then have to work out the equations to prove it."

I heard every word he said. And I think I understood. At the same time my entire body was conscious of the feel of his fingers stroking my hair. I wondered if he felt it as strongly as I did. But I asked, "Has that happened to you, that knowing in a flash?"

"Not in the way it did to Einstein, with his theory of relativity. Or to Dr. O'Keefe, with his work on limb regeneration. But in little ways with Basil, yes. He's taught me more about himself than I could have learned with just my thinking self. And Basil—Basil has taught you, hasn't he?"

"Yes. Oh, yes."

He lifted his hand and stopped stroking. "And you saw Jeb with Ynid."

Yes, I had seen Dr. Nutteley with Ynid. In the midst of his pain, Jeb had been wholly real.

"What I think"—Adam's hand began caressing my hair again—"is that if we're still around after we die, it will be more like those moments when we let go, than the way we are most of the time. It'll be—it'll be the self beyond the self we know."

At that moment there was a rip in the clouds and an island of star-sparkled sky appeared, its light so brilliant it seemed to reach down beyond the horizon and encircle the earth, a ring of pure and endless light.

I wasn't sure that Adam's words were comforting. But his arm about me was. He made me feel very real, not replete with me at all, only real, and hopeful.

He turned toward me and I thought he was going to kiss me and I wanted him to kiss me. But he just looked at me for a long time without smiling, and I wondered how much he could see in the island of starlight. His face was shadowed, and maybe it was just that more clouds opened, but it was as though his light had come on, and he smiled. "I knew we were going to be able to talk, Vicky. I knew it when I first met you. I don't talk this way to many people."

I murmured, "I don't either." Only, maybe, to people like Grandfather. But this was different. As different as being with Basil.

And I knew that if Adam kissed me it was going to be different from Zachary, with all his experience, or Leo, with all his naïveté.

Adam did not kiss me.

Yet I felt as close to him as though he had.

7

I woke up early the next morning, with the summer sun pouring across my bed and my eyes. I looked at my watch. Not yet six. Nobody'd be stirring for another hour.

I pulled my writing things from under the bed, dressed, and slipped quietly down the ladder.

The house was silent. No sound from the big four-poster bed where my parents were sleeping. No sound from the hospital bed in Grandfather's study. If he was awake he would be either reading or meditating.

Rochester rose from his battered red rug at the foot of the ladder, stretched, and followed me. Sunlight streamed across the kitchen. I wanted to write something for Ynid. I stared across the porch to the blinding early-morning light bursting across the sea. A sonnet. A sonnet for Ynid and her baby.

Ynid couldn't read. But Jeb Nutteley could, and Adam, if I wrote something I dared give them.

I stopped thinking about Dr. Nutteley and Adam and focused on the poem. It came swiftly, with lots of quick crossings-out, as new words, new lines pushed aside what I had first written down.

The earth will never be the same again.
Rock, water, tree, iron, share this grief
As distant stars participate in pain.
A candle snuffed, a falling star or leaf,
A dolphin death, O this particular loss
Is Heaven-mourned; for if no angel cried,
If this small one was tossed away as dross,
The very galaxies then would have lied.
How shall we sing our love's song now
In this strange land where all are born to die?
Each tree and leaf and star show how
The universe is part of this one cry,
That every life is noted and is cherished,
And nothing loved is ever lost or perished.

Did I believe that? I didn't know, but I had not, as it were, dictated the words, I had simply followed them where they wanted to lead.

And whether or not it was a passable sonnet I didn't know, nor whether or not I'd presume to show it to Dr. Nutteley or Adam.

But I felt the good kind of emptiness that comes when I've finished writing something. The emptiness quickly translated itself into plain, ordinary hunger.

I'd just put a saucepan of milk on the stove to warm when the phone rang.

"Vicky, I'm glad it's you. This is Adam."

"Yes. Hi!"

"I hope I didn't wake anybody. Listen, can you come over this morning first thing?" His voice sounded eager. "I want to try something new in my dolphin experiment, and I need you."

"Sure I'll come." I didn't even try to keep the rush of gladness out of my voice.

"Can you come right now? I mean, don't wait for John. Have you had breakfast?"

"Not yet."

"How about meeting me at the cafeteria and we'll have coffee and an English or something while I clue you in to what I hope to do this morning."

"Okay. Be there as soon as my bike'll get me there." I turned off the heat under my milk and left a note: "Hope somebody wants *café au lait*. I'm off to the lab. See you when."

As I got my bike out of the shed I heard someone else stirring about the house, so I pedaled off quickly to avoid conversation or explanation.

I'd grabbed my bathing suit and a towel from the line and stuffed them, still damp, into my bike basket. The early morning was cool and misty, but I sniffed the salty air and felt the warmth of sun above the mist and decided that it was going to be a fine day, and we'd be back in summer heat.

It takes nearly half an hour to get from the stable to the labs and I worked up an appetite. Adam was waiting for me at the entrance to the cafeteria, and we got trays and joined the line of early breakfasters. The line moved quickly. Adam led me to a table in the corner.

He ate impatiently. "Jeb has spent years learning dolphin language. He has a whole library of tapes, and he can slow them down so you can hear most of the sounds they make, the supersonic ones. You mentioned birds the other day, and a lot of dolphin conversation sounds somewhat like birds chirping." He paused. "Jeb figures they have a pretty sophisticated vocabulary. The real

168

problem in audible conversation between dolphins and human beings, as I see it, is that we have vocal cords and they don't. Our whole mechanism of vocalizing is completely different. To some extent they can make sounds which are recognizable as words, and it's a game with them, but it doesn't go all the way because they simply don't have the vocal equipment. And to some extent we can imitate their clickings and chirpings and blowings, but only to some extent."

"So what you're really saying"—I leaned on my elbows in my eagerness—"is that talking with dolphins doesn't really work, but maybe we should be trying to communicate with them in another way?"

"Exactly. Good girl. So—what way?"

I thought for a moment. "Two things come to my mind."

"Okay. What?"

"Deaf people—people who are completely deaf—can feel vibrations. They can hear music by putting their hands against the wood of a violin, for instance. But—"

He leaned across the table toward me. "But what?"

"Dolphins aren't deaf. But they *do* use sonar, don't they?"

"In a most sophisticated way. Go on."

"So vibrations, maybe a sort of Morse code, could take us a lot further than words."

"Who said you weren't a scientist?" he demanded.

"I'm not. Ask John or Suzy."

"You're a poet." I thought of the sonnet in my jeans pocket. "And so are most great scientists. Okay, Jeb's been working on the vibration question, and with numbers, because numbers cut across language barriers—though I've sometimes wondered about number concepts with creatures with no fingers or toes. But you're thinking about something else, aren't you?"

I was. "You won't think I'm dumb?"

Adam sounded impatient. "Come on, Vicky. I know you're not dumb."

"It sounds way out—"

"Dolphins are way out. Come on."

"Knowing," I said slowly. "Knowing without having to speak. Sort of ESP, but more—knowing, maybe even across time and space. Basil knew you were upset about Ynid yesterday. You didn't tell him. He knew. From way out at sea."

"Yes . . ."

"Basil knew you were upset because Ynid lost her baby, so he brought a friend to comfort you and take your mind off things."

"Okay. Go on."

"And she—"

He interrupted me. "How'd you know it was a female? You're right, but how'd you know?"

"I don't know how I knew. It just came to me. As though Basil had told me, in the language of knowing, not the language of words."

Adam sighed. "Yah, I'll bet Basil probably did tell you. It's a known fact that when a wild dolphin makes friends it's usually with a child."

"I'm not a child," I said sharply. "I'm almost sixteen."

He didn't even notice that I objected to being referred to as a child. "Probably one reason that Basil and his pod were so slow in coming to me is that I'm too old."

"You're not that much older than I am."

"I'm nearly nineteen and I'm in college. It makes a difference. The fact is that Basil was much easier with you than he was with John, or even with me at first. He came to you right away, without fear or hesitation. And I think you're right. He *did* let you know that his companion is a female. I don't know how he did it, but he did. What shall we call her?"

"What about Norberta?" I suggested. "We named Suzy's science-project guppy that. It means *brightness of Njord*, and Njord was the Norse god of the sea, so it seems appropriate."

"Appropriate indeed. Norberta she shall be. Okay, go on. Basil knew something I had no way of telling him. What else?"

"Ynid. She stopped beating herself against the side of the tank when Jeb got in with her."

"Why?"

"Because she loves Jeb and Jeb loves her." I felt slightly odd calling Dr. Nutteley Jeb, but since Adam did, I did, too.

"Go on."

"You told me Jeb lost his wife and baby . . ."

"Yes."

"Ynid knew. She knew Jeb was grieving and needed help even more than she did." I did not look at Adam as I said this. I gazed down at the table and the unattractive remains of English muffin and pallid marmalade.

"Vicky." His voice drew my eyes away from the plate, to meet his luminous sea-grey ones. "This summer project is very important to me."

"Sure . . ."

"John thought you might be useful to me and he

was right, more than right. You've hit on exactly my thesis. Communication between human being and dolphin is going to come about through the kind of intuitive flash of knowing we were talking about last night. I'm convinced of it. Maybe you're a—a *receiver*, because you're a poet, but also because you're still a child."

"I'm not—" I started.

He seemed determined to emphasize it. "Many children have this ability, which is, as you say, way beyond ESP, but it usually gets lost with maturity." He asked, "Want anything more to eat?"

"No, thanks."

"Let's walk off breakfast. Then we'll swim out and see what happens."

"What do you think's going to happen?" I asked tentatively. He had made me feel unsure and insecure.

"I don't know. I'm hoping Basil will come with Norberta, but we'll just have to wait and see." He took our trays out, and we left the cafeteria and went to the dolphin pens. During the night they'd been opened to each other, and the five dolphins, Una, Nini, Ynid, and her two midwives, were swimming from pen to pen. There was, I thought, something sad and subdued about Ynid's swimming.

Jeb Nutteley was there with a bucket of fresh fish. He nodded at us, and tossed a fish to Ynid. "She's eating. Not with much appetite, but she's eating."

"That's a relief." Adam watched Ynid swim to the end of the pen, holding the fish in her mouth.

"Eat it, Ynid, there's a love," Jeb pleaded.

Ynid smiled and swallowed the fish. She loved Jeb Nutteley and he certainly was not a child. I did not want Adam to think of me as a child. Not after last night.

"I'd hand the feeding over to you," Jeb said, "but Ynid might not eat."

"She needs you today," Adam agreed.

"What're you kids up to?" Jeb sounded calm, a little drained maybe, from his storm of grief the day before, but quiet now, relaxed.

"Off to work with Basil, if that's okay."

"Make sure you report to me as soon as you come in." Jeb threw several fish rapidly, one after the other, into the pen, and the great grey bodies flashed toward their breakfast.

I'd forgotten to ask Adam what his boss had thought of his taking me to meet Basil. "Was Jeb cross when you told him about Basil and me?"

Adam made a wry face. "Cross is not the word. He was furious, even when I told him I'd checked with John first. Then he was furious with John, too."

"But he's okay about it now?"

"I'm supposed to check in with him before we leave the lab and after we get back. I didn't check in yesterday because of Ynid's baby. But I did, after, and I told him about it all, partly to get his mind off Ynid. He does see that you're a valuable part of my experiment."

Maybe up to the night before I'd have been satisfied with being a valuable part of Adam's experiment.

He'd walked on and was heading toward the beach. I ran to catch up. "Why were the pens opened up?"

He paused, looking back at the pens and waiting. "They often are. Jeb wanted Ynid more enclosed for her delivery. Then he thought she might recover better if she had all her friends with her."

That made sense. "Jeb knows all about your theory?"

"Non-verbal communication? Yes. Jeb's a great guy. He's really encouraging me."

"Why did you drag it out of me at breakfast instead of just telling me?"

"If I'd just told you, I wouldn't have known how much you, yourself, understand. Having you tell me is a necessary part of my experiment, you must see that."

"Oh. Sure."

"And I had a hunch—maybe a *knowing*, as you called it—that your poet's mind had already leaped to what it's taken me all summer to arrive at."

My poet's mind. That sounded really nice. Then he ruined it.

"And you're still young enough."

I said, stiffly, "If you wanted a child, why didn't you ask Suzy?"

"I told you, Vicky. I didn't need another scientist, another pragmatist. Suzy's about as pragmatic as anyone can be. I thought I'd made it clear: scientists need poets, mystics, people who can escape our logical, linear thinking."

At first he had sounded chiding, adult to child, and I hated it. Then he was talking to me, Adam to Vicky. I didn't understand Adam at all this morning, one moment treating me like a child, the next like a reasonable human being, a peer. He was being as unpredictable as Zachary, and while I was prepared for it in Zachary, I wasn't in Adam. "Grandfather says—" I started, and stopped in mid-sentence. I'd simply run off when Adam called, not thinking about Grandfather, or helping Mother, not thinking about anything except that Adam had called and I was going to him as quickly as I could get there. I'd left the note, but that wasn't really enough. "Adam, is there any way I could phone home before we go to meet Basil? I went off before anybody else was up this morning."

"Sure. There're phone booths outside the lab."

We retraced our steps.

Fortunately, Mother answered.

"Did you get my note?"

"Yes. What's up?"

"It's Adam's experiment."

"With starfish?"

"No, dolphins. Is it all right if I stay here this morning?" If I could tell her about Basil and non-verbal communication, it would be easier.

"Sure."

"How's Grandfather?"

"About the same. Nancy Rodney's here to help him bathe and shave." Mother's voice was matter-of-fact, but I knew that Grandfather's increasing weakness had to be getting to her even more than it did to me, and that Mrs. Rodney's coming in the morning wasn't just happenstance, for one day; it was going to be part of the slowly shifting pattern of our days.

"Are you sure you don't need me?"

"Positive. Everything's fine. You stay with Adam and have fun."

I stopped myself from trying to explain that it wasn't just fun, but what was the point? No one would take it seriously. I knew that my family would find it hard to believe that dreamy Vicky, full of cobwebs, could be involved in even the smallest way in any kind of scientific project.

People were still straggling into the cafeteria for

breakfast as we headed for the beach. My damp towel and bathing suit felt chilly where I was clutching them against my shirt, but the mist had completely burned away and the sun was climbing high and hot in the sky. It was hard to realize that the night before I'd been huddled into a sweater.

The night before: Adam had certainly been talking to me as Adam to Vicky the night before, not as scientist to useful child.

I changed to my bathing suit behind the big rock. It felt clammy as I shimmied into it. I spread my damp towel over the rock to dry. As for my bathing suit, it would shortly be all the way wet.

"What I want you to do," Adam said as I came up to him, "is to call Basil."

"But I can't—" I thought of Adam's balloon and clucking noises.

"Not the way I've been calling to him. Call him the way you *knew* about Norberta."

I paused, dabbling my toes in the wavelets tracing their delicate way into shore. "Do you want me to call Norberta, too?"

"It's up to you."

"Suppose they don't come?"

"If they don't come they don't come and we try again. Stop worrying. All you have to do is try. You don't have to succeed."

I looked at his stern face and splashed into the water, which felt cool after the rain. When we got beyond the breakers, there were deep swells, topped with whitecaps. Adam swam swiftly and cleanly, soon passing me, and I followed, till I caught up with him treading water and looking not out to sea but at me.

I rolled over on my back and floated, my body rising and lowering gently in the swells. I closed my eyes, not so much against the radiant blue as against distractions, and imaged Basil. In my mind's eye I saw him clearly, butting against me and asking me to scratch his chest.

Then I imaged Basil and Norberta leaping together, coming to swim, one on each side of Adam. I concentrated on Basil and Norberta the way I concentrate when I'm deep in the world of a book, or when I'm caught up in writing a poem, the way I was earlier in the morning. I was concentrating so completely that at first I didn't hear Adam.

"Vic. Vicky! *Vicky!*"

I opened my eyes and rolled over in the water.

There, coming toward us, were not two but three dolphins, Basil and Norberta and a baby, not as small as Ynid's, but definitely a child, and alive, beautifully alive. It swam close to its mother, imitating her every flick of fluke, and making small chirruping noises.

It swam close to us, curious as to these two strange creatures who weren't fish but certainly weren't dolphins. It butted me with its little head and I reached out my hand, underwater, and very gently scratched its belly, and it wriggled with pleasure.

Norberta chirped at it, and then they swam around us, mother and baby, once, twice, thrice. It was obvious to me that Norberta was showing off her baby. Then she patted it briskly with her flipper, a sort of love spank, and turned and headed for the open sea, the baby beside her.

Basil stayed. Adam was staring after Norberta and the baby, and Basil nudged him to get his attention, gently at first, then roughly enough so that he went underwater.

He came up and grabbed Basil's dorsal fin and the two of them went into one of their great splashing wrestling matches. Then it was my turn. Again Basil dove under me and came up so that I was sitting astride his back. I did my best to hold on while he swam swiftly after Norberta and the baby. For a moment I thought he might be making off with me forever, and then I could feel him telling me to trust him, and he turned in a great slow circle so I wouldn't fall off, and swam back to where Adam was waiting. Then he leapt up into the air so that I slid off his back and into the water, and off he went, to vanish into the horizon.

"C'mon," Adam ordered, and swam shoreward.

When we were standing on the beach, with me hopping on one foot to try to get water out of my ear, Adam took my hand and shook it heartily. "You did it. Thanks. Wait till I tell Jeb."

I waited for him to turn a cartwheel or stand on his head, but he just stood there. "Did I? Maybe they'd have come anyhow."

"They've never come for me that way. And I've tried to ride Basil and he's never let me."

"I didn't try to—"

He said impatiently, "I know you didn't. It was Basil's idea. He's teaching you how to play with him. Did you enjoy it?"

I flung out my arms to the sun and the wind and the golden day. Then I started to twirl like a whirling dervish, twirled until I fell onto the sand, and the world continued to circle round me.

Adam stood over me. "Did Norberta tell you anything? Was there anything she wanted you to know?"

"I think so. But maybe it's just my imagination everybody tells me I have so much of."

Adam rode over that. "What did Norberta tell you?"

"That she's sorry about Ynid's baby. That she's happy about hers. That he's going to be my friend."

"He?"

"Yes."

"How'd you know?"

"I guess—I guess she told me."

"Did she tell you how old he is?"

"About a year."

He started at me. "Yah, that's just about right. What're you going to call him?"

"Njord, the god of the sea."

At this, Adam smiled. "Oh, you think he's pretty terrific, don't you?"

"I do. He is. Adam, would Jeb like to see him?"

Adam flopped down onto the sand. "I'll write up everything that happened this morning and give the report to Jeb. But as to bringing him to see Njord—I'm not at all sure the dolphins would come for him, for one thing. For another, I haven't taken anybody to see Basil except John and you. So, for my project's sake, I'm not inviting him to meet my dolphins. Not yet."

My dolphins. He sounded mighty possessive. *My* dolphins. *My* project. *My* child helper. I stood up, shaking sand off me. "I'd better go rinse."

"Me, too."

We splashed about in the shallow waves until the sand was off. Then Adam shook himself like a dog.

"Good morning's work, Vic." His voice was brisk and impersonal. "I'd better get on back to the lab. I want to write it all up while it's fresh. You'll be okay?"

"Sure." I thought of the cafeteria English muffins. "Would you like to come on over to the stable for dinner this evening?"

"Not tonight," he replied shortly. "I don't want to wear out my welcome, and I have a lot to do. I'll be in touch."

I was dismissed.

This wasn't the Adam who'd turned cartwheels of joy along the beach, or who had talked to me the night before as though I was a real human being, not just John's kid sister.

I'd gone to bed thinking that my growing friendship with Adam had to be part of that pattern Grandfather had talked about, and here he was throwing the pattern out as deliberately as though he'd thrown a partly finished jigsaw puzzle onto the floor.

I looked at his retreating back. I was furious. I wanted to burst into tears. I wanted to lie down on the sand and kick. All I was to Adam, obviously, was a part of his project, not as important a part as the dolphins, of course. I wasn't there because I was Vicky, but only because I was a child who was useful to him. Child, child, child. He'd rammed it down my throat.

But I was more than a mere child to the dolphins. Something in me was sure of that.

I got on my bike and pedaled home.

I felt sore, as though something inside me had been bruised.

I peeked into Grandfather's study and he was awake,

so I read to him for a while. I kept fumbling over words, which I don't normally do, and Grandfather stopped me, asking, "What's on your mind?"

"I went to the lab this morning."

Grandfather nodded. "What went wrong?"

"I'm not sure. The only thing I can think of—well, Grandfather, this sounds like blowing my own horn, but the thing is that in a way I communicated better with the dolphins than Adam did. Do you think that would make him jealous?"

Grandfather thought this over for a moment. "He doesn't strike me as the jealous type. But it might give him pause."

"Here he is, trained in marine biology, and I don't know anything about it at all, but, Grandfather, I do have a thing with dolphins. I can't explain it, but Adam's dolphins really communicated with me. I can't explain any better, because his project's sort of classified—I mean, he doesn't want it talked about."

Grandfather put his hand gently over mine. "I get enough of the picture to see that you may have made the young man do some serious thinking."

"Last night he was treating me as a—as a *peer,* and to-day he kept calling me a child, and going on about how dolphins respond better to children than to adults . . ."

Grandfather patted my hand. "As I said, you probably made him think. Just give him time to absorb whatever it was that happened this morning."

"Thanks, Grandfather. I feel better. I'll go on reading."

———

The next day I heard not a word from Adam. Leo called. Zachary called. Adam called, but not for me, for Suzy, to arrange to take her to the dolphin pens.

That night she was full of talk about the dolphins and Dr. Nutteley and Adam and the dolphins again. She'd fed Una and Nini. She'd held a fish in her teeth and Una had taken it and she hadn't been the least bit scared and Adam had said she was terrific. "He's nice, even if he is kind of square."

"He's not square," John defended.

"He's so serious-minded. Doesn't he ever do anything but study? All he has on his mind is that project of his."

"What project?" I asked sharply.

"You know, working on dolphin-human communication. He really does communicate with Una and Nini. Maybe they'll teach him not to be so square."

Which was the real Adam? The single-minded scientist, concentrating on his experiment? The philosopher of that night with me on the beach? The Adam full of fun, turning cartwheels?

At any rate, Suzy didn't mention Basil or Norberta and Njord. It was at least a small consolation that Adam had introduced her only to the dolphins in the pens.

Mrs. Rodney came daily to bathe Grandfather and help him shave. He stayed more and more on the hospital bed, though when most of us were out he would take a cane and walk slowly to the porch to be with the ocean.

When Mrs. Rodney was through, it was my time to read to him. Sometimes he paid keen attention. Other times his mind wandered. Once he interrupted me. "Sogdian."

"What?" I lowered the book.

"Nubian, Persian, Caucasian, Old Saxon."

I was frightened. "What, Grandfather?"

"I'm dreaming in languages I haven't thought of in years, haven't needed."

He smiled at me and his eyes were clear.

I asked, "You know—knew—all those?"

"In seminary. And while I was working on my dissertation. And for a few years after that. I wanted to read the New Testament in all the earliest versions— and I'm dreaming in them now, as though in tongues, and sometimes Tongues, too, which may be the language of Angels—though it's understood and spoken by the fallen angels, too, and not enough people remember that."

He paused, and I asked, "What about the fallen angels?"

"They take many guises. Demonic possession, for instance. Have you heard from young Adam?"

I shook my head.

"And how about dark Zachary?"

"I'm going out with him this afternoon."

"How are things going there?"

"At any rate *he* doesn't treat me like a child."

"And how is he, himself?"

"With Zachary it's hard to know. He gives the impression of being in control of everything. And then he opens a chink, and there's all that lostness and frightenedness within."

"It's in most of us," Grandfather said. "Perhaps we

don't cover it up as well. What are the two of you going to do?"

"He's taking flying lessons, and his teacher has a
small charter plane, and he's going to take me up in it.
I'll tell you all about it tomorrow."

Flying!

Flying was like playing with Basil, which is as great
a thing as I can say about it. I understood why Zachary
was willing to stay out of trouble during his first year
in college in order to have his own plane. For a moment I felt a little wistful about not having all the
money in the world.

Art, the pilot, was a chunky young man, a good
head shorter than Zachary, but there was something
comfortable about his muscular body and white teeth
gleaming in his dark face. He couldn't have been a
great deal older than Zachary, but he exuded confidence as he strapped me into the Piper Cub in the seat
beside his own. Zachary sat behind us, giving a running commentary.

Art flew the little plane with such loving tenderness
that I felt only the tiniest flutter in my middle when we
lifted from the runway. We flew across the water and
all the familiar buildings on the Island looked different, seen from the air. When we flew over the stable,
the pilot dipped first the left wing, then the right, and
Rob and Mother and Daddy were standing at the edge
of the bluff, waving, because Zachary had told them
approximately when we'd be there.

Then we were back over the sea again, and Art sent
the plane into swirls and dives and loops and if it
hadn't been for Basil I'd probably have been terrified.

When he righted the plane and we were flying along a straight line, Art rubbed his strong fingers through his tight black curls and gave me a steady, hard look that reminded me of Grandfather. "Hey. Sure you've never been up before?"

"Positive."

"Thought I'd scare you out of your wits."

I couldn't tell him that I might not have been up in a plane but I had flown a dolphin. "It was fun." I was excited and pleased with myself because I hadn't been afraid.

"This kid's okay," Art called back to Zachary. "Most people would have been screaming bloody murder. But she's okay."

"Told you she would be."

I wondered if Zachary'd told Art to do all that stunt stuff, and thought he probably had. Did he know it was going to exhilarate me? Or did he want to scare me? Zach being Zach, it could be either one.

Before we left the airport, we made a date with Art for the following Wednesday. Wednesday I'd come to think of as my day with Adam and the dolphins, but I hadn't heard a word from Adam. Sure, I'd love to go flying on Wednesday.

We drove from the airport to the country club for dinner. This time, because of the dance to follow, dinner was an elegant and elaborate buffet. There were more dishes beautifully arranged in silver serving pieces than I could count. Zachary offered me champagne and I turned it down—not that I haven't had plenty of sips of champagne at home, but I felt more grownup being free to refuse than I would have if I'd felt I had to prove something by accepting.

I'm a lot more at home in the water than I am on

the dance floor, but Zachary was a beautiful dancer and I found that dancing wasn't that much different from swimming, after all.

The ballroom was like something out of one of the old fairy tales of princes and princesses, dripping with crystal chandeliers, and gilt chairs along the wall, and a small band at one end, and a buffet with wines and punches and sherbets and cakes at the other. Despite the air-conditioning, which was going full blast, the long glass doors were open to a flagstoned terrace, and couples danced in and out of the night. It was lovely, but the country club was surely using more than its fair share of energy. Zachary turned me toward one of the open doors, and then we were on the terrace, and then on the short-clipped velvety green lawn, and then under the sheltering branches of an ancient maple tree.

"Let's rest." Zachary's breathing was short and shallow. "That's the most exercise I've had since . . . and I'm feeling it a bit." He dropped down to the grass and I followed. I had on the pale-blue dress, and I hoped I wouldn't get grass stains on it.

I leaned against the rough bark of the tree. Zachary, with a graceful movement, lay down with his head in my lap. Light streaming across terrace and lawn touched his black hair with strange silver lights.

"Okay, Vicky-O," he said abruptly. "What does life hold for you?"

That was a Zachary-type question, because of its unexpectedness if nothing else. "School, and then college."

"And then what?"

"I don't know. I wish I did. John and Suzy both know where they're going, and Rob's too little still."

"So where are John and Suzy going?"

"John's always been interested in space, space exploration, and everything it involves, so I suppose he'll be an astrophysicist. Suzy's going to be a doctor or a vet."

"Goody for them." He reached for my hand and put it against his cheek. "Rub my hair," he commanded. "And you don't have any idea about you?"

"Oh, I have some ideas." His hair felt silky and soft beneath my fingers. "I'm interested in writing, but not the kind you earn a living from right away, like journalism and feature articles."

"What kind, then? That feels lovely. Don't stop."

I continued moving my fingers through his hair. "Poetry." I thought of the sonnet for Jeb and Ynid still stuck in a wrinkled wad in my jeans pocket. "Stories, maybe, and novels."

"Still evading the real world, eh?"

I took my fingers out of his hair. "That's how you find the real world."

"You'd make a lousy lawyer."

"I have no intention of being any kind of lawyer. You know what Shakespeare says about lawyers?"

"Okay, egghead, what does Shakespeare say?"

"*The first thing we do, let's kill all the lawyers.* It's in one of the *Henrys*, I forget which."

Zachary stretched his arms up and pulled my head down toward his. We kissed. And then the kiss was going too far, and I pulled away.

"Why?" Zachary demanded.

"I just—I just need to catch my breath."

"I scare you?"

"No."

"We do have something very special going, Vicky.

You know that. Our chemistry really works. Why don't you just let go and enjoy it?"

"I do enjoy it, Zach, but—"

"But me no buts. I can quote Shakespeare, too, I'm not as illiterate as you may think." Swiftly, Zachary turned himself so that he was kneeling, facing me. He was right about chemistry. Ours really fizzed. It fizzed too much.

And I saw Adam's face, felt Adam's hands, not Zachary's.

Why did Adam have to intrude? He hadn't called me; he'd made it quite clear that all I was to him was a child. And even if he wasn't jealous of my communicating with the dolphins, it wasn't bringing us any closer. Adam didn't want me, and Zachary did. So why was he superimposing on Zachary, like a double negative? I did not like it, and I couldn't blot out his image.

Again I pushed his hands away.

"*Why?*" Zachary demanded, his fingers clamping tight about my wrists.

"Ouch, you hurt."

He did not loosen his grip. "Everything about you is saying 'Come on,' and then you pull away. Why?"

"Zachary." I pulled my hands away from his with a jerk. "I'm not sixteen. You could be arrested for assaulting a minor."

I thought he was going to hit me. Then he said, "Vicky, sweetie, I won't do anything you don't want to do. I thought you wanted to. Be honest. Didn't you?"

I rubbed my wrist where it hurt from his grasp. "I'm not ready. Not yet."

"Don't throw that not-quite-sixteen stuff at me. Lots of kids—"

"I'm not lots of kids, I'm Vicky. And I'm not ready. Not yet."

There was a damp edge to the breeze.

"Don't tell me I don't turn you on, because I know I do."

He did. He did, and then Adam got in the way. Does this kind of thing ever happen to other people? this being confused and torn between two people you care about? For once I was glad I was still fifteen. What would I do if I was old enough to marry, and this kind of thing, this double image, happened to me?

"Come on," Zachary said. "Let's go back in." He took my hand and we walked over the soft grass, which was beginning to be damp with dew. We passed a couple under another tree, lying together and kissing, in complete oblivion of anybody who might be passing. And I realized that Zachary and I would have been equally visible to passers-by, despite the sheltering branches of the tree.

And I realized, too, that Adam or no Adam, I would still have pulled away from Zachary.

We got in the Alfa Romeo and he drove too quickly and I hated it, and at the same time I was excited by the speed, because it was all I could think about, and I forgot my inner turmoil.

Leo and his friend were playing chess, but when Zachary said, "Hey, Leo, let's go," Leo stood up, leaving the game unfinished. We didn't talk on the trip back to the Island. I don't know what Zachary or Leo was thinking. All I wanted was to get home, to my cot in the loft, where everything was simple and uncomplicated.

But as Zachary left me at the screen door he said, "Don't fret, Vicky-O. There'll be other times and other places. No matter what, you're my sanity, don't you ever forget that." He kissed me, lightly, and said, "After we go flying on Wednesday I'll take you to a nice little French restaurant I've discovered. Only half a dozen or so tables and really beautiful food. So relax."

I let myself in quietly and went up to the loft. I was anything but relaxed, and it took me a long time to get quiet enough to go to sleep.

8

Sunday evening we cooked hamburgers down in Grandfather's cove—all of us except Grandfather. It was a clear, beautiful night, although John said that the wind was shifting and that it would rain by morning.

I tried to go back to just enjoying the evening, but flickers of the turmoil of the night before moved across my mind like small clouds. Suzy was envious of my having gone up in a plane, and wanted me to ask Zachary if he'd take her.

"And Adam said he'd take me to see the dolphins and he hasn't," Rob complained. "He took Suzy, but he hasn't taken me."

"I could take you," John said.

"But I want to see Adam's dolphins. You're working with starfish."

There was no way I could avoid thinking about Adam. Or Zachary. After a year in New York, when the boys at school had sometimes called me about the homework but none of them had asked me for a date or even walked home with me (and Suzy always had some kid carrying her books), now here I was with three, count them, three boys on my mind. It was small comfort to know that I was more on Leo's mind than he on mine, because it gave me a vague feeling of responsibility toward him.

Zachary was like being out in a storm. It was exciting and frightening at the same time.

Adam represented the grownup world, the world of the lab, and Jeb Nutteley and Nora Zand and all the other scientists there. And Adam was swimming out to meet Basil, and sharing the loveliness of Norberta and Njord. But if I was more on Leo's mind than he on mine, the reverse was obviously true with Adam and me. I thought about Leo only if he called, or I was going out with him, or he was taking Zachary and me to or from the mainland. But Adam appeared in my mind without warning or reason.

Did he ever think about me except in connection with the dolphins and his experiment? Not likely. Does it ever even out, what two people feel for each other? Or does one always care more?

I'd lost track of the conversation.

Suzy was talking about my date with Zachary.

> *"Love is a little thing shaped like a lizard.*
> *It runs up and down and tickles your gizzard,"*

she intoned.

"Don't be vulgar," I said automatically. However, her idiot rhyme wasn't a bad description of what Zachary did to me. And suddenly I didn't like it. Not the rhyme, but the way Zachary made me feel. I didn't like it because it was only a part of me, only the physical part. Zachary fascinated me, like a cobra. And I didn't want just to be fascinated. I wanted more than that.

192

Because I hadn't ever had it, I wasn't sure what that more was. I only knew I wanted it.

Daddy handed me my hamburger, just the way I like it. I slathered on mustard and catsup and put on a big slice of sweet onion.

"I want mine cooked in the middle," Suzy said, "not raw, like Vicky's. Say, John, why didn't you ask Adam tonight?"

"I did," John said.

"Why didn't he come?"

"We're not the only people he knows on the Island. He probably was going somewhere else."

"Next time we have a picnic," Suzy continued, "maybe we should ask the Rodneys."

Daddy turned the hamburgers on the grill. "Sometimes it's good to be just the family."

"I wish Grandfather could have come."

"He hasn't been up to climbing down to the beach for quite a while, Suze."

"As a matter of fact," Mother added, "he's always hated picnics. Why get all eaten up with bugs, he asks, when we can have a beautiful view of the ocean right from the porch."

John helped himself to potato salad. "Come to think of it, he probably had plenty of roughing it in Africa and Alaska."

When we'd finished eating, and burned the paper plates and cups, Mother and Daddy and Rob went back to the stable.

Suzy wanted to chitter-chatter, but both John and I wanted to be quiet and watch the stars come out, and after a while she stood up. "You two are boring. I'm going up to the stable and call Jacky and have some conversation."

John and I sat on in silence.

The stars came out, one by one.

When we were little, in Thornhill, when anything big happened, Mother would pile us into the station wagon, and we'd drive up to the summit of Hawk Mountain and look at the stars and talk. So stars have always helped me to get things into perspective. My confusion over Adam and Zachary wouldn't ease up, so I turned my mind away from them and tried to let the starlight heal something deep in me that hurt.

"Penny," John said after a while.

My mind had certainly wandered. "I've been reading physics to Grandfather in the morning. He says the physicists and cellular biologists and people like that are the modern mystics. Do you know about singularities, John?" That was a silly question. Of course John knows about singularities.

"Yup," John replied amiably. "How about the Schwarzschild radius?"

"Is that the circle you have to stay out of if you don't want to get sucked into the black hole?"

"Correct. And I think Grandfather's right—as always—about the mystics. And maybe poets, too. There's a kind of white dwarf star that's known as a degenerate white dwarf. I've always thought that would be a good title for a science-fiction story."

"Or a fairy tale. Maybe I'll make one up for Rob."

"If you do, give me a look. Also, Vic, listen to this one: a giant star with a helium-burning core turns into what the astrophysicists call a 'red giant sitting on the horizontal branch.' And do you know what a tachyon is?"

"Haven't the foggiest idea. But I love the thought of a red giant sitting on a horizontal branch. What's a tachyon?"

"They're particles that always travel faster than light."

"I thought nothing could. I thought the speed of light was the ultimate speed."

"It looks as if maybe it isn't, if tachyons exist. According to Einstein, nothing can cross the speed-of-light barrier, but it looks as though there may be tachyons on the other side of it."

"And tachyons can't travel slower than light?"

"That's the theory. You're not so unscientific after all, Vic."

"If it was all things like singularities and tachyons and dolphins . . ." I started.

And John took me by surprise. "Vic, have you and Adam had a falling out or something?"

"What made you ask that?"

"He trumped up a pretty flimsy excuse not to come to the picnic tonight."

"I thought he was going somewhere else."

"I indicated that for Suzy's benefit. He said he needed to write up his research notes. And the food's even worse on Sunday evenings than any other time."

"I don't think we had a falling out. But—"

"But what?"

"Last time I went out to the station he was suddenly completely different with me."

"Different how?" John asked gently.

"Well—when, he called to ask me to come over, he sounded all enthusiastic, and friendly, and then, all of a sudden, bang, he was being a grownup condescending to a child. And you know how he lights up? Well, the light sort of went out."

"Do you know why?" John asked.

"Well—the only thing I can think, is—well, did he tell you about my calling Basil and Norberta and Njord, and my riding Basil, and all?"

"Yes. He let me see the report he wrote up for Jeb. That's one reason I know he wasn't behind on his research notes."

"Do you think maybe he minded? Minded that they came for me, and Basil let me ride him, and all?"

"Not really," John said slowly. "Adam's got a pretty strong sense of his own center, so I don't think all that would throw him, even if it wouldn't exactly send him on an ego trip. You really do seem to have a very special thing going with dolphins."

"Yes. I know I do. I *don't* have a strong sense of my own center, but when I'm with the dolphins, I do. It's so wonderful that I hate to think Adam minds. But I can't think why else he turned me off the way he did."

"I can," John said. "He was putting the brakes on."

"Why? I thought we were really getting on okay."

"You were. That's the problem."

"Why?" I asked again.

"He had a bad experience with a girl last summer while he was working with Dr. O'Keefe in Portugal. I mean really bad."

"Do I remind him of her or something?"

"I doubt it. She was evidently an absolutely gorgeous blonde."

"Thanks."

"I don't want you to be a gorgeous blonde. I like you the way you are."

"Well, since I'm not a gorgeous blonde, why did Adam turn me off, then?"

"Vicky, you're not even sixteen."

"I'll be sixteen in November. What's that got to do with it?"

"Adam's got three more years of college, and then grad school for probably half a dozen more years before he can begin to think about being serious with anybody."

"Who said anything about being serious? Why can't we just be friends?"

"Maybe things between you were getting more than just friendship?"

I didn't answer for a while. Then: "Maybe. But can't things get a little more than just friendship without . . ."

"I don't know," John replied. "That's something you and Adam will have to work out."

"We can't work it out if we don't see each other."

"You'll have to see each other. He needs you for his project."

"It's nice to feel useful." I didn't try to keep the bitterness and hurt out of my voice.

John reached over and patted my shoulder. "Growing up isn't easy, is it, Vic? I worry about you more than I do about Suzy. Suzy's still my kid sister, and it's a funny feeling to know that you aren't, anymore. I mean, suddenly you're my contemporary."

That was nice of him. "Thanks. Thanks, John. And that's what I'd like to be with Adam. His contemporary. His colleague."

John didn't comment on that. Instead, he asked, "How are things with you and Leo?"

I sighed. "He's a really nice guy, after all."

"And what about Zachary?" John asked. "You're seeing a lot of him."

"Well, I don't think he's poison, the way the rest of you do."

"We don't think he's poison. We just don't want you getting hurt."

"I can take care of myself."

"Can you?" John asked. "Zachary's been around. How much does he—is he—"

I giggled.

"What's so funny?"

"Thanks for worrying about me, John, but isn't it sort of old-fashioned?"

"I probably am old-fashioned. So what? Anyhow, is he?"

"Sure he is. That's Zachary. But it isn't me, John, so don't fret."

"Maybe you're old-fashioned, too?"

"I'm not sure what being old-fashioned is."

"Not falling for things just because they're trendy. Not doing things just because everybody else is doing them. Not substituting what's real with what's phony."

In my mind's eye there flashed an image of one of my most unfavorite TV commercials. "You mean like that commercial for a fruit drink where the guy says with great pride that it's got ten percent real fruit juice?"

John laughed. "Precisely."

"Okay. I don't like substitutes for reality, either, so I'll go along with you in being old-fashioned. John—" I hesitated. "What about you and girls?"

"Like Adam, I have a lot of education ahead of me."

"Is marriage part of your plan?"

"Ultimately, yes. Mother and Dad have given us a pretty good picture of what marriage can be. I'd like to have a wife and kids. When I'm in a position to support them."

"That *is* old-fashioned," I commented. "Lots of women have careers right along with their husbands. What about your own boss this summer? And you don't think Suzy's going to give up being a doctor or a vet when she marries, do you?"

"Okay, you got me. Maybe I'm just not ready yet."

"Have you been dating anybody?" I looked up at the stars and hoped John wouldn't be offended.

He replied calmly, "There's a couple of girls I like in Boston. And Izzy and I've been corresponding. I'm not sure how I'll feel about her when we get back to Thornhill and I see her again. Okay, so maybe I am old-fashioned, but I don't want just a relationship. Relationships aren't real unless they end in bed, and they don't have to go any further than that. What I want is the real thing, and I'm not ready for it yet."

John, I thought, not only looked like Grandfather, he *was* like him. "Oh, John—thanks for talking to me as though I'm real. Zachary thinks our whole family's nuts."

"Everybody's nuts except thee and me," John said lightly. "And I'm not at all sure about thee. Maybe we'd better get back up to the stable."

"It's so nice out here . . ." I continued to look up at the

sky sprinkled with stars. Galaxies. Singularities. Red gi-
ants sitting on horizontal branches.

The ocean sang sleepily. The breeze stirred the
bushes. Then a star flashed across the sky and appeared to fall into the sea.

"That was a big one," John said, and stood up.
"Let's go."

The best thing about this talk with John was that it
made me feel grownup without adding to my confusion. And if Adam was putting on the brakes, it meant,
it had to mean, that there was something between us
big enough to make him do it.

John was right. I woke to a slow and steady rain,
and I wasn't quite warm enough.

There went Leo's plan for a day at the beach.

I got up and dressed, without waking the others, and
went down to the kitchen, and just as I got there the
phone rang and I picked it up on the first ring.

It was Adam. "John said you're usually the first up,
so I risked calling. How about coming over?"

I looked at my watch. "I could come for a while. I
want to be home in time to read to Grandfather at
nine, and then Leo's picking me up."

"Okay. Why don't we just meet on the beach?"

I went to the shed for my bike. It was barely six, so
Adam and I'd have plenty of time.

He was waiting. He greeted me in a normal, friendly
sort of way, and I went behind the big rock and
changed to my bathing suit. We swam out, and then I
lay on my back in the soft swells, feeling the rain
falling gently on my face and making small dents in

the water. *Basil*, I called silently. *Basil, my friend, my friend who makes me feel real, Basil, come.*

He came. He greeted us both exuberantly, and then he dove down and I was on his back, riding him. This time he didn't just swim with me, he rose from the water and we were flying, and it was glorious.

Then he went to Adam, and they had one of their rough games, with Basil winning as usual, throwing Adam up into the air so that he belly-flopped into the water. Basil thought this was enormously funny.

Adam righted himself, sputtering. He swam over to me. "Ask Basil something. Not out loud. Something simple."

Can you do a cartwheel?

Basil butted me, and then he flashed out of the water and made three big circular flips, as close to a cartwheel as can be managed on water.

"What did you ask him?"

"To do a cartwheel."

"Get him to ask you something."

"He is, right now. He wants me to scratch his chest." Which I did, and Basil wriggled and beamed pleasure.

"Are you sure he was asking you?"

"Adam," I said desperately, "I'm practically never entirely sure about anything."

"Okay, okay, relax, sweetie."

Sweetie. He called me "sweetie." Did he mean it? Or was it just the way some people call everybody "darling" or "dear" and it doesn't mean anything?

No, Adam didn't do or say things that meant nothing, which was maybe why Suzy thought he was a square.

"Maybe another cartwheel?" Adam suggested. "Just to be sure it wasn't coincidence?"

I turned to Basil, and almost before I had time to think, he did a backward cartwheel.

"Oh, terrif, terrif," Adam applauded. "Once more."

Once more, I urged Basil. *For Adam. Don't be cross. Just once more.*

A forward cartwheel. A backward cartwheel. One more forward, and then he took off, flashing his way into the horizon.

He reminded me of Mother saying, when we were little, "Too much is enough."

We swam in. Dressed. Adam strapped on his watch. "Not seven-thirty yet. You're in plenty of time."

"Adam—I wouldn't have missed that, with Basil."

"I know." He delighted me by standing on his head.

I bent down. "It's sort of beyond words. I mean, it's beyond anything that's ever happened to me."

He flipped onto his feet again.

There was a funny sort of embarrassment between us.

"I guess you'd better hurry now . . ."

"I guess I had . . ."

"I'll call you."

"Thanks."

When I got home I went in to Grandfather.

He had the back of his hospital bed raised, but his eyes were closed.

"Can I bring you some coffee, Grandfather?"

He shook his head slightly. "Nancy Rodney is convinced that her coffee carries special benefits. Perhaps it does."

I looked at him and thought that he needed any special benefits she or anybody else could give him. It struck me how much weaker he had grown in a short time. I thought of the big four-poster bed where Mother and Daddy were sleeping now, with its view of sea and sky, and realized that it was so high that Grandfather couldn't have managed, any more, to get in and out of it by himself. The hospital bed was easier for him because he could push the controls and get it just the right level for getting in and out.

"Did I interrupt you?" I asked. "Were you meditating?"

He smiled at me, his welcoming smile, so I pulled up the chair and sat down. "I was meditating. But I'm glad to see you." His eyes twinkled. He looked relaxed and very much himself.

"What *is* meditation, Grandfather? How do you do it?"

"It isn't exactly something you do."

"What, then?"

He was silent a long time, and I thought he wasn't going to answer. I was beginning to get used to his removing himself as completely as though he had left the room; suddenly he just wasn't there. Sometimes he seemed to retreat deep within himself; sometimes he would mumble as though he didn't quite know where he was, as though he was trapped in a bad dream. But now he said to me, and I wasn't sure whether or not he was answering me, or if he was changing the subject, "You like to go down to the cove by yourself, don't you, Vicky? And sit on the rock and look out to sea?"

"Yes, and usually at the wrong moment, when Mother or Daddy needs me to do something else."

"But *you* need to go to the rock and look out to sea, don't you?"

"Yes, and sometimes I think you're the only one who understands why."

"What do you do when you go to the rock?"

"I don't do anything. I sit."

"Do you think?"

"Sometimes. But those aren't the best times."

"What are the best times?"

"When I sit on the rock—and I feel—somehow— part of the rock and part of the sky and part of the sea."

"And you're very aware of the rock and the sky and the sea?"

"Sometimes."

"And sometimes?"

"Sometimes it seems to go beyond that."

"And then what is it like?"

I thought for a moment. "It's hard to explain because it's beyond words. It's as though I'm out on the other side of myself." I thought of what Adam and I had talked about the other night. I tried to tell Grandfather some of what we had said, and ended, "And it's being part of everything, part of the rock and the sky and the sea and the wind and the rain and the sun and the stars . . ."

"And you, Vicky? Are you still there?"

No. Yes. How do you explain no and yes at the same time?

"I'm there—but it's as though I'm out on the other side of myself—I'm not in the way."

"There's your answer," Grandfather said. "That's meditation."

I didn't say anything. I was thinking.

He went on, "People like me spend years learning the techniques of meditation. But you're a poet, and poets are born knowing the language of angels."

That sounded nice, almost too nice. "I didn't even begin really to write poetry till last year . . ." I started.

But Grandfather said, "Get your father." Blood was pouring down his face.

I ran out of the stall, yelling, "Daddy!"

And Daddy came running and so did everybody else.

"Out," Daddy said to us all, including Mother. As we left, I saw Grandfather, streaming with blood.

My heart was pounding and I was shaking and my hands were wet and cold. No wonder Rob had been terrified.

Mother, walking as though in her sleep, went to the kitchen and began wringing out towels with cold water.

"I'll take them," John said.

Mother pressed her knuckles against her lips. "No."

The screen door slammed and Mrs. Rodney came in, shedding a dripping poncho and a sou'wester. "Problem?"

"Hemorrhage," John said.

"Something told me to come on over early this morning." She reached for the wet towels and Mother handed them to her, meekly, like a child. "Don't fret." There was solidity in her voice as well as in her chunkiness. "We'll have it under control in no time."

Rob took Mother's hand, but this was not Rob, my baby brother, reaching out to Mother to be comforted; this was Rob taking Mother's hand to give her comfort.

Suzy opened the refrigerator. Her hand was trembling.

"Is all this too much for you kids?" Mother asked. And her voice, like Suzy's hand, trembled.

"No," John said firmly.

I poured milk into the little saucepan. "It doesn't matter whether it's too much for us or not. This is where we want to be. With Grandfather. No matter what."

On her way home, Mrs. Rodney came to me and said that Grandfather would like me to read to him.

He was in the hospital bed, looking transparent. Mrs. Rodney whispered, "He'll probably fall asleep. Don't mind, it's the best thing you can do for him. We'll give him a transfusion later today. He's not up to it right now."

There was no sign of the bloodied bedclothes. Mrs. Rodney had bundled them up and taken them with her; she had a washing machine and could soak the blood out in cold water and then run the sheets through the regular cycle; she wouldn't hear of our using the laundromat in the village.

Grandfather and I were reading a book called *Lives of a Cell,* so I pulled up a chair and sat down by him. He turned slightly toward me and smiled, and fluttered his long fingers on the clean white coverlet.

I started to read and, sure enough, when I finished the chapter I saw that his eyes were closed, and his breathing was the quiet and rhythmic breathing of sleep.

I tiptoed out.

Leo was sitting with Mother and Daddy in the

dining stall, drinking coffee. The rain was driving into the porch, and the porch furniture was shoved back against the wall. It was the first time this summer that we'd had to eat indoors.

"Where's everybody?" I asked.

Leo answered, "John's at the lab. Suzy and Jacky are cleaning out the boathouse."

"And Rob's gone down the road to the big house to play with the Woods' grandson," Mother added.

The rain lashed against the stable walls. The hanging brass kerosene lamp swayed a little, as though the stable were a ship at sea. It was raining much harder than when I'd gone to meet Adam.

Leo put down his coffee cup. "First thing we'll go over to the mainland to get blood for Mr. Eaton. I'll give some, too."

I looked at Daddy. "Can I give some blood for Grandfather?"

Daddy nodded thoughtfully. "You're his blood type, and you're in good condition. I'll have to give you a note because you're a minor." He rose and headed for the science stall and his desk.

Leo and I said goodbye and walked out into the rain. The little birds were huddled into their nest. They looked much too big for it.

"Are they nearly ready to fly?" I asked.

Leo looked at them without emotion. "Probably not."

"Think they'll make it?"

He looked at the subsidiary nest we'd prepared on the stone step. "Wait and see."

It was lovely to walk in the rain, to feel it against all

of my body. I lifted my face to it and began to drink the drops.

"Better not," Leo warned.

"Why not?"

"Rain water's not pure any more. It used to be the purest water there is, but that was before we were born. It's got lots of nasties in it now from the gluck we've put in the atmosphere, strontium 90 and other radioactive horrors."

"I hate it!" I was as violent as Suzy about the thousand porpoises, and somehow it was all part of the same thing, a wrongness that was deathly. "Is that why the swallows are so stupid about their nests?"

"I think it goes back a long time further ago than that," he said gently.

"John says there's lots more leukemia than there used to be and pollution is one of the causes."

"Could be." Leo led the way to a little VW bug. "Mom said I could take the car today. On the other hand, people used to die a lot earlier, of plagues and pestilences and pneumonias."

"Okay, I know. Things have been kind of heavy this summer." And Leo's father's death was part of that heaviness.

We drove to the dock without saying much, and I found that I was quite comfortable being silent with Leo. He also drove a great deal less flashily than Zachary.

Jacky had the launch ready for us, with a canvas-tarp sort of thing to protect us from the worst of the rain. Suzy stood on the dock looking cute, instead of funny, in a huge mackinaw.

It was chilly on the water with the rain blowing in, under, around, through the canvas tarp, slipping between sou'wester and poncho and slithering down my neck. I shrugged up my shoulders to try to keep dry. The water was rough and we went up and down, both rolling and yawing, as though we were on a marine roller-coaster. I was grateful I don't get seasick.

Once I asked, "When we get to the mainland, how do we get to the hospital?"

"Cor says I can use his pickup."

"Cor?"

"Cornelius Codd. The old bloke I play chess with."

"Cornelius Codd—I don't believe it."

"It's his real name." Leo pushed the back of his hand across his face to get the rain out of his eyes.

"I love it, I really do. Not many people have names that fit them so perfectly."

"How about Leo Rodney?" He turned briefly toward me, his pale lashes trembling with rain.

Leo's not exactly a lion type. More like a basset hound puppy. "It's a nice name," I evaded.

He turned back to the sea, his light hazel eyes narrowed as though against sunlight, though the day seemed darker than ever.

Cornelius Codd was waiting in the doorway of a weathered lean-to. He had an unlit pipe in his mouth and wore a shiny yellow slicker. His old woolen cap was pulled down over his hair. He gestured with the pipe. "Car's out back."

"Thanks, Cor." Leo shook his hand. "This is Vicky Austin."

Cornelius Codd took my hand in both of his.

Although his hands were callused and horny, his grasp reminded me of Grandfather's.

The pickup looked to be about the same age as Cornelius. Leo took my elbow and I put my foot on the high step and jumped into the cab almost as though I were getting on a horse. The leather of the seat was cracked, with bits of stuffing coming out, and the springs had long since sprung. But it still drove. Quite a change after the Alfa Romeo.

We reached the cement-block cube of the hospital and as Leo drove around to park I saw that behind the modern building were several much older and lower brick buildings, and it was as though the island were light-years away from this drab place of city noises and smells.

We drove around until we found a place in the crowded parking lot. I stayed close by Leo's side. The only time I'd ever been in a hospital was after my bike accident at home in Thornhill, and it was a small hospital and of course Daddy knew everybody and because I was his daughter I got all kinds of special TLC. This huge complex with its jumble of ancient and modern buildings was very different. I dropped slightly behind Leo, so I could follow. "Do you know where to go?"

"I'm not sure. I should have checked with Mom. We might as well go in through the emergency room."

Does picking up blood constitute an emergency? I knew even less than Leo, so I didn't say anything. We went in through the emergency-room door, which was, in fact, the door closest to us, and Leo pointed to an empty seat. "Wait here. I'll go see what's what," he said, and went to stand in line in front of the nurses' desk.

The room was filled with rows of wooden benches and there were folding chairs against the wall. I looked around at people of all ages and degrees. A nurse was moving along the rows, and I heard one young man say, holding out his finger, "This squirrel just up and bit me, so I thought maybe rabies . . ."

An old woman on the bench in front of me was moaning, "God help me, O God help me, do you have to be bleeding to death before anyone pays any attention?"

A doctor came out of one of the cubicles, a nurse called out, "Norris," and an old man with a bloody bandage around his hand followed the doctor into the cubicle.

A woman came in, carrying a limp little girl, maybe three or four years old. A nurse looked at them, touching the child lightly. "Sit down. I'll come take her history in a few minutes."

The woman found a seat. Was the child already dead? Surely death would constitute an emergency—or maybe it wouldn't, being too late. I couldn't see whether or not the child was breathing. How long would they have to wait?

I thought I was going to be sick. I swallowed, swallowed.

Leo was threading his way back across the room, gesturing. I followed him through an inner door and out into a long corridor. I took a deep breath of cool air and my stomach quieted.

We went up a flight of stairs and down another corridor and into an office where someone told us to wait. I felt that we were in a nightmare.

Leo nudged me toward a chair. "Leo, I think there's a dead child there and the nurse didn't pay any attention."

Leo tried to explain. "Mom says there's a nurse trained to look at people and make a quick assessment of who can be helped and who's too late and who's a real emergency and who can wait."

"Doesn't she ever make mistakes?"

"Sure. Mom says that's inevitable. Still, it's the best system they've come up with."

I thought of the old woman who said you had to be bleeding to death before you got any attention. How can anyone, no matter how specially trained, tell who's a real emergency and who isn't?

A nurse came in and greeted us pleasantly and took Daddy's note saying it was all right for me to give blood. I lay on a high, narrow bed, and a nurse wrapped some rubber tubing tightly around my upper arm, had me make a fist, and then dexterously inserted a needle into a vein on the inside of my elbow. The needle was attached to a tube leading to an empty plastic container and I watched, fascinated, while it began to fill with my blood.

When it was over, the nurse said, "Sit up slowly now, hon. Sure you don't feel faint?"

I didn't. Not in this small, clean, uncrowded room. It smelled like Daddy's office and that was a home smell, a good smell.

The nurse patted my shoulder. "Brave girl. Now I want you to drink this good hot broth before you leave. Your young man's all through, too. He's in the waiting room just outside."

"Does he have the blood for my grandfather?" I sipped the broth and looked at the calm, kind face of the nurse over the rim and wondered if she could stay this kind and calm if she worked in the emergency room.

"Everything's all set. Drink slowly, there's no rush.

'Bye, now, dear. You may feel a little dizzy but it will pass, and your blood will give life to someone else."

I finished the broth. When I stood up I did feel a little dizzy, but it lasted only a moment, and I hurried out to Leo.

He rose to greet me. "You all right?"

"Sure. Fine. You?"

For answer he indicated the parcel in his hand. "Let's get the blood for your grandfather back to the Island."

Cornelius Codd was waiting in the door of the shack, as though he hadn't moved the entire time we were gone. His woolen cap was dripping rain.

We delivered the blood to Mrs. Rodney, and Daddy asked us if we felt all right, and we said we were fine. "But the emergency room—" I looked at Mother.

"As I think back on it, though," Mother said, "I marvel that the nurses were as patient as they were . . ."

Leo looked at me. "When I come home from the hospital I want a swim to clean off."

Mother glanced at her watch, "It's time for lunch."

Leo, too, checked his watch, as though synchronizing time. "We'll just go for a quick swim and then I'll take Vicky to the drugstore for a sandwich if it's okay. We did plan to do something together today."

"Of course, Leo. And thanks for giving up your morning—and your blood. We're very grateful."

"I'll just go put on my bathing suit," I said, and left to get away from the pain in Mother's voice.

Leo and I slithered down the steep path to Grandfather's cove. My bathing suit felt wet and clammy from the morning's swim. The rain was falling softly now, and the beach was cool and wet. There were dents in it the size of silver dollars from the heavy rain that had fallen earlier. But now the wind had dropped and the ocean surprised me by murmuring its way quietly into shore.

I looked out to the horizon and saw the flash of a dolphin. Basil? Norberta? I felt a yearning ache. "How far can we swim?"

Leo was breast-deep in water. "I'm not sure. There doesn't seem to be much pull."

"I saw a dolphin, so we don't need to worry about sharks."

Leo flung himself into the water and started swimming. He called back to me, "The tide's turning. It'll be on its way in shortly. We can have a good swim."

I followed after him, slowly. The water was much warmer than the air. I swam, swam, letting the water cleanse me of the lingering horror of the emergency room. I needed desperately to wipe out of my mind's eye the images it retained, so I replaced them with images of Basil, of Norberta, of Njord. I needed the reassurance of their smile. I needed to be assured that the world really isn't like the emergency room of a hospital, that there is hope and goodness and love . . .

I called them silently, hardly realizing what I was doing.

Leo was swimming parallel with the shore now, as though racing someone. I'd swum quite far beyond him. Then, just as I realized how far out to sea I was and that I ought to turn back, I saw them:

Norberta and her baby.

They didn't swim up to me as they did when I was with Adam. They flashed up out of the water in unison, leaping, diving, leaping, beaming at me. They rose up out of the water, standing on their flukes, and then they dove down and disappeared.

Leo, still racing his invisible opponent, had not even seen.

I felt a surging sense of relief and elation. I hadn't set out deliberately to call them, but they had heard my need, and they had come in answer to it, but they wanted to reveal themselves only to me, not to Leo. I felt absolutely sure of that, and absurdly happy.

How can one person be so frightened, and so sad, and then so joyful, in such a short time?

Even in the rain, it was hot work climbing back up to the stable. I took a quick shower. The bathroom is next to the double stall with the four-poster bed, and when I turned off the shower and was rubbing my hair dry I heard a sound I couldn't identify at first. Then I realized that it was muffled crying.

I had never before heard Mother cry that way. I didn't know what to do.

I decided to do nothing. If I went in to her she'd feel she had to stop crying, and I thought maybe she needed to cry. Sometimes if I need to cry I want to do it all alone, without anyone to bother me, even with comfort.

And I thought that if Mother needed someone to cry with, the way I'd cried with Leo, it should be Daddy, not me.

Maybe I was just being a coward. I don't know.

There were quite a few other kids in the drugstore when Leo and I got there. I knew some of them and of course he knew them all. It's always been the hangout for the high-school kids. Leo greeted or waved to them as we went by, but led me firmly to the last booth, which was still empty. We ordered chicken-salad sandwiches and coffee milk shakes. I was hungry, and it tasted good.

"Vicky, when I'm at Columbia, can I write to you?"

"Well, sure."

"I mean, you know all about that part of the city. And I just want to write to you."

"I'd like to hear from you. But Adam knows lots more about Columbia than we do."

"If there's some kind of a football weekend or a special prom, do you think you could come?"

"I don't think either of us can afford that kind of thing." I touched my jeans pocket, where I'd shoved a couple of dollars to pay for my lunch. "But I'll write to you."

"Okay. Want anything more to eat? Ice cream?"

"No, thanks."

"There's a pretty good movie on tonight," Leo said, "and I've saved enough money to take us to dinner at the Inn. Want to go out in the boat now?"

"Leo." I didn't want to hurt him after all he'd just done for Grandfather. "I'd love to go to dinner and the movies with you this evening—but I just want to be home for a while now. It's—it's hard on my mother seeing Grandfather get weaker and weaker, and so quickly."

"Okay. Sure." Leo dropped some change on the table and we pushed out of the booth.

"Hey, Leo." I reached in my pocket. "I want to pay for my own lunch. I brought the money."

"No."

"Yes," I said. "Come on. Don't let's fight about it."

"I bet you don't offer to go dutch with Zachary."

"That's different."

"How? Except that Zachary's loaded and I'm not."

Basically, when we go out with kids we go dutch. If we let someone pick up the tab it usually means something serious. I realized that with Zachary the usual rules didn't apply. "As you so rightly remarked, he's loaded and you're not." I stuck my money out at him.

He took it. "Okay. Lunch, then. But tonight's on me."

I decided to think about that when the time came.

I didn't want anything to get complicated between Leo and me, but I hoped I'd always have him for a friend. He was the kind of person, like his mother, who could always be counted on to be there when you needed him.

The stable was quiet. Grandfather was asleep, the book of Henry Vaughan's poetry open beside him. Mother was in the kitchen making crème brûlée.

"I'm like my mother," she said. "I cook for therapy. And it's as much of an art form, I believe, as painting or writing or making music."

"Crème brûlée's an art form all right. Yum. Anything I can do to help?"

"I don't think so. Except keep me company. But I thought you were off with Leo for the day—"

"A full day's an awful long time with Leo. He's coming back and we're going to the Inn for dinner and then to a movie. Mother, should I let him pay for me?"

She turned slightly toward me, still stirring something in a small saucepan. "Is it being a problem?"

"Sort of. He did let me pay for lunch, but he was very insistent about dinner. The thing is, I don't want to hurt his feelings, but I don't want to lead him on."

Mother turned back to the stove. "Are those the only alternatives?"

"That's what I'm not sure about."

"I'm afraid that's something nobody can tell you, hon. You have to sense it out for yourself. As long as you don't make a production of it, I have a hunch you could probably let him pay for one evening. Leo needs to feel that he's a man right now."

"Yeah. That's what I thought. Thanks." I looked at her and her eyes were just a little puffy, as if she'd been crying. But her voice was her own voice, without any tension behind it.

"I've unplugged the phone by your grandfather's bed, but grab for it here if it rings. Sound carries only too well in the stable."

At which moment the phone did ring, and I dashed across the kitchen and grabbed for it.

"Hi, Vicky. Adam. Glad it's you. I forgot to check this morning. Are you coming over on Wednesday?"

"Oh, Adam—I can't. I'm sorry. I promised Zachary I'd go flying with him."

There was a pause. Then: "Guess I can't compete

with that. My own fault for not being more clear about it."

"Adam—" I lowered my voice, speaking softly into the mouthpiece. "I saw Njord and Norberta today."

"Tell me." Then: "Are you alone?"

"No."

"Okay. Maybe I could come over this evening after dinner."

"I'm going to the movies with Leo—I'm sorry. Could I come over to the lab tomorrow morning?"

"Why not?"

"How—how early?"

A pause. Then: "Come along whenever you get up and we'll have breakfast. The cafeteria opens at six-thirty."

"Okay. I'll be there." I hung up, and my heart was thumping. I hoped nothing in my face would betray me. I asked Mother, "Is it okay if I have breakfast with Adam tomorrow? I'll be back in time to read to Grandfather."

Mother bent down to set a pan of water in the oven. "Vicky, you don't need to feel obligated to read to your grandfather every morning. He wouldn't want it to be a burden for you."

"I know. But it isn't. I really like doing it."

"All right. But if you're having a good time with Adam, don't worry about getting back."

Would I have a good time? It all depended on Adam.

I went down to the beach and sat on my rock. The rain seemed to be slackening off with the drop in the wind. I watched the waves breathing quietly. Adam's call had left me churning, and I thought perhaps if I meditated I'd see more clearly.

Mother says my seesaw moods are part of my adolescence and they'll moderate as I grow older. The hospital had thrown me into a pit of darkness; then Norberta and Njord, responding to my need, had lifted me back up to the light. Maybe you have to know the darkness before you can appreciate the light.

Meditation, I thought, sitting there on the rock in Grandfather's cove, has something to do with that light.

I let my mind drift toward the dolphins, and as I stared out at the horizon there was the lovely leap I was half expecting, and I was sure it was one of my friends. My breathing quietened, slowed, moved to the gentle rhythm of the sea. The tenseness left my body until it seemed that the rock on which I sat was not embedded deep in the sand but was floating on quiet waters.

My mind stopped its running around like a squirrel on a wheel, and let go. I sat there and I didn't think. I was just *being*. And it felt good.

I wasn't sure how long I sat there, letting go and being, when a sea gull flew directly above me, mewling raucously, and reminded me that I'd better get back up to the stable.

As I reached the top of the cliff, Daddy and Rob got out of the station wagon, our nice, battered old blue station wagon completely unlike Zachary's hearse. I followed them into the porch and shook the rain out of my hair.

Mother came hurrying out of the kitchen, putting

her finger to her lips, and Daddy held the screen door so it wouldn't slam. "Father still asleep?"

"Yes." Mother put her arms around Daddy and he held her. Our parents are not the kind who never kiss in front of their children, but there was something very special about the way Daddy put his lips against her hair, her cheek, her lips.

"C'mon," I gestured to Rob, and we went into the stall which held the children's books.

"Why aren't you with Leo?" he asked.

"I'm going to dinner and the movies with him later. I wanted to come home for a bit. It's pouring again."

Rob was witness to that piece of obviousness, standing dripping in his yellow slicker. He shucked it off and put it over a chair.

"Vicky, there're probably lots of planets besides us with people on them, don't you think?"

I sat down on one of the low round leather ottomans. "John says we'd be pretty megalomanic if we thought we were the only inhabited planet in all of the solar systems in all of the galaxies."

"Mega—"

"Megalomanic. It means thinking you're the most important."

He nodded, looking solemn. "So maybe there's a planet somewhere where nobody has any eyes."

I looked at him, and I thought his own eyes were shadowed, and I wanted to hug him and pull him onto my lap the way I sometimes did when he was little. But he was sounding as though he felt very grownup. "Could be, I guess."

"Well, if nobody had any eyes, they'd all get along all right without them, wouldn't they?"

"Sure, I guess they'd compensate."

"They'd get along with hearing, and smell, and touch, but they wouldn't have any idea what anything looked like."

I wasn't sure what he was driving at, but I knew that it was important to him. "No, they wouldn't."

"And if someone from our planet went to the planet where no one had eyes, and tried to describe something to them—the way the rain looks falling on the ocean, or the lighthouse beam at night, or the sunrise—it couldn't be done, could it?" He sounded anxious.

I tried to understand. "No. It just wouldn't be possible. If you didn't have eyes, if you lived in a world of touch and sound, then nobody could tell you what anything looks like. Why, Rob?"

He pulled up another ottoman and sat, elbows on knees, chin in hands. "Well, maybe when the people on the planet with no eyes die, then maybe they get sent to planets where there *are* eyes. But you couldn't tell them about it ahead of time."

"That's right."

"So, maybe when we die, we'll get something as important as sight, but because we don't know what it is, nobody could tell us about it now, any more than we could explain sight to the people on a planet with no eyes."

I still thought of Rob as a baby, but he wasn't a baby any more, and he made a lot of sense. Maybe it wasn't the kind of thing you'd hear in most churches, but it made more sense to me than a lot of sermons. And I thought Grandfather would like it. I asked Rob if he'd told him.

"Not yet. I just thought of it. But I will, sometime when he's—he's at home."

I knew what he meant. Grandfather had been more at home earlier in the morning, before the hemorrhage, when we'd talked about meditation, than he'd been in quite a while.

Daddy put his head around the partition of the children's bookstall. "Mother's making tea. Want to come join us?"

Leo borrowed his mother's VW again to take me to dinner.

"Is Zachary still staying at the Inn?" he asked.

"I think he sometimes stays at the Inn, and sometimes on the mainland at one of the guest apartments at the country club."

"I'd just as soon he's not there tonight. I want you to myself."

I didn't know whether I wanted Zachary to be there or not. I definitely did not want Leo to get cosmic about me. And yet everything that was happening, our weeping on the beach, our morning at the hospital, was bringing us closer together, whether I liked or wanted it or not.

He said, "In a way I suppose Zachary and I could be friends. His mother's dead. My father's dead. I think he's just as mixed up about life as I am, though he shows it in a different way. But he has all the money he needs. And I don't."

"Hey, you have enough to take me to dinner at the Inn," I reassured him. "And you're going to Columbia in the autumn." The wheels of the little car *hished* on the wet macadam. I was glad I was driving with Leo, not Zachary.

"That's not much in the way of competition, when he can charter the launch any time he wants, and keep rooms at both the Inn and the country club, and feed you on champagne and caviar."

"Leo—you don't have to compete. With all his money, Zachary's a lot more mixed up about life and death than you are."

"He knows what he's going to do after college—law school. And he's got the money to go there. And the brains."

"If he's willing to use them, and that's a big if. It took him all this time to get out of high school." The windshield wipers on the little VW whizzed away, as though joining in the conversation.

"Okay, then," Leo said. "I really didn't mean to spend this date talking about some other guy."

"Conversation about Leo only," I promised.

"And Vicky." He drew up in front of the Inn. "You get out, and I'll go park."

I scurried in through the rain.

And looked at the Inn through Zachary's eyes. After the country club, it did seem pretty dingy. There wasn't anyone to take my coat. There wasn't, as far as I could see, anyone to do anything. The paint, which should have been white, was greyish. There were cracks in the plaster. The lighting wasn't intimate, it was just dim.

Leo came in, and took my jacket. "I made a reservation," he said. "Zachary clued me in to that one. I wouldn't have thought of it otherwise."

"No more Zachary," I reminded him.

We had a table by the window, and even in the rain the view across the little green to the beach was lovely. The rain slanted against the tall street lights, glowing with golden droplets. And reflected in the night windows, but not blocking out the view, were the lights of the dining room.

The menu that was given me, unlike the one at the country club, did have prices. I chose filet of sole because it was the cheapest thing on it.

"Hey, Vicky," Leo said, "please have anything you want. I'm going to have steak." That was the most expensive.

"I really like sole," I said.

"Well, okay, if you're sure. Then I think I'll have it, too." He didn't offer me anything to drink.

While we were waiting for our order, the waitress brought in some crackers and cottage cheese and relish. I kept nibbling crackers because I didn't have anything to say.

Leo did. "I know you don't play around, and I don't, either, but can't we be friends?"

"We are friends."

"You know what I mean."

I drank a few sips of water. "I told you, Leo, I don't feel that way about you."

"Yet . . ."

I didn't answer. If I told him I *did* feel that way about someone else it wouldn't solve anything, it would only create more problems. He'd know it had to

225

be either Zachary or Adam, and I had a hunch Leo suspected Zachary. As for Adam, the last thing in the world I wanted him to know was that I thought of him as more than a friend. I had enough sense to know that if Adam suspected how I felt he'd more than put on the brakes; he'd get out of the car and run.

"As far as feeling *that way* is concerned," Leo said, "I think Suzy and Jacky do, and I agree with Mom that they're much too young."

"So're we."

He leaned earnestly across the table. "Half the Island kids are married out of high school."

That was true in Thornhill, too—not nearly half, and half was undoubtedly much too high an estimate for the Island—but enough, enough so that I'd used it as an argument in my own mind in thinking about Adam and me.

I'd missed part of what Leo was saying; he was talking about Jacky and Suzy again. ". . . and Jacky said they had lots of fun."

"Lots of fun" can mean more than one thing. "What do you mean?" I demanded. "What kind of fun? How much fun?"

"Don't get all excited. Not *that* much. I mean, not all the way or anything."

The idea of my little sister and Jacky; it wasn't that impossible. "If it's not that much, and I'm certainly glad it isn't, why are you bringing it up?"

"I don't know. It was a dumb idea."

"It was." I looked at Leo and said swiftly, "Let's just forget it. One more thing. I'm not Suzy. I don't work the way she works. She's always been pretty and cuddly and I've always been elbows and knees and not cuddly. But when

I cuddle it will be really important. And I don't want it till then. But I do want to be friends with you, Leo, real friends, who can talk to each other and be there for each other, no matter what."

He started to speak, then stopped as the waitress came in with our filets of sole. There was broccoli with hollandaise, and parsley potatoes, and it smelled good.

"Why have I been so hungry all summer?" I asked.

"Because eating is part of life. So is loving."

It rang true. "Let's concentrate on eating, then. For now." Then I asked, "Have you been hungry, too?"

"Famished. I talked to my mom about it, and she explained about it being an urge to live. When Dad's father died—he had a heart attack unexpectedly, just like Dad—they wept, and then they made love. And she showed me that this wasn't being disrespectful but a—what did she call it? Oh, yes, an affirmation of the goodness of life."

I thought of Mrs. Rodney, short, stocky, sensible, unglamorous. Commander Rodney was more like a movie star. And I couldn't visualize them making love. Or even kissing the way Zachary and I had kissed. And my parents? Could I visualize it with them? Sooner or later I was going to have to see them as separate people, not just Mother and Daddy. John hasn't called Daddy anything except Dad for a long time. Somehow, calling him Daddy this summer was trying to keep him—well, maybe not exactly omnipotent, but the daddy of my childhood who could kiss a hurt and make it all right. The daddy who ought to be able to cure Grandfather's leukemia. And I realized that part of the pain of this summer was in letting the old mother and daddy go, because that was part of my own growing up. They had to be free to weep, to hurt, just as I did. Daddy had to be free to be human and not able to cure all diseases. And they had to be free to make love, whether I could picture it or not.

Leo had been talking through my thoughts. ". . . and faith that God will never abandon any of his creatures. Vicky, where do you think my father is now?"

I thought of Rob's planet with no eyes. "Well—I do think he's somewhere."

"And what about Zachary's mother?"

"Frozen?"

"Yeah—frozen. That keeps getting in the way when I try to like Zachary. Much more than the fact that my dad died after he pulled Zachary out of the water."

—Leo, you're nice, I thought,—you're lots nicer than I am.

I said, "I don't know whether I think freezing her's holding her back or not. I guess if she's really dead, it isn't."

"But what if—in a few centuries or so, it should happen the way Zachary thinks, and someone does bring her back to life?"

"I don't know. I suppose it's possible. Adam says that anything human beings can think of has to be possible sooner or later."

"So what does that do to her now?"

I took three bites of sole without tasting them. "I don't know. I guess I think God can cope."

"You do believe in God?"

"Some of the time."

"Not all of the time?"

"No. But whenever anything goes wrong or I'm frightened I shout for God to help. So I guess when it comes to the pinch I believe."

"You don't feel you have to be strong and self-sufficient enough to be able to do without God?"

"Do you?" I countered.

"My mom says it isn't either strength or self-sufficiency, and I think she's right. And I guess if she can believe, with all she's seen as a nurse, it's got to be real. That she believes."

I thought of the emergency room that morning. To work in an emergency room and still believe in God would be a real test of faith, and I wasn't sure I'd pass it.

Zachary would say that needing God is all self-deception, a cowardly illusion. But Adam hadn't hated me for being afraid that night when we sat together on the beach.

"If it isn't real"—Leo pulled me back into the present—"then nothing makes any sense. It's all a dirty joke. If we get made with enough brains to ask questions, and then die with most of them unanswered, it's a cheat, the whole thing's a cheat. And what about all the people who die of starvation and poverty and filth—is that all there is for them, forever?"

I picked at my salad. "Maybe it's like school. And this life we're in now is probably like being way back in kindergarten. And I want to go on all the way through school, and college, and everything. But when you're in kindergarten you don't have any idea what college will be like. And when you're four or five years old you're not able to understand things that will seem simple later on."

"I like that." Leo smiled, and when he smiled his whole face smiled, even his summer's sprinkling of freckles. "Maybe that's what's wrong with freezing people. You arrest them in the kindergarten stage and they can't grow up."

The waitress came and asked if we wanted a sundae or pie. Leo chose lemon-meringue pie and I decided on a chocolate sundae with coffee ice cream, nuts, and whipped cream. I hadn't gained any weight this summer as far as I could tell, and Leo was right, or at any rate his mother was. It was an affirmation.

9

It rained all night, as though the heavens were having a gigantic weep. The ocean soughed and sighed and susurrated. It wasn't a storm, with waves crashing roughly into shore, just a slow, steady emptying, rain onto earth and sea, sea onto sand.

It made me want to weep, too, and yet I didn't know just what I wanted to weep about.

When I woke up in the morning, a little after six, I was bathed in blue and gold. Everything was washed clean; the sky looked as though somebody had scrubbed and swept it; there wasn't a cloud in the unblemished sweep of blue. The ocean sparkled with diamonds; it wasn't a bit like Homer's "wine-dark sea." The beach seemed to have absorbed the gold of the sun, and the grass was green, with a burnishing of brass.

The bike ride was cool in the early-morning air, and the breeze blew my hair back from my face and the air was sparkling. It was like music. Mother says there are certain pieces she can't play or sing and feel sad or sorry for herself, and this day was like that. I was in a tingly way apprehensive about seeing Adam, but I no longer felt rejected.

I parked my bike and walked toward the cafeteria.

Adam hurried along the path from his barracks, or whatever the dormitory-type building was called. He waved and I waved back.

We didn't talk until we'd put out trays on a window table, and the silence was heavy. I tried to concentrate on choosing breakfast.

"Okay, tell me."

So I told him about the hospital, and then swimming in the rain to wash off the terror, and then crying out for the dolphins, not deliberately but instinctively, and then Norberta and Njord coming to reassure me and waving their flukes at me and disappearing without Leo's even seeing them.

"You're sure it was Norberta and Njord?"

"Who else? You don't mind, do you? that they came when you weren't there?"

"Mind?" Adam seemed to chew the word along with his pancakes. "I admit to a pang of what I suspect is jealousy. But it does bear out my thesis. Okay. Now, you haven't shown me anything you've written yet."

I tried not to sound stiff. "I did write a poem for Jeb and Ynid. But—" I dribbled off.

"You mean I haven't been very encouraging?"

"Not very."

"I'm going to get more coffee. Want some?"

"No. Thanks."

I'd made a big production about paying my own way with Leo. What about with Adam? There wasn't a cashier at the cafeteria. Food went along with the salary and housing. What about guests? I'd have to ask him.

He came back and sat down, and stirred approximately three grains of sugar into his coffee. "Maybe you'll let me see the poem you wrote for Jeb and Ynid?"

I reached into my jeans pocket. "As a matter of fact . . ." I pulled out a very crumpled piece of paper. "I'm not sure it's still legible."

"Let me see." He reached across the table and took the paper, smoothing it out. I felt my bands going cold and clammy while he read; he looked back up at the top of the page and read again. "Hey, Vicky, I really like that, it's good," he said at last. "*Nothing loved is ever lost or perished.* Okay if I show it to Jeb?"

"Is it too messed up? Should I copy it again?"

"No, it's fine. Is this your only copy?"

"I have the original scrawl."

"Thanks. Thanks for showing it to me. Listen, don't ever change."

I tried raising one eyebrow the way John and Daddy can do. "Is it all right if I grow up?"

He grinned. "It really teed you off, my calling you a child, didn't it?"

I found myself grinning back. "It did."

"Okay, let me try to explain. It isn't just chronology. It's a quality, too, that I don't think you have to lose when you're fully mature physically. Your grandfather has it, and he's one of the most mature people I've ever met. It's a kind of freshness that cuts through shams and sees what's really there." He paused and took a gulp of coffee. "In this psych course I took, it's called *archaic understanding.*"

"What's that?"

"It's understanding things in their deepest, mythic sense. All children are born with archaic understanding, and then school comes along, and the pragmatic Cartesian world—"

"Cartesian?"

"After Descartes."

"Oh. Yeah." I felt stupid, so I added, "*I think, therefore I am.*"

"That's the guy. The thing is, the Cartesian world insists on keeping intellectual control, and that means you have to let go your archaic understanding, because that means going along with all kinds of things you *can't* control. Does all this make any sense?"

"When dolphins went back to the sea, and gave up hands, did they keep their archaic understanding?"

"That's a good question. I'll have to think on it. Okay, now. When you write, you go with your writing, where it wants to take you, don't you?"

"I try."

"So you let go your own control."

"I guess. Yes."

"So, if you're lucky, you'll still keep that willingness to go into the unexpected even after you're grown up. It's easy for you now because you're still as close to childhood as you are to adulthood."

"Hey, wait, it's not all that easy. And chronologically you're still an adolescent, too," I pointed out.

"Yah, but I'm closer to the other side than you are. And I'm a scientist, not a poet. Even when I was a kid I read *Scientific American,* not fairy tales. My academic parents didn't encourage fairy tales. And I think it was my loss. You *did* read fairy tales, didn't you?"

"Fairy tales, fantasy."

"And you communicate with dolphins. Don't you

see that it's a bit humiliating for me to have my dolphins come more quickly and respond more fully to you than to me?"

"I'm sorry."

"That's the way things are. It's nothing for you to be apologetic about. A lot of discoveries come through teamwork, with two completely different types of imagination working together and being far more than either one alone. We make a good team." And just as I was feeling warm with happiness, he went on, "But we also have to face the fact that after this summer we'll probably never see each other again. Berkeley's all the way across the country."

"There is, after all, the mail," I ventured. "Some letters actually do get delivered."

"I'm a lousy letter writer. But sure—we'll write." He didn't sound at all sure.

"What about next summer?" I was afraid I was pushing it, but I couldn't stop myself.

"I have a good grant here for this summer. I'll take whatever's the best offer I get, for next summer. I'd like to work with Dr. O'Keefe again, for instance. And what about you? Will you be coming to the Island when your grandfather's not here?"

"I don't know. But, Adam, this isn't next summer. It's this summer. And we're here, now."

"Yah, you're right." He changed the subject. "We'd better wait for a while before we go swimming. And there's something I want to try . . . C'mon." Adam pushed back from the table.

"Adam—when I eat here, do you have to pay for me?"

"It's minimal."

"I can afford to pay my own way."

"Don't be stuffy. It's the least I can do, for all the help you're being to me. We've got Jeb really excited."

I followed him out of the cafeteria, into the lab building, through the big room with the tanks of fish and starfish and lizards, and along to a corridor lined with doors. Most of the doors were open, so there'd be a cross-draft. Adam went to the last door on the left and knocked on the door frame.

Jeb Nutteley's voice called out, "Come!"

He was sitting at his desk, his swivel chair tipped back, his feet up on the desk. When he saw me he stood up. His office was small and crowded; three walls were covered with bookcases jammed with books, papers, all kinds of electronic equipment, snapshots of dolphins, whales, sea lions. The fourth wall was window, and light from the ocean sparkled all over the desk, splashing the mess of books and papers with sunshine.

"What's up?" Jeb asked.

"Okay if we have Vicky listen to some of your dolphin tapes?"

"Sure. Take over. I'm just off to the dolphin pens. Have fun." And he ambled out.

Adam had me sit down in Jeb's chair. He fiddled with a big reel-to-reel tape machine, and then fitted headphones on me. I leaned back in the chair and listened, and heard chirpings and cluckings and all the dolphin noises I'd become familiar with.

Adam asked, "Can you tell what they're saying?"

I lifted the phone from one ear and he repeated his question. "No," I answered. "I haven't any idea."

"Not any?"

I couldn't tell whether or not he was disappointed. "Adam, they're not talking to *me*."

"Yah. Listen a little longer."

I listened, but it was just noise. I looked around the room, at the desk, and there in a silver frame was a picture of a young woman and a small boy: it must be Jeb's wife and child. I felt a wave of cold wash over me, as though the sun had gone in, but light continued to splash brightly all over the room and onto the picture.

"Does it make any sense at all?" Adam asked.

I lifted the earphone again, and he repeated his question patiently.

"No. And I don't think Basil could understand *me* if he just heard my voice on a tape. Anyhow, this is a lot of different dolphins, not Basil or Norberta."

"Okay."

"Let's go pay them a visit."

When we'd swum out, the water dazzling our eyes, I asked, "Do you want me to call all of them, all three?"

"Try calling just Basil, since you saw Norberta and Njord yesterday."

I turned on my back and floated, closing my eyes against the glare, against Adam, against outside thoughts. Basil. Basil. Basil.

I tried to put myself outside of time passing, tried not to think whether it was taking a long or a short time, tried to be in the very moment.

"Here!" Adam called, and I rolled over.

He came first to Adam, then quickly to me with pleased nudgings and chirrupings of greeting, then back to Adam, and the two of them went into a noisy wrestling match. Finally Basil flung Adam from him, so that he splashed into the water, laughing.

Then Basil came to me.

What shall we do? I asked him silently, and listened for his response with my inner ear. I seized his dorsal fin and we went flying through the air. Then he dove into the water, what must have been a shallow dive for the dolphin but was deep for me, and up, up into the air again. He was much gentler with me than he was with Adam; it was, in fact, a completely different game. He wasn't trying to dislodge me, but to see how high he could leap into the air with me holding on, how deep he could go without my having to let go and surface. Leap, dive, in a regular but increasing rhythm, so that each time we were longer out of the water, deeper under the wrinkled skin of the surface.

He seemed to know just when it would have been impossible for me to hold my underwater breath one moment longer, for he broke up into the air and gently flipped me off. Then he swam rapid and widening circles around Adam and me, then came back and nudged me, as though wanting something.

I began to scratch his chest, gently but firmly, and he wriggled with pleasure.

"Right," Adam said. "Playtime's over. Ask him something."

I pushed slightly away from Basil and he bathed me with his smile, and my hand almost automatically reached for his dorsal fin, and he did a dolphin cartwheel with me holding on.

Now a backward one with Adam. Aloud, I said, to Adam, "Take his dorsal fin."

And Basil flipped over, backward.

"Terrif," Adam said. "Try something else. Simple. In a few minutes you can try something more complicated."

Swim, dear darling Basil, and I mean every bit of the dear and darling because you're very dear and darling to me. Swim out to the horizon and then turn around and come back to us.

Like a flash he was gone, and then as he was about to vanish from sight he was back.

"Right," Adam said. "Now maybe you could try something a little more subtle."

What I wanted to do was to ask Basil to give me all the answers to everything, as though he weren't a dolphin but some kind of cosmic computer. And I knew that that was not only not realistic, it wasn't fair. But I wondered . . .

I thought of Ynid and her grief at her dead baby, and I asked Basil, *Is Ynid's baby all right? (Is Commander Rodney all right? Is my grandfather all right? Am I? Is it all right?)*

Basil pulled himself up out of the water and a series of sounds came from him, singing sounds.

And what it reminded me of was Grandfather standing by Commander Rodney's open grave and saying those terrible words and then crying out, full of joy, *Alleluia, alleluia, alleluia!*

Then Basil was gone, flashing through sea and sky, to disappear at the horizon.

Adam beckoned to me, and turned to swim into shore. I followed.

He was standing on his head when I splashed in. "Good for the brain," he said, upside down.

I sat down at the edge of the water, letting the little waves lap about me.

Adam gave a dolphin-like flip and stood on his feet instead of his head. "I wish . . ."

"What?"

"Oh, several million unobtainable things." He came and sat down in the water beside me. "When it occurred to me to involve you in my project, I was thinking of John Austin's kid sister, who was a bit at loose ends and available. I did think of you as a child, at least in comparison to John and me. And then—"

I didn't look at him. I looked down at the water and traced the pattern of a wavelet with my fingers.

"You're full of surprises, Vicky. First, there's that incredible rapport you have with dolphins. And added to that, you very quickly stopped being just my friend's young sister. You're very much Vicky. Very special Vicky. And it's too soon."

"Too soon for what?" It simply *was*, and sooner or later didn't have anything to do with it.

Adam, too, dabbled his fingers in the water. "Added to which, you've gone far beyond my wildest dreams in my project . . ."

"Is that bad?"

Now he sprang to his feet. "It's so good I don't quite know what to do about it."

"Why not do as Confucius advises?"

"Relax and enjoy it?"

"Right."

"Yah, I should be able to. But I'm confused."

"So join the club," I said bitterly. "Zachary tells me he's confused. Leo tells me he's confused. Now you tell me you're confused. So what's new? I'm confused, too. Life is confusing."

"Is John confused?" he asked me.

"He hasn't told me he is, but John's human, so he's confused. Anyhow, he's old-fashioned."

"You mean conservative?"

"I think John thinks of it more as being radical."

"John and I feel the same way about a lot of things; that's why we became good friends so quickly. Okay if I invite myself to dinner tonight?"

"Sure, that'll be fine."

"Listen, will you do something for me?"

"What kind of something?"

"Will you go home and write about you and Basil, and you and Norberta and Njord?"

"Write how?"

"I've been keeping very detailed notes, but it's all from my point of view. So what I want is to have you write it all out from your own point of view: how you feel about them; how they feel about you; how Basil answered your questions; how he tells you things. I realize I'm asking a lot of you, but would you try, please? It could be invaluable."

"If you don't want anything formal, I've already written a lot about them. Since I can't talk to anybody except you about them, and I go home bursting with wanting to talk, I write it all out in my journal. I could copy some of that for you."

"That would be great! And it is okay if I show your sonnet to Jeb?"

"Why not?" Suddenly I wasn't afraid of having Jeb see my work.

"See you tonight, then," Adam said.

As soon as I got home I went in to Grandfather. His eyes were glittery, as though he had fever.

"Are you all right?" I asked. "Should I get Daddy?"

"I just have a small cold. Don't bother your father. Are we going to read?"

"That's what I'm here for." And I opened the book we'd just started, *The Limitations of Science*. I was deep in it, and so I was startled when Grandfather burst out: "Why all of this, my Lord and my God? Either bring the world to an end or remedy these evils! No heart can support this any longer. I beseech Thee, O Eternal Father, do not permit any more of this—"

I dropped the book. "Grandfather!"

"Teresa of Avila said that, in the sixteenth century. It should comfort me that there have always been outrages to the Divine Majesty. But it doesn't."

"Grandfather—what's the matter?" I was frightened, I'd never heard Grandfather talk wildly like this before.

He pointed to the newspaper on his hospital table. The headline was a plane crash, a big one, with everybody killed.

"It's not so much the crash itself"—Grandfather's voice had returned to its normal quietness—"though that's bad enough. It's the vandalizing of the dead bodies for money and jewelry. The National Guard had to be sent for to protect the corpses, and thirty people were arrested. It seems that there are no depths of depravity the human creature cannot sink to. Sorry I startled you . . ."

242

"Oh, Grandfather—" I said helplessly. I'd avoided newspapers as much as possible this summer, and after pointing out the article on dolphins, Daddy had kept what was in the paper to himself. And if Mother and John saw any horrors they didn't pass them on. But not reading the paper only kept me from not knowing things; it didn't keep them from happening.

Grandfather reached for the box of tissues and blew his nose. "Maybe instant information isn't good for us. We can't absorb it."

"So we drop out," I said. "At least that's what I've done this summer."

"Perhaps I shouldn't have pulled you back in. Oh, Caro, is dropping out what I was doing when I left Boston and went to Alaska? Are anyone's motives ever pure?"

I hated it when he thought I was our grandmother even more than when he thought I was Mother.

He continued, "And perhaps, my dear, my vocation in my last days is simply to pray. To pray for the broken world. To pray for people so lost they can rush to steal from fragments of dead bodies of their fellow human beings. I can no longer go bodily to where I think I'm needed. And prayer may in the end be stronger than all my actions. But I need your support, my Caro."

I didn't know how to handle it. I went and called Daddy.

Grandfather did have fever.

Daddy gave him a shot of penicillin.

But the fever didn't cause the horrible things in the newspaper.

Mother and Mrs. Rodney and Rob came in. They'd been doing errands in the village. Mrs. Rodney said she'd give Grandfather an alcohol rub to bring the fever down. She sounded calm and undisturbed.

"His defenses are very low and he's open to infection," she said to Mother. "Don't worry. This is just a cold and we'll take care of it."

If anyone could take care of it, Mrs. Rodney could.

Mother nodded, but she could not disguise the strain in her face. I felt helpless, but I asked, "Anything I can do to help?"

"Yes, Vic. It was hot and sticky in the village. It'd be a big help if you'll take Rob for a swim."

So I took my journal and my wet bathing suit and Rob and went down to the beach. After we'd had a swim Rob started to build a sand castle, and though I knew he wanted me to do it with him, I said, "Start off by yourself, Rob, while I copy out something for Adam he asked me to do, okay? Then I'll help you with the moat."

I looked at Rob and he was happily concentrating on his sand castle. So I started copying out everything in my journal that referred to the dolphins and my meetings with them.

And when I had finished, I remembered that he was coming for dinner and I hadn't told Mother.

But first I'd help Rob finish his sand castle.

10

After lunch Rob had a nap. I'd promised to sit with him till he fell asleep, which he did almost immediately. His face was flushed and angelic and he had one arm flung over Elephant's Child. He looked like my baby brother, but he wasn't. Not any more. He hadn't been a baby for a long time.

Instead of going back down, I took my pen and notebook and started a story about a degenerate white dwarf trying to make a red giant fall off his horizontal branch.

That cheered me up and when Rob woke up I was out of my gloomy mood.

And we had a good evening.

Adam seemed cheerful and easy, though after I'd given him my sheaf of papers and he said he would read them as soon as he got back to the station, he talked more to John than to me.

After dinner Mother read, and we all relaxed and listened and laughed, and then we sang, and without saying anything we all chose things that Grandfather particularly liked so he could hear them from the hospital bed in his study.

And the world had somehow righted itself again.

In the morning Suzy woke up with a sore throat and a runny nose and Daddy told her to stay home.

"But Jacky and Leo need me!"

John and I looked across the breakfast table to each other but we didn't laugh, and we didn't say anything. For me, at any rate, that was progress.

Daddy said, "Better miss one day and get rid of your cold than go to work and get really sick. I'll phone them for you. I don't want you getting germs on the phone."

She started to protest, then said, "But tell them I'll be there tomorrow, for sure."

Mother poured her an extra glass of juice. "And, Suzy, I don't want you to go near Grandfather."

Now she did protest. "Why not? He has a cold. I probably got it from him!"

Daddy, on his way to the phone in the kitchen, stopped in the doorway. "Suzy, your grandfather's resistance to infection is very low. You ought to understand that."

She blew her nose and looked down at her plate. "Oh. Yes. I forgot."

Daddy simply nodded and went to the phone.

Mother pushed a nonexistent wisp of hair back from her forehead. "Rob, you've been invited to the Woods' again for the day. In the afternoon they'll take you to the docks when the lobster boats are coming in, and you can bring us home lobster for dinner."

Rob's face brightened at the mention of lobster. He'd seemed very unenthusiastic till then.

Suzy asked, "What're you doing today, Vic?"

"Reading to Grandfather this morning if he's up to it. This afternoon I'm going flying with Zachary, then dinner."

"You have all the luck!"

Mother said, "I'm really not totally happy with the flying—"

"Oh, Mother—" I started. Then, more quietly, "Zachary isn't doing the flying. It's a trained pilot." I did *not* mention the stunt flying.

Suzy said, "I bet it's terrifically expensive."

"Money's not Zachary's problem."

"Or is it? People like Zachary don't give away something for nothing." Suzy's eyes narrowed. "What's he want of you?"

"Suzy," Mother remonstrated.

"I think," I said, "that he wants me to believe in him." And I know that Zachary did want that, that it mattered. "He needs me."

"Oh, c'mon," Suzy said, "a guy like Zachary's catnip for someone like you. Anyhow, don't get too beholden to him."

"I don't feel any more beholden to Zachary than I do to Leo or Adam. Money isn't what makes people beholden."

"It helps." She sniffed and blew her nose again.

"Come on, Suze, give me a hand with Mother and Daddy's bed."

We made the big beautiful bed in silence. The bed takes up most of the room, and the east wall is all one huge window, right down to the floor, so that when you're in bed there's nothing between you and the ocean. I broke the silence. "Grandfather must miss this view."

Suzy burst out, "Vicky, you haven't talked to me all summer."

I turned from the ocean and looked at my sister.

I love her. Because she's my sister. I can't imagine the world without her. But I've never talked to her much. I've shared more with Rob than I've ever shared with Suzy. Maybe because Suzy's always been so much better at everything than I have, even little things, like playing catch or spud. Have I been, am I jealous?

Jealous. It's an ugly word. It's an ugly feeling. I don't feel ugly about Suzy. But I don't feel close. So, yes, maybe I am jealous. It's not that I don't want Suzy to have everything she has. But when the gifts were being distributed I'd like to have had a few more.

"I'm sorry," I muttered.

"You talk to everybody, but you never talk to me."

"Oh, Suze—" but I didn't find anything to say.

"I mean, look at you this summer. You've got *three* guys interested in you."

"That's a switch, isn't it?"

She overrode this. "And you let Leo do everything for you and you don't do a single thing for him."

"That's not true—"

"You let him date you. You let him pick up the bill—"

"I paid for my lunch—" If we'd been a few years younger this would have turned into a fistfight. As it was, Suzy continued the attack verbally.

"Big deal. And I don't think you even realize you're shortchanging him. You take it all from him and you don't give him anything. Jacky and I think it stinks."

I almost did hit her. "Leo and I are friends. That's all."

"Does Leo know that's all?"

"Of course he knows that's all! What do you think I am!"

"I don't *know*!" I saw tears trembling in her eyes. "I might as well not be here as far as you're concerned."

"That's not true . . ."

"I'm miserable," she burst out, "and you haven't even noticed!"

I hadn't. I'd envied her going off to clean brass and paint the boathouse and have fun with Jacky. "What's the matter?"

She was really crying now. "I've wanted to be a doctor all my life."

"You and John have always known what you were going to do. You're lucky."

She brought her voice back into control. "It's one thing to operate on dolls. But I'm too old for dolls. And I don't think I can be a good doctor for people. Or animals."

"Why not? Whenever there's been an accident you've known exactly what to do, and you've done it, the way you did with that kid who fell and cut her artery on a piece of broken glass last summer, and everybody else fell apart, and you went right ahead and did what you knew was right till Daddy got there."

She blew her nose again. "I know I could be helping Mrs. Rodney with Grandfather's blood transfusions, or even helping him bathe, but I can't. I can't do it! All I want is to get out of the house, and so I run away to

Jacky, to anything that will keep me from seeing Grandfather."

I responded quickly, off the top of my head. "Suzy, you know perfectly well that when a surgeon's spouse or child has to have an operation the surgeon doesn't do it. Another doctor who isn't emotionally involved does the surgery. You're emotionally involved with Grandfather, that's why you can't help take care of him."

"Daddy's emotionally involved."

"Yes, but not by blood. He's related to Grandfather as an in-law. You're related by blood. And haven't you noticed how much time Daddy spends at Grandfather's desk in the science stall? He takes himself away, too."

"Yes, but he's working on his laser book. He has to get it finished this summer."

"I know, but he still makes himself scarce. Anyhow, you're biologically involved with Grandfather."

"So are you."

"But I don't want to be a doctor."

"But you haven't run out on Grandfather and his illness. I have. You're much stronger and better than I am, and I hate you for it. I hate you!" She began to cry again. "And John, too. I hate him. He's always best at everything, and he's always going to be voted the most likely in his class to succeed. But you know what? Statistically the people voted most likely to succeed usually end up alcoholics, or flops, so there!"

I patted her, clumsily, astounded by her words. "Don't cry too much. It isn't good for your cold. You'll make your nose all stuffy."

"It already is."

"And I'm not strong and I'm not good. Any time I'm alone with Grandfather and he does anything peculiar I call for Daddy. I'm just as miserable about Grandfather as you are."

"I'm not miserable about Grandfather, I'm miserable about *me*."

"Suze, if Jacky was hurt or sick, or somebody who wasn't in the family, you'd be able to handle it, wouldn't you?"

"Sure, but—"

"I just *told* you, doctors aren't supposed to take care of their own families when it's anything serious."

"They don't run out on them."

"You haven't run out on Grandfather any more than John has. He works even longer hours than you do."

She looked at me hopefully. "You really think that? Honest?"

Who was I to differentiate between a "real" job and a "made-up" job? "Honest."

Even when she was crying, even with her nose red from blowing, Suzy was beautiful. She looked at the big wad of tissues she was holding. "Thanks. I feel better. I'll go to the incinerator and burn these. Then I'll wash my hands with yellow soap."

I watched after her as she left.

It was one thing to be surprised by Leo, someone I hardly knew.

It was something else again to be surprised by my own sister.

Mrs. Rodney told me that Grandfather would like me to read to him. "But not for long—maybe half an hour. His fever's down, but he's very weak."

He looked even paler than usual, but his mind seemed clear. "I'm not up to science this morning. I need to be amused." He indicated his Bible. "Read me the Book of Jonah."

I'd never realized before what a funny story that is. We both laughed.

When I was through, Grandfather said, "Funny how we hate to have God be more forgiving than we are, isn't it?"

"You're forgiving, Grandfather."

"Not always, not easily, not if anyone hurts someone I love. By the way, how are things with you and that black-haired young man?"

"Pretty good. I think. I'm going flying with him to-day."

"Is he still giving you his burdens to carry?"

"Not really. Not so much. He does need someone to believe in him."

"Do you?"

"About a lot of things, yes. I mean, he has a good mind if he wants to use it, but nobody's really cared about making him use it. That's why he took so long getting through high school. Grandfather, I do remember what you told me. I'm really not trying to save Zachary or anything like that. But I *am* trying to believe in him, because I know being believed in helps. It's helped me a lot in my writing to know that you believe in me."

"I hope he won't let you down." Grandfather closed his eyes. "I think I'll rest now, child. Tell Caro to wake me in an hour."

I put the Bible down, within easy reach, and walked out.

Shortly after lunch Zachary came to pick me up. He appeared to be in an odd mood, a wild mood, and he drove much too fast.

Finally I had to shout at him, "Zachary, if you're going to drive like a madman, stop the car and let me out. *Now*."

He took his foot off the gas pedal and put on the brake. "Don't you trust me? I'm an excellent driver."

"Nobody's an excellent driver at that speed on these roads."

"Scare you?"

"Yes."

"Fun to scare you."

"Not to kill me. Or yourself." But suddenly my stomach lurched. For Zachary it might be fun.

But he kept on driving at a reasonable speed. As we neared the docks an old woman was crossing the road, using a cane, and hobbling along slowly. "She's no use to society. Shall I mow her down?" He put his foot on the gas pedal.

"Zach!" I screamed.

He slammed on the brakes, but not before he'd given the old woman—and me—a good fright. He was grinning.

"That wasn't funny."

"Oh, come on, Vicky-O. You know I wasn't going to hit her."

I tried to keep my voice light. "With you I never know."

"Keep you guessing, don't I?"

"That's your intention, isn't it?" I parried.

We were at the dock now, with Leo waiting for us. Jacky stood in the doorway of the boathouse, carrying a can of paint. There was a big smear of paint across his upper lip, like a white moustache.

"How's Suzy?"

"Very coldy."

"Tell her to take care."

"I'll tell her."

Leo helped me into the launch and we took off.

Zachary didn't talk much and I hoped he was over his manic mood.

When we got into the little red Alfa Romeo he said, "I've really come along with my flying lessons. Want to see me fly?"

"Not till you get your pilot's license," I said firmly. "And not then unless you're less crazy in a plane than you are in a car."

He glowered. "You think I'm crazy?"

"I didn't mean it literally. But I don't like it when you drive as though zombies were chasing you."

"Sometimes I think they are."

"Driving like a bat out of hell is not going to help you escape them."

He started the Alfa Romeo noisily, but the thunderous look was gone. "You were right when you said you've changed from last summer. You have."

"An improvement?"

"Like most people, I don't want anything I like to change. Let's say you're more of a challenge."

He drove at a reasonable speed till we got to the airport, and he didn't try to knock off any more pedestrians.

Art greeted us amiably.

To my consternation, I was strapped into the seat behind the pilot. In this plane there were double controls up front, which meant that Zachary was going to fly, and I was certain my parents wouldn't be happy about that. Neither was I.

"Don't worry," Zachary called back to me. "I've been taking two lessons a day and Art says I'm a natural."

Art tapped his controls. "If he goofs, I can correct it. I've also made it clear that before he can do any fancy flying he has to know how to fly conservatively." And to Zachary: "No tricks."

"I'll be good, teacher, honest."

"Can you take her up, or do you want me to?"

"I'll do it."

I wanted Art to do it. But I knew that if I protested, or if I showed how frightened I was, that might make Zachary do something wild.

It was a good takeoff, I had to admit that. Even if it was only my second time in a plane, I knew that the smooth lifting from the ground into the air, almost like Basil leaping from the sea, was well done.

Zachary did whatever Art told him to do, and did it well. But despite the soaring takeoff I didn't feel as though I was riding Basil. Maybe I was blocking the pleasure of the ride because Zachary had frightened me when he nearly hit that old woman. There was a gleam in his eyes when he was manic which kept me tense, and which told me that I was a fool if I thought that someone with my lack of experience could possibly be of help to someone like Zachary.

At one point Art took over the controls because a big

jet was coming in for a landing. I could see it far above us, and then getting larger as it came closer. Art pulled on the stick to keep us well out of the way. He and Zachary both had on earphones and I relaxed when I realized that they were hearing instructions from the control tower and we really weren't in any danger of having the jet crash into us, and that we were much farther away from it than it seemed.

Art let Zachary take the plane in. It seemed to me that Zachary brought her to the ground gently and without much bouncing, and I wasn't surprised when Art complimented him.

Without consulting me, Zachary said he'd be back for his regular lessons and that I'd be with him again on Saturday.

—Well, I thought,—we'll wait and see about that.

The rest of the day was unexpectedly lovely.

The French restaurant was up in the hills, nearly an hour's drive, and Zachary didn't speed but drove slowly enough so we could enjoy the scenery. We ate outdoors, on a tiny flagstoned terrace looking into a pine forest. There were only two other tables on the terrace, and we were shaded by an enormous maple, the biggest one I've ever seen, with a massive trunk that was almost as big around as a redwood.

At this restaurant there wasn't even a menu. That's the ultimate in elegance. The proprietor hovered over us, murmuring suggestions in French.

We had snails, which I expected to hate, but which I loved. It may have been the garlicky butter sauce which sold me, and the crusty homemade bread to soak up the sauce.

Then we had boeuf Wellington, which is beautiful

rare beef coated with pâté and baked in a flaky pastry, and watercress and endive salad, and for dessert we had crepes suzette, prepared and flamed especially for us on a little table. Zachary didn't badger me to have a drink, but set out to prove to me how much Shakespeare he'd read, ". . . a lot more than either of your other two swains."

I'd started out the afternoon being afraid of Zachary, and here he was making me feel glamorous, something I don't often feel like, and it was a very pleasant feeling.

A sliver of a new moon was setting, slipping behind the terrace, as the sky darkened, and the waiter brought out candles in silver candlesticks with glass globes.

"Vicky-O." Zachary leaned across the table toward me and the candlelight brought out the purply-blue highlights in his hair and warmed the whiteness of his skin, which never seemed to tan. "You're so good for me, so good."

I could only murmur, "I'm glad."

"You're getting better about slapping me down when I try to show off. I only show off because I'm insecure."

"We're all pretty insecure."

"Your brother John doesn't strike me as being insecure. He strikes me as being repellently secure. My shrink says I've been deprived of proper familial interrelationships."

That sounded like jargon, but I thought it was probably true.

"You're good for me because you're so different from anyone else I've ever known. But you've got to watch out for those 'come hither' eyes."

I had to laugh at that. "Don't put me on, Zach. Suzy's the one with the 'come hither' eyes. You said so yourself."

"Hers are so obvious you don't have to pay any attention. You're much more dangerous because you're so completely—shall we call it subliminal?"

"Flattery will get you everywhere."

"No, I'm serious."

The proprietor came up just then, to see if we'd enjoyed our meal, to see if we needed anything else. Zachary asked for the check, and when he got it, I was horrified by the bills he put down. Zachary acted as though he were paying for a hot dog.

"Come along, Vicky-O. It's over an hour's drive to the dock, if you want me to creep like a tortoise. It's hard on the Alfa Romeo to be held in check, but for you I'll do anything."

He did put one arm around me while he drove, but he didn't speed, and I wasn't afraid of him. I felt a vague kind of tenderness, a sensing that he needed to be protected.

Protected from what? From himself, mostly.

When he said goodbye to me at the stable, he kissed me, a long, slow kiss, but he didn't try to make anything more out of it than that, and I was grateful.

Why did Adam have to keep getting in the way when Zachary kissed me? Adam had never shown the slightest indication that he wanted to kiss me, though I'd stupidly thought he was going to that night we'd sat together on the beach.

I turned off the light Mother'd left on for me and climbed the ladder to the loft. I saw a slip of paper lying whitely against the grey of the blanket and picked it up. Enough light came in as the lighthouse beam swept around so that I could read it.

I DON'T HATE YOU, SUZY.

Neither Suzy nor I is good about apologizing. That note meant a lot, coming from Suzy.

11

I went to the lab with Adam on Friday. We fed the dolphins in the pens, then went to the beach and swam out. He had me call Norberta and Njord, and they came. Njord and I played, and Norberta hovered maternally.

Adam had me ask Njord to swim to the right, to the left, and he would do what I wanted him to do and then he'd butt me and make it quite clear that all work and no play would make Njord a dull boy and he wasn't having it. We alternately played what Njord wanted to play and worked, for about an hour.

Then Norberta butted Adam and me, and then Njord, as though to say, 'School's over for the day,' and they took off.

Without consciously realizing what I was doing, I turned my mind toward Adam. *Do a cartwheel in the water, like Basil.*

I held my breath.

Adam dove down. Up came his legs. Flip. Head and arms were out of the water. Just like Basil.

Adam, do you really think of me as nothing more than a child? I realize I'm naïve and backward for my age in lots of ways, but I don't feel about you the way a child feels. I've never felt about anybody else the way I feel about you, touched in every part of me . . . *Is it only my feelings? Doesn't it touch you at all?*

He broke in, saying sharply, "Vicky, what are you *doing?*"

I could feel heat suffusing my face. "N—nothing."

Now he was shouting at me. "Don't *do* that!"

"Why? Why not?"

"Because—because—" He clamped his mouth shut. But he was telling me without speaking, *Because it's too intimate.*

I had felt, down on the beach with Leo, when we were holding one another and weeping, that this kind of sharing was more potent than kissing. But that was nothing compared to this, to the merging of two minds. The power in this was explosive.

But I did it with the dolphins. Why was it all right with the dolphins?

And the answer came lapping gently into my mind like the water lapping about my body. Because this is how dolphins are, all the time. They're able to live with this kind of intimacy and not be destroyed by it.

Our family is close, but in comparison with this other kind of closeness the distances between us are greater than the distances between galaxies.

I had, without asking permission or assent, totally invaded Adam's privacy.

And yet, although he had shouted at me, stopped me, he was not angry at *me.*

Without saying anything further, he turned and swam in. When I joined him, he was standing on his head, so I knew everything was all right.

But I didn't know what to say. I waited.

Still standing on his head, he spread his legs into a

V and said, "I have to keep reiterating that I don't think you realize quite what a special thing you have going with—with dolphins. Have you ever had precognition?"

"You mean knowing something's going to happen before it happens?"

"Yes."

"No. I don't think I'd want it. I think it would scare me."

"How about teleportation?"

"You mean thinking with things and making them move, the way I do with dolphins?"

Adam flipped over onto his feet. "More or less."

I thought about it for a moment. "I've never tried it. It would certainly make tidying my room easier. Do you think it's possible?"

"I didn't, till I got involved with my dolphin project and did some reading. There've been some cases which seem authentic. I just wondered . . ."

"What?"

"This summer, with Basil, and Norberta and Njord—is this the first time you've had this kind of experience in any way, shape, or form?"

I wandered slowly back to the water's edge and dabbled my toes in the foam. "Maybe there've been—hints—if I look back on it. But nothing I've recognized. And with the dolphins, it's just seemed so *natural* . . ."

Adam splashed along beside me. "It's natural for dolphins. It's not natural for people."

My skin prickled. "Well. It feels natural to me."

"Sorry. I didn't mean to upset you. It *is* natural to

you, and that's terrific. It's nothing to be afraid of. The dolphins are to be trusted."

"And people?"

He looked down at the froth on the little waves. "Some are. Some aren't."

"Are all dolphins to be trusted?"

His grey eyes were sober. "There hasn't been enough research for me to answer that. Let's just say that, proportionately, dolphins are more trustworthy than people. Want a Coke?"

"Sure. Work always makes me thirsty. My treat this time."

Adam had to kick the Coke machine to make it work. We sat at the table by the window I'd come to think of as our table, and he talked about some of the research he'd been doing in connection with his project. It was being a good day in a way because he was treating me like a colleague, not like a child; and it was a frustrating day in another way because Suzy's little lizard was running up and down me as I looked across my Coke glass at Adam's alert smile, and while I preferred being a colleague to being a child, I also wanted more, much more.

And I thought of that incredible moment of intimacy after Njord and Norberta had left, and it both scared and excited me.

Adam didn't call me "sweetie." Mostly he didn't call me anything, not even Vicky. But there was electricity between us.

Real electricity. When he took my hand to say goodbye we made an electric shock and I could almost see sparks.

But all Adam said was, lightly, "You're dangerous,

Vicky. I'd better steer clear of you. Except among the dolphins. See you Wednesday?"

"Sure. Wednesday."

I went home, and all the rest of the day I remembered the workout with Njord, and the electric moment of contact with Adam afterward. I wondered if he thought about it, now that it was over, and if so, what.

On Saturday I went flying with Zachary again, and I had to admit that he handled the plane beautifully. Art told him that he could end up a professional pilot if he wanted to.

"I can make more money as a lawyer. I'd rather fly for fun."

Art, looking dark and chunky in a brown leather jacket, asked, "Aren't you going to inherit a lot of bread?"

"Enough so Uncle Sam'll take most of it. Anyhow, as my pop could tell you, there's a certain seductive pleasure in making it."

Instead of driving me someplace for dinner, Zachary took both Art and me to the airport restaurant—not the coffee shop, but the posh restaurant with wine lists, and large menus with high prices.

Zachary and Art talked flying. Art told us about his experiences as a fighter pilot. I hated it.

Well, so did Art. "War made more sense when people fought with swords, or even clubs, and you knew who you were fighting. Now when we kill we don't even see who we're killing and mostly it's civilians, women and kids and old folks who have no way to defend themselves. If I ever get called up again I'm going to be a C.O. I've had it with killing. Never again."

I almost asked, 'You mean you've really killed

somebody?' and stopped myself. He had, though not face to face, and he probably didn't even know who he'd killed or how many.

He began to tell us about the early days of flying, because both his father and his grandfather had been pilots, and he told me to read Antoine de Saint-Exupéry's books about flying.

"I've read only *The Little Prince*, and that's one of my favorite books in the world. I didn't realize he was really a flyer."

"One of the great ones."

We lingered over dinner and coffee, and Zachary and Art drank a bottle of wine. Sometimes while they were talking my mind would flicker away from them, to the dolphins, to Adam. Adam the square; the philosopher; the cartwheel turner and headstander. The colleague. Adam, who had, for a moment, heard me in the silence as the dolphins heard me—

"Vicky-O!" Zachary snapped his fingers in front of my face. "Where were you?"

"Oh—off in dreamland."

"Come back to Art and me. Want some more coffee?"

"No thanks."

It was a good evening with Zachary and Art. Around Art, Zachary was more real than I had ever seen him before.

Adam came for lunch on Sunday. We had beautifully messy BLT's, with the bacon crisp and the tomatoes dripping juice so that the toast fell apart and we were licking our fingers not to miss any of it, and then using up half a dozen napkins.

After lunch, Adam said, "Got to be getting along. Want to come, Vicky? We might have a swim."

"Sure." I looked toward Mother and she nodded.

"If you'd like to come back for dinner, Adam, we're having moussaka."

"Sorry to be ignorant," he said, "but what's that?"

"Ground lamb and eggplant and cheese and sauce and other goodies. If you don't like eggplant, you won't like it."

"I've never had much eggplant. It's worth a try. I've never eaten anything here that wasn't delicious. Thanks, Mrs. Austin."

We got out our bikes and rode side by side except when a car came along.

I thought at him, trying not to invade his privacy, but still trying to reach him: Talk to me. Talk to me about yourself. Why are you afraid to be friends with me? Why do you keep trying to push me back into childhood just when I'm feeling most ready to be grown up? Talk to me. Really talk. Please.

When we neared the station he stopped and leaned his bike against a stunted, windblown tree on the ocean side of the road. He beckoned me to follow, so I parked my bike by his, something we couldn't possibly have done in New York if we'd ever wanted to see our bikes again, and we crossed to the dunes and slithered down to the beach.

He sat where the sand was soft and warm, and began sifting small grains through his fingers the way he had the night we sat on the dunes and talked. "Vicky, this is definitely just between the two of us. I mean, John knows I had a problem with a girl, but that's all."

I nodded, looking at his sea-deep eyes, and waited.

"I was responsible for someone's death while I was in Portugal, far more responsible than anybody was for Commander Rodney's . . ." He paused, and his jaw was clenched, and the same little muscle was twitching that had twitched at Commander Rodney's funeral.

"What happened?" I asked at last. I was almost afraid to speak, and yet I thought it was better at this moment to ask the question out loud than to think it at him. He was doing as I'd silently begged him, really talking, and I nearly held my breath.

At last he said, "Dr. O'Keefe had some very important papers about the regeneration of limbs in human beings, and unscrupulous people were out to get them, and in the wrong hands they could have been disastrous." Again he stopped, and I remembered our first conversation in the lab, when I asked about human limb regeneration, and he'd more or less turned it aside without answering.

Finally I whispered, "Did they get them?"

"No. But Joshua was killed in saving them. And it was because of me. I believed a beautiful girl I should never have trusted, and if I hadn't, he might not have been killed."

"Who was Joshua?" I kept feeling that if I raised my voice I'd stop him from saying what he had to say.

"He worked for the Embassy in Lisbon. But more than that, he worked with people who really care about what goes on in the world, what happens to all the little people." He swallowed. "He called it caring about the fall of the sparrow. I guess that's somewhere in the Bible."

"Yes."

"He wasn't interested in money or prestige or knowing the right people in the Embassy. John reminds me of him." He turned toward me briefly, swallowing again painfully, as though he had a sore throat. "After Joshua died no one tried to make me feel guilty and they wouldn't let me do it to myself. When something happens, you can always say afterward, from hindsight, that it wouldn't have happened if only . . ."

"I don't blame Zachary any more. I know that's a dead-end road."

"Yah. It's easier to stop blaming someone else than to stop blaming yourself, though. The thing is, I did stop, because I finally understood that the best thing I could do was to get on with the business of living, and to care about the things Joshua cared about. But, up until the moment Josh died, I'd never thought about death at all, or what happens after death, because it simply wasn't part of my world. If anybody'd asked me, I'd have said that death is death and that's that. But when Joshua died, I simply could not imagine him not being. It wasn't that I got religion, I just couldn't imagine all that was Joshua being lost forever." He lay back on the sand and closed his eyes. "What I did was shelve it, because I couldn't cope. And now I'm wondering again. Because of your grandfather. And because of the dolphins. And you."

I was looking out to sea, at the sun sparkling on the water, and a great shadow of dark lying across the water from a heavy cloud, and I did not dare turn to look at Adam. But I felt close to him, much closer than touch could bring us.

He said, "I guess it's something poets are born thinking about."

"Well, yes. Death has always bothered me, as far back as I can remember."

We were both silent for a long time. I, too, began to let sand trickle through my fingers. I felt shivery and happy and frightened and alive.

Adam said, "See, sweetie, if we think too much about what happens when we die, we'll stop being able to live, to live right now in the very minute."

"Like when I'm with Basil, or Norberta and Njord."—He called me 'sweetie' again . . .

"Yah. That's the way it should be all the time. You and the dolphins—Oh, Vicky, Vicky sweetie, after Joshua died I swore I'd never trust another female again, ever. I find myself trusting you, and that scares me. That's why I cut you off when—"

"No, you were right to," I said. "I shouldn't have done that, not without asking you first. And, Adam—I trust you."

To my surprise, because I didn't think this was the mood or the day for it, he stood on his head. "I thought I could keep this scientific, just part of my project—" And then he flipped upright and turned a cartwheel. "Hey, I'll race you along the beach to the big rock and then you can change into your bathing suit and we'll go out and communicate with Basil and Co. And—each other."

"I'll have to get my suit out of the bike basket." I scrambled to my feet.

"I'll get it for you."

I padded along the beach, and then speeded up as Adam came along with my bathing suit.

We swam out and I floated and thought: Njord.

Njord.

He came, but not alone.

Norberta was with him, and as they approached she flapped her flukes at me, splashing me with great deliberation, as though to scold me for summoning Njord without her, telling me in no uncertain terms that Njord was not old enough to go off on his own.

I burst into laughter.

"What's so funny about being splashed?" Adam asked.

I told him.

He laughed, too. "You're absolutely right. That's just what she was telling you."

Njord flicked toward me and nudged me. I caught hold of his dorsal fin and away we went, like a tachyon, toward the horizon.

Speed.

Much faster than Zachary with his foot down on the gas pedal.

I was gloriously excited and frightened at the same time. A baby dolphin may be a lot smaller than a grown one, but it's a lot bigger than I am, and Njord was stronger than he realized. He would never hurt me on purpose, but he might overestimate my strength.

Norberta wouldn't let him.

If I trusted him to come when I called, I had to trust him all the way.

He swung around so suddenly that I almost let go, but not quite, and we went racing back to Norberta. Njord dove and dumped me, and I came up to the surface, sputtering, and both Njord and Norberta began to splash me, making loud laughing noises.

"Calm them down," Adam said. "Tell them you want to ask them some serious questions."

What should I ask? What would be serious to both the dolphins and to me—and to Adam?

Dearest Norberta and Njord. Do you live in the now, or do you project into the future, the way I do, far too often?

I felt a gentle puzzlement coming from Njord.

Maybe he's too young to understand about the future. When Rob was a baby, everything was *now* for him. Now embraced both yesterday and tomorrow.

Norberta?

Again I felt puzzlement, not puzzlement about her understanding, but my own. Norberta wasn't sure I'd be able to understand.

Try me.

I rolled over onto my back and floated and Norberta moved her great body toward me until we were touching, and I was pressed against the beautiful resiliency of dolphin skin. And a whole series of pictures came flashing across the back of my eyes, in the dream part of my head.

The ocean.

Rain.

A rainbow, glittering with rain.

Snow, falling in great white blossoms to disappear as it touched the sea.

And then the snow turned to stars, stars in the daytime, drenched in sunlight, becoming sunlight.

and the sunlight was the swirling movement of a galaxy

and the ocean caught the light and was part of the galaxy

271

and the stars of the galaxies lifted butterfly wings and flew together, dancing

And then Norberta, with Njord echoing her, began making strange sounds, singing sounds, like the alleluia sounds Basil had made, and they did something to my understanding of time, so that I saw that it was quite different from the one-way road which was all I knew.

Norberta was right. There was much she understood that was beyond anything I'd ever dreamed of.

She and Njord slapped the water with their flukes in farewell and vanished over the horizon.

I rolled over and began to tread water.

"What did you ask them?" Adam swam to me.

"About time. Adam, their time and ours is completely different."

"How?"

"Norberta tried to tell me, but it was in a language I didn't know, and it translated itself into images, not words."

Treading water, he held out his hands to me. "Hold. And try to tell me what she told you."

I held his hands tightly. Kept moving my legs slowly. Closed my eyes. Imaged again what Norberta had imaged me.

I heard Adam sigh and opened my eyes.

"Nonlinear time," he said. "She was trying to tell you about nonlinear time."

"What's that?" I was still holding on to the beauty of Norberta's images, so it didn't quite hit me that Adam and I had communicated in the same way that I communicated with the dolphins.

"Time is like a river for most of us, flowing in only

one direction. Get John to explain it to you. Physics isn't my strong point. But there's a possibility that time is less like a river than a tree, a tree with large branches from which small branches grow, and where they touch each other it might be possible to get from one branch of time to another." He let go my hands. "I'm not explaining it well."

"Do you mean maybe for dolphins time is less—less restricted and limited than it is for us?"

"Isn't that what Norberta was trying to tell you?"

"Yes. Adam, did you see the butterflies?"

He nodded. "Like the one we saw at the cemetery."

"You saw it, too?"

"And so did your grandfather."

"And Grandfather would know what Njord and Norberta were singing."

"Dolphins don't sing." Adam's voice was flatly categorical. "Only humpbacked whales sing."

"Call it what you like," I said. "To me it was singing."

He was staring out to the horizon, where they had vanished. "Granted I've never heard dolphins sound like that before. Hey, are you sure you don't want to go in for marine biology?"

"It's a thought," I said, "but somehow I have a hunch that if I went scientific about them I might not be able to talk with them."

"You may be right. Maybe that's why I resisted you, because I'm too scientific."

"No," I replied quickly. "I was wrong. I went at you without thinking what I was doing."

"And today?"

My body felt as though the water had instantly

dropped several degrees. "Did you really see what Norberta showed me?"

"I think so. You're cold, sweetie, and your lips are blue. Let's swim in and have some tea and then we can check it out."

"Okay." He'd called me "sweetie" again. It was as beautiful as the dolphins singing.

"Then I have to spend the rest of the afternoon working on my report. Forgive my repetition, but you've thrown my project for a loop."

"Do you mind?"

"Minding doesn't have anything to do with it. I simply did not expect that John Austin's kid sister would be thunder and lightning and electricity."

Cautiously, I asked, "Not—not like whoever it was last summer?"

"Not like. Very definitely not like. Okay. I'll come along back over to the stable in plenty of time for that moussie or mucksie—"

"Moussaka."

"Yah. I'll be there for it." Imitating the dolphins, he dove down and swam underwater, emerging yards away.

The song of Norberta and Njord echoed in my ears.

And it was joy.

And joy, Grandfather would remind me, joy is the infallible sign of the presence of God.

But I couldn't tell Adam that. Not yet.

When I got home, Mrs. Rodney wasn't there.

Almost imperceptibly, we'd become used to having her around most of the time.

Mother asked me to take a glass of iced tea in to

Grandfather. He had the back of the hospital bed up high, and his Bible on his lap. I pushed the table tray close to him for the iced tea.

His smile radiated sunshine, like Rob's. "Thank you, dear my Caro."

"I'm Vicky, Grandfather." Usually I just let him go on thinking I was whoever it was he thought he saw, but there was something about him this afternoon that made me feel I had to be Vicky, not my mother or grandmother.

"Vicky—Caro—it doesn't matter. I want you to do something for me, something only you can do."

Despite the heat, my hands felt cold. "What, Grandfather?"

He put his hand up to his brow. "I get fuzzy. Sleepy. Not aware. I'm afraid—"

"Of what, Grandfather?" If I kept on calling him Grandfather he might remember who I was.

"That I won't know when to let go. That through inertia I'll hold on to these mortal coils when I should be shedding them. That I'll hold on and be a burden. Caro." He reached out for me and his grip was strong about my wrist. "When it comes time for me to let go, you must tell me. Promise me."

"Grandfather—"

He dropped his hand. "This disease is affecting my mind. I didn't expect that. No one told me that would happen. So, if I don't know, if my time comes and my mind won't—Caro, you'll know when it's time for me to let go."

"Grandfather, I'm only Vicky, please—"

For a moment he looked at me with recognition.

"Vicky. Yes. But you must ask Caro, then. She'll tell you."

"Grandfather, she's dead," I said frantically. "I can't ask her."

"You can, you can." He stretched out his hand again and gripped mine tightly. "The line on the other side of time is very fine; it is easily crossed. We are *not* bound by linear time." For a moment I was flashed a vision of Norberta sending me images. Did Grandfather somehow know what had happened?

He reiterated, "Ask Caro. She'll know. I'm not afraid of dying. I'm as eager as Paul."

"Paul?" Paul who? I was almost as confused as he was.

"Of Tarsus. The tentmaker Paul. I'm ready. I'm just afraid that if my mind blurs I won't be able to let go at the right moment."

"Oh, Grandfather, you will, you will." Tears began sliding down my cheeks.

"Don't cry, Vicky." Again for a moment he was himself, completely with me. "When you're a little older you'll write about it. But you must tell me. If you listen carefully, Caro will help you. Do you promise?" His eyes glittered as they held mine.

"I'll—I'll try, Grandfather."

"Listen to the deep and dazzling darkness and you'll know."

"I'll try."

"Don't be afraid. The ring of pure and endless light is coming closer, closer . . ." He closed his eyes. "Caro will help you listen."

What was I to do?

He was asking something impossible.

I couldn't go to Mother with it. It would hurt her. The only person I could tell was Adam.

He came at six and there wasn't a moment to be alone with him. I called across the singing to him, and saw only that he was engrossed in the music, and his baritone was warm and rich and happy.

Rob went up to bed, then Suzy. Adam rose. "I'd better be getting along. Vicky, walk me out to my bike, will you, please? I want to ask you something."

When we got outdoors, the screen door shutting softly behind us, I asked, "What?"

"You want to talk to me?"

"Did you know?" Of course he knew, knew my need in the same way that the dolphins knew.

"Can you come to the beach for a while now?"

"It's late—I'm not sure my parents—"

He looked at his watch. "Can it wait till morning?"

"Yes." It could. Now that I knew I could talk to Adam, the burden did not feel quite as heavy. "I'll have to come early, because of reading with Grandfather, and then I'm going out with Leo."

"How's Leo doing?"

"He's hurting. But he's growing, too. I'm getting really very found of him. As a friend."

"Friends are what make the wheels go round, Vicky. See you tomorrow, early. Can you make it at six? Down on the beach by the big rock."

"I'll be there."

He was waiting for me.

The morning was cool and pearly.

"What happened," he asked, "to upset you so deeply?"

I told him.

He started walking along the beach. I walked beside him. Finally he said, "That's a rough one."

I told him about Grandfather and the Eskimos, and how they knew when to say goodbye and let go.

Adam looked down at the sand, scuffing it with his bare toes, and nodding. "We're out of touch with death. I think the Eskimos are right. And your grandfather."

"But, Adam—for once I *do* feel like a child. I'm not old enough to know things like—like when it's time for someone to die."

"I don't think it has anything to do with age. And, Vic"—he reached for my hand and held it in a strong clasp—"I know it's hard to face, but remember that your grandfather's slipping in all kinds of ways. To tell him when it's time to die is something he never should have asked you to do, and if he had been himself, he wouldn't have asked it."

Grandfather—when he *was* himself—had quoted John Donne to me: Other men's crosses are not my crosses. But that was about Zachary, warning me not to take on too much.

Adam was right. This wasn't my cross. It was something Grandfather would never have asked me to pick up and carry. Or—

I said, slowly, "How do we know how much we're to do for other people? Or for how long? I mean—like Simon of Cyrene carrying Jesus' cross for a while, and then putting it down."

"I suppose that's somewhere in the Bible?"

"Yes. All I mean is, we are meant to help each other, but not to feel that we have to do it all, all by ourselves. I guess maybe dolphins are more like Eskimos than we are. Maybe they don't think about death coming, the way we do. Maybe they just know. And maybe, when the time comes, Grandfather will know."

"Let's hope," Adam said. "I haven't been much help."

"Yes, you have. I'm back in perspective again."

"Good. Can you stay there?"

We both began to laugh. "For at least five minutes," I promised.

He turned a cartwheel. "I'll call you tonight."

I went home, holding on to the promise of hearing his voice in not too many hours, and accepting just how much that voice meant to me. I went down to Grandfather's cove and sat on my rock for a while. To meditate. To be. Like the dolphins. Like Grandfather when he was fully Grandfather.

And what I knew was that when the time came, if I was meant to say anything to Grandfather, then I would know. It was like meditation. It wasn't something I had to *do*.

I packed a picnic lunch for Leo and me. We went in his launch to the mainland, borrowed Cor's pickup, and went to the hospital to get blood for Grandfather. It was too soon for the two of us to give blood again, but Leo assured me that more than enough had been donated by the Islanders.

This time he'd checked with his mother and we

didn't go in through the emergency room but by the main entrance.

Leo had me sit in the lobby, on a deep leather sofa that nearly swallowed me in its embrace. I lay back and watched people coming and going. Visitors carrying flowers. Going into the gift shop. Coming out with packages. People being discharged, coming out of the elevators in wheelchairs, little suitcases or pots of flowers in their laps. People coming to be admitted, some carrying their own cases, some clinging to someone else. Some looked tired or pale, but they could all walk in.

Suddenly I recognized the woman I had seen in the emergency room with the limp child, the child I'd been afraid might be dead. The child was holding her mother's hand, pale, with deeply shadowed eyes, but very much alive. I think the woman recognized me, too, because she smiled at me and pushed the child toward me. "Sit there, hon, and wait. Momma'll be right back."

The child sat down, almost disappearing into the soft cushions, and turned to smile at me. She wasn't as much younger than Rob as I'd thought, and when she smiled she reminded me of my little brother.

"Hi," I said. "My name's Vicky. What's yours?"

"Robin."

We sometimes used to call Rob Robin when he was little.

"Momma and Poppa call me Binnie. Are you sick?"

"No, I'm fine. Leo—my friend—and I've come to pick up blood for my Grandfather."

"He's the one that's sick, then. I've had lots of transfusions. There's something wrong with my blood."

I wondered if she had leukemia, and I knew that any kind of cancer is much worse in children than in old people, because cancer cells grow at the same rate as the body cells. Somehow I found myself very relieved that she was called Binnie and not Robin. Even her voice sounded like Rob's, and it was scary because her paleness was in such contrast to the golden tan Rob's skin had turned in just a few weeks.

"My poppa doesn't want me to have transfusions," Binnie confided. "It's against his religion. So Momma smuggles me in and we keep it a secret. This morning Poppa flushed all my pills down the toilet. He said it was God's will. If I don't have the pills I get all jerky and then I pass out. So Momma's come for more. My poppa loves me, though. He and Momma just don't agree about God."

Leo came out of the elevator and his hands were empty and his face looked pasty-white and his eyes had faded to almost no-color. His voice was muffled with rage. "The inept, incompetent idiots don't have the blood."

"Why?" I asked incomprehendingly.

"Some kind of emergency last night and they used up all their supply. I thought we'd contributed enough to take care of the entire state."

"I got blood last week," Binnie said, "but Momma says I don't need it today. Just my pills."

Leo's voice was muffled. "That's good, kid. Vicky, some nincompoop of a technician said your grandfather isn't an emergency, and until the supply of blood comes up to normal we'll have to bring him up to the hospital. In other words, it has to be an emergency or it doesn't count. You'd think they'd be glad to have us *prevent* an emergency, but no. I'm going to call your father." He turned on his heel and vanished into a phone booth.

Binnie's mother came around the corner. "Okay, Binnie lovey, I have your pills." She patted her handbag. "Thanks for looking after her, Miss—"

"Vicky Austin. She reminds me of my little brother. His name's Rob."

"Let's hope he doesn't have as much wrong with him as my Robin."

I felt almost guilty.

"It's her grandfather who's sick, and they won't give him any blood because he's not a mergency."

The woman clucked. "Some people's idea of an emergency . . . Come along, Binnie-bird. We'll go to the water fountain and you can take a pill. 'Bye— wha'd you say your name . . ."

"Vicky," Binnie said quickly.

"'Bye, Vicky. I'm Grace. Come on, Bin." And she took the little girl's hand.

As they left, Leo came out of the phone booth. "Your dad says he'll see what he can do. Meanwhile, we're to come on back to the Island or whatever we want."

"Leo—" I pulled myself up out of the sofa. "It's nice of you to do all this for Grandfather."

"I told you. I love him. I'd do anything for him. Listen, how about if we go to one of the little islands with that super picnic of yours, and swim and relax?"

"Sure, that sounds like fun."

"You don't sound very enthusiastic."

"Oh, Leo—I was just worried about Grandfather and what would happen if he hemorrhaged . . ."

"We'd bring him here."

"I don't want him to come here. I hate it."

He took my hand. "Don't borrow trouble, Vicky. Your dad will get blood as soon as possible."

"I know. I'm sorry. I shouldn't project frightening things. Grandfather once told me that the reason I do this is that I have a storyteller's imagination, and that it's both blessing and bane. Thanks, Leo. Let's go."

We returned the pickup to Cor, who was indignant about the blood.

"Dr. Austin'll fix it," Leo said. "Thanks, Cor. I'm bringing a group to the mainland tomorrow for shopping. How about a game?"

Cornelius Codd's face brightened. "I'll lick the stuffing out of you."

"Unh-unh," Leo said. "This time I'm going to win. Wait and see." To me he said, "I win just often enough so Cor can't relax."

We left Cor cackling as we went to the launch.

Leo chose one of the small, uninhabited islands. There was a curve of beach where we landed. Otherwise, the island was largely rocks, with a few stunted trees driven into strange shapes by the wind. We scrambled about the rocks till we were too hot. Then we had a swim. The thought of the dolphins flicked against the corners of my mind, but something told me (did they?) not to call them. Anyhow, we didn't swim out far because Leo wasn't sure about the undertow.

We sat on a rock, barely shaded by one of the trees, and ate our picnic. We talked about Leo's going to

Columbia, and how strange living in a big city was going to seem to him. We talked about the sea, and about ships. And when it was time to go he asked, "Can I kiss you?"

I shook my head. "I'd rather not."

"Why?"

"I keep telling you."

"I bet you let Zachary kiss you."

"I don't 'let' him."

"But he kisses you?" Leo pursued.

I didn't answer.

He grabbed me and pressed his lips fiercely against mine, and I shoved him hard and broke away. "Don't spoil things!"

He shouted, "Who's spoiling them?"

"You are. Leo, friendship's the most important thing in the world. Please, please, let's just be friends for now."

"Do you let Adam kiss you?"

"Adam doesn't kiss me."

"Never?"

"Never. Okay? Adam has all kinds of schooling to get through before he can get serious about anybody. He and I are friends. You and I are friends. Zachary feels he has to kiss everyone. It doesn't mean anything. I think it's just a substitute because he doesn't know how to be friends. I want to go home now, please. I want to make sure Grandfather's all right."

As we shoved off, I said, "If I can't go out with you without having it turn into a wrestling match, then I'm not going out with you again."

He put one hand lightly over mine. "I'll play it any way you want."

"Honest?"

"Honest."

But I wasn't sure, and Suzy's accusations echoed in my ears. Leo was super as a friend, but he didn't make that little thing shaped like a lizard run up and down me anywhere at all.

Zachary called on Tuesday to tell me about his first really solo flight. All the blasé sophistication was gone; he sounded as excited as Rob. He asked me to come flying with him on Wednesday, but Adam had already called about Wednesday.

"Saturday, as usual?"

"Okay, sure." But was anything ever "as usual" with Zachary?

Whenever the phone rang we thought it might be the hospital saying their supply of blood was replenished and we could pick it up. Daddy explained to us that drastic blood shortages were not that uncommon, and if the worst came to the worst we could always take Grandfather to the mainland.

I told him about Binnie, and he said it sounded as though she probably did have some form of leukemia, though what kind or how bad he couldn't tell. The pills might well be for epilepsy, which could be the least of her problems, unless her father kept flushing her medication down the toilet.

"These religious nuts." Suzy sounded ferocious. "They ought to be put in jail."

"Hold on, Suze." John used his most reasonable voice. "I don't agree with throwing out the pills which would control epilepsy, but what about keeping somebody whose central nervous system has blown, say, from an aneurism, on life-support machines? Keeping an irrevocable vegetable alive is against *my* religion."

Suzy stuck her underlip out stubbornly. "It's not the same. What Binnie's father's doing should be against the law."

"It probably is. But so is unplugging a vegetable from a life-support system against the law. Right, Dad?"

"True," Daddy agreed. "And we can't go making value judgments against Binnie's father, because we aren't positive of her diagnosis."

"When I'm a doctor," Suzy said, "I want medical decisions to be a lot clearer than they are now."

"So do we all, Suzy," Daddy sighed. "So do we all."

Adam and I worked with Norberta and Njord Wednesday morning. That is, we worked for as long as they were willing to work, which meant that when it stopped being a game for them, they invented games of their own for us to play. At one point Njord and I were turning somersaults together in the water, with me clinging to him for dear life.

Norberta interrupted us, nudging me, and I put my arms around her and closed my eyes. Listened. Saw. Ocean, with no land in any direction. A night sky dipping down to the water on all four horizons, a sky alive with stars which moved in a slow and radiant dance, rising from the east and dipping down into the west, so that I felt the turning of the planet, and that this, too, was part of the dance, and so were the dolphins, and so were Adam and I.

I pressed my cheek against Norberta's vibrant coolness and shivered with the beauty of it. Finally

Norberta gave me a goodbye nudge, called Njord with a small slap of her fluke, and they were gone.

I tried to show Adam some of what I had seen. "The problem *is*, what seems a big deal for us is the way they do things all the time."

Adam did a Basil-type water cartwheel. "C'mon, Vic. Jeb's asked us to have lunch with him. I've shown him all our reports, and he wants to talk with you."

I felt a flutter of nervousness and excitement. But even though I didn't know Jeb very well, I trusted him.

He took us across the Island to the Inn for lunch, saying we'd have no privacy at the cafeteria. We had the same table at the Inn that Leo and I had had, but it was bright daylight instead of rainy darkness, and the dining room was stuffy.

We ordered salads and iced tea, and Jeb thanked me for the sonnet. "I read it to Ynid," he said, and smiled at me. "You know, Vicky, there are not many people who would understand my doing that, and there are not many people I'd tell it to. But I assume Adam has made it clear to you that your ability to understand dolphins is unusual?"

"It seemed so—so—"

"I know. So natural. But it takes most of us months if not years to be in tune with dolphins as you are."

"So right," Adam agreed. "And her reports of the experiments with the dolphins are much more vivid than anything I could write."

"Puts you in your place, eh?" Jeb said.

Adam screwed up his face in a funny sort of grimace. "I'm not sure what—or where—my place is."

Jeb handed his empty iced-tea glass to the waitress.

"In marine biology, that's clear. But it's an extremely wide field and widening daily. You have a few more years before you have to decide precisely where to specialize . . . My thanks," he said to the waitress who had refilled his glass.

Her face had been tired and cross when we ordered. Now it untensed and she smiled. Jeb had that effect on people, with his warm brown spaniel eyes with the pain not quite hidden behind them, and a smile that made you feel he understood and liked you, just the way you were.

"And you, Vicky?" The generous gaze turned to me.

"I guess I'm glad I have a lot of years before I have to decide. This day and age doesn't make much provision for poets in garrets."

"Judging by the reports on dolphins you wrote for Adam, your prose is excellent. You never use a word you don't need, and your imagery is precise and vivid. Read a lot?"

"Oh, I do."

"And when you get to college, major in English. The great writers are your best teachers. If you take my advice, you won't go in for those so-called creative-writing courses. You'll write anyhow, and you'll never again have a chance like the four years of college to soak yourself in writers of all kinds and sorts. And a lot of people who teach creative writing tend to be manipulative, or to want to make the young writers over in their own images. By the bye, your prose in your dolphin reports reminds me of O'Keefe's, and I consider him a latter-day Lewis Thomas or Loren Eiseley."

I could feel my face getting hot. "Oh—wow—" I

murmured inanely, and added, "My father's writing a book on his laser research."

"I've read a few of his articles," Jeb said. "He lacks your sense of the poetic, but his language is tidy, and his experiments are breaking new and important ground. Yet I understand he's not going to continue his research?"

"Not full-time. He's always done some, and corresponded with other researchers in his field, like Shasti and Shen Shu. But he's a people doctor."

Jeb rubbed his hand over his bald spot. "God knows we need those. People doctors, as you call them, doctors with both skill and human compassion, are becoming an endangered species. Anyhow, Vicky love, keep on with your writing. You've got the gift, and a gift is to be served."

"I'll try," I promised. Jeb was talking to me as though I were as old as Adam or John. As though I were a grownup. As though I mattered to him.

Then he began asking me questions about Basil, about Norberta and Njord, and before I knew it we were the only ones in the dining room.

"Better go before they throw us out." Jeb handed Adam some bills. "Here, pal, you go do the work, and bring Vicky and me each a mint. Two mints, please." While Adam was at the cashier's desk, Jeb said, "You're good for him. He was pretty badly hurt a year ago."

I nodded.

"How much did he tell you?"

"About—about Joshua being killed. And he felt responsible for it because of some girl."

"He's learned to trust you then. Good. Adam's a very private person by nature, and last summer intensified it. I'm a friend of Dr. O'Keefe's, so I already knew most of the story, and it was through O'Keefe that we got Adam here this summer. He'll make a brilliant scientist if he even begins to fulfill his promise. I'm glad he has you for a friend."

Me, Vicky. Not "all of you Austins" the way it usually is, but me, myself. And Jeb's warm look made me feel very me.

And before dinner I had a full half hour to go down to the beach and sit on the rock and absorb the goodness of the day, and be part of the rock and the sea and the sky.

Friday night while we were drying dishes the phone rang. Suzy, as usual, grabbed for it. "Adam!" She sounded pleased; then, "Adam, what's wrong?" She turned from the phone. "John?" John was out on the porch, wiping the table. "Vicky—" Suzy sounded surprised. "He wants to speak to you."

I started to snap at her, then shut my mouth and took the receiver she was thrusting at me. "Hi— Adam?"

He sounded hoarse. "Jeb's in the hospital."

"What—"

"He was in the village, walking back to his car, and a motorcycle hit him."

"Oh—Adam—"

"He has a fractured skull and he's unconscious and we can't get a thing out of the doctors. Listen, is your father there?"

"Daddy—" I gave him the phone.

There was a long pause while he listened. Then he

said, "The CAT scan was all right? That's a big weight off our minds then, no worry about a subdural hematoma . . . He responded to the pressure of your fingers? Are you sure? . . . All right, hold on to that good thought."

John had come in from the porch. He squeezed out the wet sponge and stood leaning against the sink, listening. He and Suzy were probably understanding everything Daddy was saying. He touched Daddy's arm. "Tell Adam we're all with him. And we'll get Grandfather's prayers going. They're sure-fire."

Suzy gave John a funny look.

"We'll all pray," Mother said quietly.

Daddy said, "Let us know if there's any change. Are you back on the Island? . . . Feel free to call us any time. And try to sleep."

When he hung up, I asked, "Is Jeb going to be all right?"

"We won't know for a while. The sooner he regains consciousness, the more hopeful the prognosis."

I didn't like the sound of his voice. A shadow seemed to move across the kitchen windows. I kept on wiping the knives although they'd been dry for a long time. "Well, but—" I said at last. "You don't think he's going to die?"

"A skull fracture's pretty critical, but as long as the CAT scan was okay he's got a good chance if he doesn't stay unconscious too long."

John added in a low voice. "Better he die than—" His voice trailed off.

"Be a vegetable?" I asked.

John simply nodded.

Mother turned off the water, which had been running all this time. Even though the Island is surrounded by water, Grandfather's drinking supply comes from a well and we're careful not to waste it.

'Wonder who'll be the next to go?' the woman had asked at Commander Rodney's funeral. Maybe it wouldn't be our grandfather after all. Maybe it would be Jeb Nutteley, struck down as wantonly as his wife and child. I had an irrational desire to run across the Island to the dolphin pens. But if Ynid needed to be told, she would surely know from Adam.

"I'm going to help Father get ready for bed," Daddy said.

Suzy demanded, "So, are you going to ask him to pray for Jeb?"

"Why not?" Daddy responded mildly.

"You mean, it may not do any good but it probably won't do any harm?"

Daddy's voice was still mild. "I think it well may do good."

Suzy snorted and turned away from Daddy, so that she was facing Mother.

Mother put her hand against Suzy's cheek. "I believe in prayer. You know that."

"But you don't even know Jeb! You've never even met him!"

"What's got into you?" John demanded sharply.

Suzy still sounded angry. "Prayer didn't keep Jeb from being hit by a motorcycle. It didn't stop Grandfather from having leukemia."

"Prayer was never meant to be magic," Mother said.

"Then why bother with it?" Suzy scowled.

"Because it's an act of love," Mother said.

Adam called again in the morning. Jeb was still unconscious, but his vital signs were stable. John's boss, Dr. Nora Zand, was at the hospital and would stay all morning. Someone else would take over in the afternoon. Adam had been asked to remain at the station and care for the dolphins.

Suzy had answered the phone as usual and was relaying the information. Now she thrust the phone at me. "He wants to speak to you."

Adam simply asked, "How's your grandfather?"

I knew what he meant. "Daddy spoke to him last night. I'll go in to him in a few minutes. He's usually clearest in the morning." And I trusted Adam to know what I meant. "How's Ynid?"

"She's not eating."

"Oh, Adam—" If Ynid was not eating, that meant that Jeb was not all right.

"I'll call again if there's any news. Or send a message by John."

We hung up and I went in to Grandfather. I thought he looked very pale. "Grandfather—"

He looked up from the Bible and lavished his smile on me.

"Adam's boss, Jeb Nutteley, was hit by a motorcycle and he's got a fractured skull and he's unconscious."

"Your father told me." He rubbed his finger lightly over the open page of the Bible.

"Will you pray for him?"

Prayer. An act of love, Mother had said.

"Of course," Grandfather replied.

"How *do* you pray for someone like that?"

Grandfather held out his open hand, palm up. "There are many different ways. I simply take him into my heart, and then put him into God's hand." Again he smiled. "That sounds like rather an athletic feat, doesn't it? Nevertheless, it's as close as I can come to telling you."

For a moment I had a flash of understanding. "Thanks, Grandfather. That helps. I'll come read to you after breakfast."

In the kitchen Mother was opening the oven door. "Where're the hot pads?"

Rob handed her one.

"Okay, breakfast," John said brusquely. "I'll bring out the butter."

There was something comfortingly normal about sitting around the big white table. It was hard to realize that Jeb was lying unconscious in the hospital, instead of standing by the dolphin pens, throwing fish to Ynid. I closed my eyes and thought of Jeb and his gentle kindness, and then I imaged Ynid, and Una and Nini. They understood acts of love. They would know how to pray for Jeb.

"What's the *matter*, Vicky?" Suzy asked.

I opened my eyes. "I think I was praying."

"Do you have to look as though you're dying?"

I didn't answer back. I helped myself to a blueberry muffin. Rob pushed the butter toward me, asking, "What're you doing today?"

"Read to Grandfather. Then nothing till this afternoon. I'm going flying with Zachary." This was not the time to be telling Mother that Zachary was likely to be doing most of the flying. If I hadn't told her after the first time Zachary was at the controls, I couldn't very well tell her now. And there wasn't anything to tell, really, with Art right there at the dual controls, able to correct anything Zachary might do wrong.

Suzy interrupted me. "Are you praying again?"

"Why are you so hipped on the subject?" I snapped back. "I was just thinking."

When I went in to Grandfather the clarity his mind had had earlier was all muddied. He called me Caro, and he thought he was in Africa. "It's time we sent Victoria away to school," he urged. "She's been having too much dysentery and I'm worried about her."

"Grandfather," I asked loudly, "do you want me to read to you?"

He moved his fingers restlessly over the sheets. "I can't find the notes I made yesterday . . ."

I opened the book and started to read, hearing the words but having no idea of the content. I read for about five minutes and Grandfather's hands quietened and his eyelids drooped.

I tiptoed out.

By the time Zachary came for me, I knew how Suzy felt about getting out of the house. I wanted to get away from Grandfather's confusions. I wanted to get away from the two worry lines between Mother's eyes. Mrs. Rodney had remarked on Grandfather's pallor and called the hospital. They hoped the supply of blood would be replenished by Monday. Meanwhile, in an emergency we could always bring Grandfather in.

"Not yet," Mother said. "Not unless we absolutely have to."

"I agree." Mrs. Rodney still had her hand on the phone. "Leo can go get blood first thing Monday morning."

And I wanted to get away from Daddy, who had shut himself in the science stall. He'd received a bulky load of scientific tomes and was working hard on his book.

Mrs. Rodney went in to Grandfather to give him a haircut, "to boost morale." Whose morale?

Rob was in the children's bookstall, reading. He'd been slower to read than the rest of us, probably because he's the youngest and had so many people to read to him. Even now it was difficult for me to understand that he was old enough to lose himself in a book all by himself. I looked to see what he was reading: *The Secret Garden*.

"I like it better when Mother reads it," he said.

The phone rang. I stood frozen, listening. It might be news about Jeb. It might be the hospital saying they had blood for Grandfather.

"Vicky," Mother called. "It's Adam. Nothing new on Jeb's condition."

"Hi," Adam said. "No news—except I wanted to tell you that I coaxed Ynid into eating a little."

"That's hopeful." I was ready to cling to any straw.

"Yah, but I don't want to count on it too much."

"Ynid wouldn't eat, if—" I held the phone between my ear and shoulder so my hands were free. Pulling the cord to its fullest length, I turned on the cold-water tap and poured myself a glass of water.

"What're you doing this afternoon?" he asked.

"Going flying with Zachary." I rinsed out my glass and put it on the drainboard.

"Oh. Yah. That will take your mind off things."

"I'm not sure I want it taken off."

Zachary's horn tooted outdoors, and I heard Mrs. Rodney running out to shush him. "Zachary's here."

"Yah, I know you have to go. Maybe we can get together tomorrow."

"Let's hope. These things can string out. Adam— what do you think his chances are?"

"From what I can gather, about fifty-fifty."

"Adam—things seem to keep piling up."

"Things have a way of doing that. They usually unpile eventually. Let's hold onto good thoughts about Ynid's eating, and our getting together tomorrow."

I hung up and went out to the porch. Mother said, "Have a good time."

"Sure you don't mind if I go?"

"Sure I'm sure."

"If Adam calls—"

She gave me a little hug. "It won't help Jeb for you to turn your back on a good time. Just take care, will you?"

"I will." The thought of Zachary at the controls of the plane flickered against the corners of my mind. No. This was not the time to say anything about that to my mother.

I went out to Zachary, glancing at the swallows' nest. The little swallows were still clinging in there. I had half expected to find them dead on the step.

Zachary was in high spirits. I told him about Jeb and he made polite noises. After all, he didn't know Jeb.

"You're looking better," I said. "Not such dark circles under your eyes."

"O-ho, so you notice what I look like."

"I notice."

"That's one kindly thing in an unkind world. Maybe that's why I'm baffled and fascinated by you Austins. Most people are predictable; they're out for number one, and they don't give a damn about anybody else, and if they have to step on you to get where they want, they don't even notice you lying in a pool of blood—literal or figurative. It's the only way to get on in the world. I'm not knocking it."

I thought of Zachary's father and all that money.

"So you intrigue me. Your father's never going to get anywhere and you don't even seem to care."

"I think my father *is* somewhere." I didn't need to defend Daddy to Zachary. If I looked at Daddy, and then looked at Zachary's father, that was obvious.

"He's never going to make any money."

Daddy's salary at the hospital in New York was probably double what he'd make as an overworked general practitioner in Thornhill, but "you can be just as miserable with money as without it."

"Yes, but you can be miserable a whole lot more comfortably. There's that old woman again. This time I'm going to get her."

"Zach!" I could not control my reflex of screaming, stiffening, and pressing both feet down on imaginary brakes.

"Idiot." He laughed. "I didn't come anywhere near her."

And he really hadn't, not anywhere near as last time. "Zachary, this kind of thing does not amuse me."

"My, my, aren't we pompous, though."

"I mean it. If you do anything like that once more, I'll never go out with you again. I'm serious." My heart was still thudding. Probably whoever was on that motorcycle hadn't meant to hit Jeb.

Zachary held the steering wheel lightly with his left hand, put his right hand over his heart. "No more trying to rid the world of obsolete old women. Promise. Cross my heart and hope to die. No more old women."

He was so full of high spirits and so talkative on the launch between the Island and the mainland that Leo whispered to me, "Has he been drinking or something?"

I shook my head. "I don't think so." He certainly didn't smell of alcohol. "I think it's just one of his manic days."

Zachary turned toward us. "What?"

Leo pointed to the horizon. "That freighter, there, can you see it?"

"What about it?"

"It's carrying a huge load of fireworks. I was wondering what it would look like if she blew up."

"That's a royal idea. Okay, skipper, ram 'er."

Leo gave Zachary a pale look. "Fortunately, this tub couldn't catch up with her."

"Come on. You know you get a good bit of speed."

"Not that much. The freighter's nearly over the horizon. Anyhow, dying in a blaze of fireworks doesn't appeal to me."

"It does to me," Zachary said.

Leo's eyes lost even more color. "We have Vicky with us, in case you've forgotten."

"How could I forget. Wouldn't it make noble headlines: Young Lovers Go Up in a Blaze of Glory."

"Lovers?" Leo demanded.

"Only a figure of speech, despite all my efforts to make it more."

We left Leo at the dock. "What time will you be back?"

"Oh, the usual," Zachary said. "Around eleven."

"Let's make it ten, please," I said. "I'd like to get home early . . ."

"Anything you say, princess. Ten, then, Leo."

"Right." He was still angry and his eyes hadn't regained their color. He disappeared into Cor's shack.

Zachary helped me into the Alfa Romeo with a flourish. "Off we go, into the wild blue yonder."

At first he drove moderately. Then, suddenly, he swerved to the left. "Let's pretend we're British."

"Zachary, please."

"You're absurdly easy to frighten." He continued driving on the left, even when we saw a car coming toward us. As it drew closer, the driver slowed down.

"Zach, get over."

"I will, I will," and he did, just as I thought a headlong crash was unavoidable, because the other driver was nervously starting to pull over to *his* left.

"Zachary, you are not funny. I don't enjoy being terrified. And you promised."

"I promised not to go after any more old women. And I haven't."

"You're not to go after anything, not old women,

not fireworks, not drivers who're on the right side of the road. Not anything."

"Don't get hysterical."

"I will, if you don't stop behaving like a lunatic."

"A selenophile, that's me. Are you a selenophile or a heliophile? A lunar lover or a solar lover?"

"Zachary, I'm asking you please to drive like a reasonable human being."

"Vicky-O, you're not going to be a spoilsport today, are you?"

"If you call not wanting to be terrorized being a spoilsport, yes."

"Didn't we have a good time last Saturday?"

"Yes."

"So let's have a good time today."

"I want to."

"And stop worrying about this Jeb character. After we go up with Art I'll take you to a Polynesian restaurant I think you'll like. And, Vicky-O, sorry I frightened you. Truly."

He sounded sincere, but I wasn't sure. I was never sure with Zachary. However, I was a lot firmer with him than I'd have dared to be a summer ago. Both Adam and Leo had given me a kind of self-confidence that Suzy was born with and I'd been afraid I'd never attain.

We reached the turnoff to the airport without further conversation. Art was waiting for us.

This time I was prepared to be strapped into the back, but I still wasn't completely happy about it. Art didn't even ask Zachary if he'd like to take off. Looking almost as intent as Rob building a sand castle, Zachary lovingly touched the instruments, and we lifted, easily, gracefully.

Art began giving soft instructions, and Zachary followed them without effort. Flying did seem natural for him, and the tenseness started to leave my muscles. I looked out and down at a strange and beautiful carpet made of the interlocked tops of trees. Lost in loveliness, I was able to forget that it was Zachary, not Art, at the controls. Trees, farms, villages, moved by below us. I began to feel the words of a poem moving in my mind. I forgot to be anxious about Jeb, about Grandfather, and drifted like the breeze, moving with the plane, with the air, with time.

I closed my eyes, so that I didn't see Zachary or Art, I didn't see the plane, there was only the movement of flying, with nothing between me and the clouds.

"Vicky-O."

I opened my eyes.

Zachary looked back at me and there was a glitter to his eyes I didn't like. "I promised you I wouldn't hurt any more little old ladies. I hope there are no little old ladies on that plane."

"Watch it," Art said sharply.

"Zach!" The scream tore out of my throat. "Stop!"

I couldn't see the approaching jet. I could hear it, sounding like thunder above us, but I couldn't see it. "Zach!" I screamed again. I thought I would die of terror.

Art reached for the instruments with a swift and furious gesture and our little plane dropped like a stone and then veered sharply to the left. I could still hear the thunder of the jet, and my heart seemed to be trying to rip my body apart as I waited for the jet to crash into us.

"What the hell do you think you're up to?" Art shouted.

Zachary looked very pale, paler than Grandfather. His jaw was set.

"Zachary!" Art repeated. "What were you trying to do?"

Now Zachary shrugged. "Nothing. Just a little fun."

Art's voice continued loud and belligerent. "Fun! Do you realize that you could have killed not only the three of us but well over a hundred people in that jet? Do you realize you probably scared the pants off that pilot?"

"Oh, cool it. I was only giving Vicky a little thrill." But his voice had a tremor in it.

My heart was still galloping, my voice frozen in my throat.

Art glared at him. "Scared yourself, did you? Came a little closer than you meant to? My God, kid, play with death by yourself if you have to, but leave the rest of us out of it. It'll be a far day before I let you up in a plane again."

"Aw, Art, you know I didn't mean—"

"Get your hand off those controls. I'm taking us in."

When we landed, Art helped me out of the plane. My legs were so shaky I couldn't have managed on my own.

The big jet sat across the field, nearer the airport, with people streaming out, carrying flight bags, tennis racquets, golf clubs.

Zachary unstrapped himself and climbed out.

Art was still furious. "You stupid, smart-assed kid. Do you realize a trick like yours could cost me my license?"

"Art—I'm sorry—"

"Someday you'll be sorry too late. Don't come around tomorrow looking for a lesson."

"Art, please—"

"Goodbye, Vicky," Art said. "It's been a real pleasure meeting you. Any time you feel like a ride, let me know, and I'll take you up free, gratis." He waved at me, ignored Zachary, and strode off.

Zachary started toward the Alfa Romeo. "Come along, let's get going, Vicky-O."

I planted my feet solidly on the tarmac. "I'm not going anywhere with you. I'd rather walk."

"Don't be stupid. You know it's much too far."

"I'll get Art to drive me."

"Oh, come off it. Nothing happened."

"You wanted it to."

"If I'd wanted it to, it would have."

"If it hadn't been for Art, it might have."

"I'd never hurt anybody. Not on purpose. You know that."

"As Art said, if you keep on going this way, you're going to hurt somebody whether it's on purpose or not."

He put his hand on my shoulder and I drew away.

"Relax, Vicky-O. You just scare easy."

"You scared Art, too. *And* the pilot of the jet."

"Art was just saying that. The pilot probably never even saw us. Listen, if you like, I'll drive you to the hospital and you can see how your friend's doing, and maybe even visit him."

I shook my head. "No. There's someone from the lab with him. I'd just be in the way. No."

He got down on his knees on the hot tarmac. "Vicky. I'm sorry." He turned his most haunting Hamlet look on me. "I apologize. From the heart. Honestly. I don't know what got into me, or why I thought it necessary to frighten you. Please. Let me drive you to that Polynesian restaurant and put some food in you. Please. I'm sorry. Truly."

Was he? Was Zachary ever truly sorry?

But how else was I to get home? Art was gone. We were standing alone on the landing field.

He helped me into the car and unhooked the seat belt. Then he got in on the driver's side. Now that he had me in the car he sounded more like himself. "Maybe I thought a few drastic measures were needed to wake you up."

"I'm not asleep."

"You live in a dream world." He started the car and we drove away from the airport, in the opposite direction from the hospital and the city. "I wish your dream world could be the real world, but it isn't, and the real world's going to be a shock to you."

"I'm not a child, Zach. I know there are bad things. But the horrors aren't all the world. I know they're there, you don't have to make it a life's work proving it to me." My voice was tight and tense and higher than usual; I was still not over the terror. "The bad things are there, but they aren't all of it."

"More than you're willing to admit."

"I told you I'm willing to admit the horrors. You're not willing to admit the good things."

"I read the papers. I don't keep my head buried in the sand." He took one hand off the wheel and put it on my knee. With one of his abrupt and total changes he said, "You're a good thing, Vicky. You're the most good thing that's ever happened to me."

He melted me only moderately.

"Say, do you think Art really meant it about no more lessons?"

"I don't think Art says things he doesn't mean."

"He'll cool off." But Zachary's voice held a tinge of anxiety.

"Don't count on it. Not soon."

"I'm not going to quit flying. If Art won't teach me I'll find someone else who will, even if I have to drive a hundred miles to another airport."

"Speaking of the real world," I said, "most people don't have enough money to buy their way out of things or to get them whatever they want, no matter what it costs."

"Money's what makes it possible to cope with the real world. If you don't get it, it'll get you."

I leaned back and closed my eyes and let the wind blow against my face. Terror had seemed to make me exhausted. Maybe my worlds weren't very big, the worlds of Thornhill and the Island and my family, but they were, I thought, just as real as Zachary's.

The Polynesian restaurant was fun and different, and Zachary was on his best and most charming behavior, calling me princess and treating me like one. It was after nine when we left, and it was nearly an hour's drive back to the dock.

When we got there Cor was sitting on his keg in front of the chessboard, but Leo wasn't opposite him. As Zachary slowed the car to a stop, Cor stood up and moved stiffly toward us.

"Where's Leo?" Zachary demanded. "We told him ten."

Cor took his unlit pipe out of his mouth and cleared his throat. "Leo, he got a hurry call to get back to the Island."

"Listen!" Zachary was indignant. "I hired Leo for the afternoon and evening. I'm paying him for his

306

services." He looked to where Leo's launch was in its regular berth, waiting. "So where is he?"

Cor cleared his throat again and put his pipe back in his mouth, speaking around it. I'd never seen it lit. "Money can't buy everything. Leo was needed."

"What for?" Zachary demanded. "His boat's right here, so where is he?"

Cor was having a hard time saying whatever it was he was trying to say. "Coast Guard ambulance left the Island. Some woman starting labor a month early."

Zachary's irritation mounted. "What's that got to do with it?"

Suddenly I was frightened.

Cor mumbled around his pipe. "It's Miss Vicky's grandfather. He needed blood."

"Hemorrhage?" I asked.

"I guess. Leo was off in a flash to get him and bring him back here to the hospital."

I looked at the launch, rising and dipping against its moorings.

Cor said, "Leo went with your folks to the hospital to see if he could give blood. Said you'd probably want to get right over to the hospital to see your grandfather."

"Zach—" I turned to him.

He was already hurrying to the car and I ran after him, calling out thanks to Cor.

I didn't say anything as the needle of the speedometer crept up, past sixty, past seventy. All I wanted was to get to Grandfather, to Mother and Daddy, as fast as possible.

There were only a few cars in the parking lot. We ran to the main entrance and it was dark and closed. AFTER 9:00 P.M. USE EMERGENCY ENTRANCE, the sign read.

Zachary grunted, took my hand, and we ran around to the emergency entrance. Zachary pushed open the door and we went in to the smell of fear and misery. It wasn't as crowded as it had been the morning Leo and I'd been there, but it was bad enough. I didn't see Grandfather or Mother or Daddy.

We stood in line at the desk.

It seemed like forever. There was a mother ahead of us, with a child with its arm twisted in an odd position, obviously broken. There were a couple of young men who looked completely normal and I couldn't see why they were in the emergency room. There was an old woman who was wheezing. Several nurses were moving about, checking, and I had to admit that they did not lose their tempers, even with people who must have tried their patience to the limit. One woman was scream-ing in Spanish what was obviously abuse, and I couldn't see that there was anything wrong with her at all.

Behind us I heard a siren and a flurry, and a stretcher was pushed into the emergency room, followed by an-other, and then another. The flashing lights of the ambu-lances were brighter than the interior lights as they whirled round and round, but they carried none of the comfort of the lighthouse beam, only more terror. This was the kind of scene my father had to face frequently, that Suzy would have to learn to face—

"Either a car crash or a tavern brawl," Zachary said. The line at the nurses' desk stalled as everybody rushed after the stretchers. Finally one of the nurses returned to her place.

"Why don't you sit down?" Zachary suggested. "I'll keep your place in line."

"No. I'll wait here."

Time crawled as slowly as a slug creeping along the path to the stable, and I thought of John and Suzy and Rob waiting there.

At last it was our turn. "My grandfather—" I stumbled over the words in my anxiety. "Mr. Eaton—my parents brought him—my father's Dr. Austin—they brought him in for a blood transfusion."

"Oh, yes, I remember," the nurse said. "Internal bleeding. They'll be admitting him. It's all being taken care of, so you just sit here and wait till your parents come for you."

"And J-Jeb—Dr. Nutteley," I stammered. "He's a patient here, with a skull fracture, and I wondered if he's regained consciousness—"

"I wouldn't know about that, and I'm too busy to—" The nurse looked around the room. The Spanish woman was still going at the top of her lungs. "Just sit down and wait for your parents. I'm sure they'll be along as soon as they get your grandfather comfortable."

I realized that she was being kind and patient with me, yet all I felt was fear and impatience. Internal bleeding—what did that mean? How bad was it? I turned to ask, but I knew that she wouldn't—or couldn't—tell me, so I said thanks and went and sat on one of the benches.

Zachary wrinkled his nose. "What a stench. I suppose I was brought in through here. I'm glad I don't remember any of that part of it." He didn't sit down but stood in front of me, shifting his weight from side to side in a trapped way. "I can't take—" he started, then said, with a change of tone, "I'm going to go see what I can find out. I'm sure some of the nurses will remember me. Wait here."

I didn't protest. I just watched him leave through the

inner door that led into the main body of the hospital. It was very clear to me that he was running away, abandoning me to this terrible place he couldn't stand.

Adam. Adam wouldn't have run out on me.

And there was nothing for me to do but wait.

Wait.

I felt as exhausted as though I'd been running up and down mountains all day, but whether they were exterior or interior mountains I did not know.

I closed my eyes and it was as though I were up in the plane again, feeling the jolting drop and swerve as Art grabbed the controls—

I opened my eyes, to see Grace coming in. She was carrying Binnie. When she saw me she hurried over and thrust the child at me. "Here. Hold my Robin for me." She dumped her on my lap. "She always passes out after a seizure. This time I'm not going to be made to wait forever." And she rushed frantically to the nurses' desk, thrusting into the line.

The little girl stirred slightly and shifted position. It was like holding Rob. I put the back of my hand against her cheek and it was cold and clammy.

Once again I heard the scream of an ambulance and then shouting and cries and stretchers being rushed in and everybody running. I heard one of the doctors groan, "My God, what a night."

Again the child stirred in my arms and a strange animal sound came out of her throat and her legs began to flail. I'd never seen anybody having a convulsion before, but there was no question in my mind as to what was happening to Binnie, and all I knew was that you were supposed to keep people who were having seizures from swallowing their tongues. I grabbed

Mother's filmy wool shawl with one hand, trying to hold Binnie with the other, and stuffed a wad of the shawl in her mouth.

Pinkish foam was coming from her lips, her nose. The horrible animal sounds continued, and the jerking. It was all I could do to hold her. I looked frantically around but everybody was busy with the people coming in on stretchers. At the nurses' desk Grace was gesticulating and crying.

And then all my attention had to be on keeping Binnie's wild jerking from throwing her out of my arms and onto the floor. Desperately I held her. And then the noises from her throat, the flailing of her limbs and the arching of her body stopped as suddenly as they had begun, and I remembered Grace saying, "She always passes out after a seizure."

The inner door opened and my parents came in and I could not get up and run to them because I was holding Binnie's limp body. I saw that my mother's cheeks were wet with tears, and with hearing suddenly grown acute, I heard her say, "I don't want him kept here. They'll plug him into a life-support system—"

"I won't let that happen," my father said.

"You can't help it." Mother spoke through sobs. "They'll do it when your back is turned. I don't want to leave him here. They won't let him stay human—" I had never before seen my mother like that, totally out of control.

"Victoria," Daddy said sternly, "right now what we have to do is find Vicky and Zachary. Leo said he left a message at the dock for them to come here." He began looking around the crowded room, and just as he saw me and started toward me, Grace and a nurse came hurrying from the opposite direction.

I looked down at Binnie's body, which felt heavy in my arms. The shawl had fallen out of her mouth and was flecked with blood. Her face was dead white. "She had a convulsion," I said. "I put the shawl in her mouth to keep her from swallowing her tongue."

"Good girl," the nurse said.

Binnie's mouth was open, her tongue lolling like a dog's. There was blood on her teeth, her lips. Her mouth closed, then opened again in a tiny sigh. The heaviness of her body became a different heaviness, although she had not moved.

The nurse reached for her wrist, fingers tightening where the pulse should be.

Grace started to scream. "My God, I'll kill him, it's his fault," and her words dribbled off into shrill, agonized screaming.

I did not need anyone to tell me that Binnie was dead.

I, too, screamed, but mine was an interior scream, because there was no sound.

12

The darkness closed in.

Someone took Binnie away.

Someone told me that I'd done the right thing. She had died not from the seizure but from her weakened heart. A nurse put her arm around Grace and led her across the stilled room and into one of the cubicles.

The ambulance lights were still flashing around but they could not cut through the dark.

I think I saw Leo, but then again it might have been Zachary, because I could not tell in the dark whether I was seeing the picture or the negative.

Leo.

He was saying, "Mrs. Austin's right. We can't leave him here."

And then Daddy was speaking but I couldn't hear what he was saying, and then Leo was squatting down in front of me and reaching for my hands.

I pulled them back. "Don't touch me till I wash—"

I had held death. I was still holding death. There was blood on my hands, the blood of a little girl who might almost have been Rob.

A nurse came with a wet cloth and alcohol and cleaned my hands.

Mother had stopped crying and was Mother again, her arms around me, comforting me. "We'll take you home now, Vicky. Leo's waiting."

"Not without Grandfather. We can't leave Grandfather in this place."

"We won't leave him," Daddy said. "I promise." Daddy's promises, unlike Zachary's, were to be trusted.

"The internal bleeding—"

"It's stopped," Daddy said. "For now. He's had a transfusion. We'll get him home as soon as he's rested a bit."

"How—"

"The Coast Guard ambulance boat can take him on their way home."

"Come," Mother said.

But her words were a dim roar against my eardrums. I was lost in a cloud of terror, with dim pictures transposing themselves one on top of the other, a falling plane, Binnie, Rob, Grandfather . . .

There was no light.

The darkness was deep and there was no dazzle.

There was no point in being human in a world of emergency rooms where a little girl could die because there weren't enough nurses or doctors

in a world where desperate fishermen clubbed a thousand porpoises to death

in a world where human beings stole from dead bodies, from pieces of dead bodies

Maybe Zachary was right after all

and I was wrong

and Basil and Norberta and Njord were wrong

and Adam

and Jeb and Jeb might now be dead

or a vegetable—

"Vicky!" Daddy was shaking me. I tried to look at him but I couldn't focus.

"Vicky, where's Zachary?"

I shook my head.

"We need him to drive you to the launch so Leo can take you and Mother home."

"Grandfather—"

"I'll stay with Grandfather till he's ready. We'll be home almost as soon as you are."

I closed my eyes again.

"Vicky, where is Zachary?"

"He—left." I jerked one shoulder toward the inner door.

Leo said, "I'll get him."

I heard Mother and Daddy talking but it was in nightmare darkness, and sound only added to the darkness. Mother was sitting on the bench beside me, her arm around me.

I had to make some kind of response.

"My dress," I said. "We have to burn my dress."

"It'll wash out," Mother said.

"No. No. We have to put it in the incinerator. Binnie . . ."

Mother's arm tightened around me. "You did all the right things, darling, and she wasn't alone when she died. She was with someone who cared about her."

Daddy said, "It was just as well for Binnie, sweetheart. The resident said she couldn't have lasted more than a couple of weeks, no matter what. You were a brave, wonderful girl, and we're very proud of you."

"Grace—where's Grace?"

"Her husband came to take her home."

"She said it was his fault."

"It wasn't anybody's fault. Even regular medication and blood transfusions wouldn't have helped her for long."

"She—reminded—me—of—Rob." I let my head drop down against Mother's shoulder as my words dropped into the dark.

Leo stood in front of us again. "I can't find him. And that sports car of his isn't in the parking lot."

So he was gone. Run out on me.

It figured.

I closed my eyes.

I didn't hear what any of the voices said.

Then my hands were held firmly. Not my parents' hands.

Adam.

"You called me," he said.

He'd come in the Coast Guard cutter, the one he'd used when he'd first tried to make contact with Basil and his pod. He'd borrowed Cor's pickup and driven as fast as the old truck would go.

When he'd heard the call he was sleeping. At first he thought it was Jeb, and he knew he had to get to the hospital as quickly as possible. Halfway across the water he'd realized that it wasn't Jeb's voice but mine.

"But you couldn't possibly have heard anything," Leo protested.

"Vicky called me and I came."

And then Zachary strolled in.

When everything was over he came back.

The darkness came down on me again.

I am told that Adam took me home, but I don't remember anything.

I am told that Zachary drove Mother and Leo to the dock, and Leo took Mother home.

But all I remember is darkness, and going out in the darkness to the incinerator and thrusting my dress into it, and Mother's shawl.

It wasn't Binnie I was burning, but death, death which had come and taken her out of my arms.

"Vicky!" I heard Suzy yelling at me. "Speak to me! What happened?"

In darkness I moved away from Suzy, and to the shower.

It wasn't Binnie I was washing away, but death, death stifling the darkness, blinding dazzle.

I heard Adam's voice. "She's had a terrible shock. She'll be better when she's had a good sleep."

Through the darkness I climbed the ladder and fell onto my cot. Fleetingly I saw Rob sleeping in the cot next to mine.

Rob.

Robin.

Rob.

I woke to hear sounds below, and then both Mother and Daddy were standing by me. It was still night.

"Grandfather's home," Daddy said. "He's much improved."

"Sleep, my darling," Mother said. "You'll feel better in the morning."

"I—burned—the—dress—and—your—shawl—" The words echoed in a hollow chamber.

"That's all right. I understand."

You don't. No one understands. It's too dark and

heavy. It's piled too high and I can't bear the weight. I'm crushed under it.

But I didn't say anything aloud.

Daddy gave me something to drink and it tasted bitter and it did not bring back the light.

I woke up because sunlight was streaming across my face, but there was no light in it, only heat and discomfort. And there was a large, dark blankness in my mind, a deep fog of unknowing.

Something terrible had happened, but I could not think what. I was in the familiar loft in Grandfather's stable. Rob's and John's and Suzy's cots were empty.

Rob.

Something had happened to Rob.

I sat up and the loft tilted and swirled and everything started to go dark. I lay down quickly as a wave of nausea broke over me. I closed my eyes and the dizziness and sickness went away. Exhausted, I slid back into sleep.

I woke up to a timid tapping against my arm.

Go away. Something terrible has happened but I don't know what.

Rob.

I opened my eyes.

Rob was standing by my cot, smiling down at me.

And it came flooding back.

Binnie in my arms. Dead.

The remembering stopped there and the blank cloud moved back in.

I sat up, cautiously, but the dizziness did not return. "Rob, you're all right—"

"Vicky, I've got something to tell you."

I interrupted him. "How did I get home?"

He looked at me in surprise. "Adam brought you."

"He couldn't have. He wasn't there. Only Zachary and Leo."

A shadow moved across the room, and John and Suzy emerged, up the ladder. "Zachary came back," John said. "And Adam did bring you home."

"How—"

"He said you called him."

"Vicky!" Rob bounced impatiently on his toes. "I have something to tell you! The baby swallows—"

Dead. Of course they were dead. All dead.

"They flew! They all flew! They're all right! They made it!"

It was the biggest present he could give me. Somewhere deep in me I knew that he was giving me life, and that was Rob's gift, just as it was Grandfather's. And had been Binnie's. And Binnie was dead and I couldn't accept the gift. It was outside the ring of endless light. Or perhaps I was caught within it, caught in a black hole in the center, a singularity where no light would ever come, a place of annihilation.

Nothingness. Despair.

"Vicky," John said. "Grandfather wants to see you."

I shook my head and lay back down.

"Vicky, *talk* to us," Suzy urged.

I closed my eyes.

John's voice was rough. "Who are you to think you can wallow this way?"

You don't choose it. It happens, like flu.

John went on, "You're not being asked to bear more than the ordinary burdens of life, the things that come to everybody, sooner or later."

Suzy sounded cross. "You're not hungry. You have a roof over your head and lots of people who love you. And you've got three men after you! That's more than I've ever had. Snap out of it!"

"Grandfather wants to see you," John said again.

"And you're the one who always can—when I can't—" Suzy added.

Still I didn't move.

"Grandfather has asked to see you." John's voice held almost as much authority as Daddy's and it did not touch me.

Rob bent over me anxiously. "He *wants* you." The joy which had radiated from Rob because of the swallows was gone.

I could not resist him. Slowly I swung my legs over the bed, my feet onto the floor. "I'll get dressed and come down."

I went to the big communal dresser and got clean underclothes, shorts, shirt. Now I remembered that I had burned my dress and Mother's shawl. What did I think I was doing? You can't burn death.

I dressed slowly, and then went to Grandfather, not stopping at the kitchen or the porch.

He was lying on the hospital bed, propped up slightly on a couple of pillows. He looked at me questioningly. "What's wrong?"

How could I tell him? "Don't you know?"

"I know what happened last night, yes."

"To Binnie?"

"Yes. That's a hard one, Vicky, and you're young to learn it, but it's part of life."

"Not life. Death."

He looked at me steadily. "It is time, Vicky, for me to give you my last instructions."

"Grandfather—"

"This morning I'm strong and clear enough. Later on, I may not be. Vicky. You will not need to tell me when to let go. Asking you that was part of my weakness and confusion and it was an intolerable burden to put on you and I apologize."

"Oh, Grandfather . . ."

He smiled. "*Other men's crosses are not my crosses* . . . remember? Perhaps holding Binnie while she died was a cross prepared for you at the foundation of the world. But telling me when to let go is not. I cannot ask that even of your father, because even a doctor does not necessarily know."

"But—"

He held up his hand for me to stop, and again the loveliness of his smile washed over me. "Caro." But he was not confusing Caro with me. "I am at that place where the wall between here and hereafter is so tenuous that it is no longer a barrier. Caro will tell me when it is the right time. She will let me know. Vicky, are you hearing me?"

"No," I said flatly.

He reached out with one frail hand and pressed the button that raised the head of the bed. When he was in a half-sitting position he said sternly, "You may not think you are hearing me, but you will not forget. When I am on the other side you will remember, and you will be able to let me go."

"No—" My whisper was so faint it was almost inaudible.

Grandfather's voice was quiet but strong. "Empty yourself, Vicky. You're all replete with very thee."

No, no. Not with me. With darkness.

Grandfather reprimanded. "You have to give the darkness permission. It cannot take over otherwise."

But I hadn't given it permission. It had come, as suddenly and unexpectedly as death had come and taken the child in my arms.

"Vicky, do not add to the darkness."

I stood at the hospital bed, still alien in Grandfather's study, and looked at him, thin and translucent as an El Greco—

Where had I thought that before?

At Commander Rodney's funeral.

I heard him and I did not hear him.

"Vicky, this is my charge to you. You are to be a lightbearer. You are to choose the light."

"I can't . . ." I whispered.

"You already have. I know that from your poems. But it is a choice which you must renew now."

I couldn't speak.

He reached out and drew me to him, kissing me gently on the forehead. "I will say it for you. You will bear the light." He kissed me again. "Now go." He lowered the bed and closed his eyes.

Rob was waiting for me, hovering anxiously. "Mother's made you some *café au lait*."

Blindly I followed him. Everybody was on the porch. So it must still be early. The sun struck violently against the ocean. How can anyone bear the light? It burns, burns.

I couldn't drink the coffee. I took a sip and another wave of nausea swept over me and I put my hand over my mouth, gagging.

Daddy took my temperature.

What for? I didn't have any fever.

Only darkness, and darkness is cold. And maybe it's better than the burning of the light.

The phone rang. Suzy went for it.

"That was Leo, to see how you are. Zachary called, too."

I made no response.

"It's time to go to work. John, aren't you going to be late?"

"I'm not expected for a while."

"I thought Dr. Zand had such a thing about promptness."

"She doesn't expect me till later this morning."

"Well, Jacky expects me to be on time, and I'm going."

Mother brought me a cup of tea, sweetened with honey, and I managed to sip at that.

The screen door opened and Adam came in. "Hey, those little birds are all sitting on the roof and squawking for breakfast."

John asked, "Jeb?"

"Nora says he opened his eyes. There's hope. Vicky, come along to the station with me."

I wanted to emerge from the darkness into consciousness, and I couldn't. I couldn't even answer him. I opened my mouth and nothing came out.

Vaguely I heard John saying, "I really don't think she can ride her bike."

I heard them talking, John and Adam, Mother and Daddy, but I heard only snatches. I heard Daddy saying that he wasn't going to take Grandfather to the hospital again, or give him more blood transfusions, and I knew what that meant, though I couldn't formulate it in words. Then they were talking about me.

Adam's voice: " . . . sounds crazy, because I swore her to secrecy about my project . . . real thing with dolphins, especially . . ."

Daddy: ". . . worth a try . . ."

Mother: ". . . but she might . . . careful . . ."

John: ". . . never get her in her bathing suit . . ."

A kaleidoscope of sound, shifting patterns, but the patterns made no sense.

I tried to listen, to let the pieces of the kaleidoscope fall into shape.

John was saying something about my bathing suit again.

Adam—or was it Grandfather? no, it couldn't be—replied, "Never mind. Just get her in the car."

"Why not right here?"

"She can't call them in this condition, and they may come more easily in the usual place."

"It's worth a try. D'you think she'll swim?"

"I'll swim with her."

"Think you can manage?"

"I'll manage."

John's anxious voice: "I'd better come."

A blur of John, Daddy, Mother.

And at the end, Adam's voice: "No. Just Vicky and me."

I heard their words hitting at me like tacks being hammered in. But there was no meaning to the words.

There was no meaning.
To me.
To Adam.
To Adam and me.
He was right.
Wrong.
Right place.
Wrong time.
I'm too young and the world is too old
a degenerate white dwarf
"Vicky!"

I felt them propel me out of the house and into the car.

I heard Adam telling Mother and Daddy not to worry.

I heard John saying it would be all right.

I heard Rob reassuring me once more that the little birds were flying.

I heard the phone ring, shrilling across the darkness.

Suzy wasn't there to run for it.

John and Adam, holding me between them, stood still, waiting.

Daddy came to us. Jeb had regained consciousness. He was going to be all right.

What for? Why be conscious in a world like this?
Why bother
it doesn't matter
because nothing matters

Somehow or other I was in the front seat of the station wagon beside Adam.

We drove through darkness
and a horrible silence

and then I was standing on the beach because Adam
took me and pulled me out of the car and across the
road and down the path
"Take off your clothes," he said.
I felt him pulling my shirt off over my head,
roughly ripping
dropping my shorts on the sand
pushing me into the ocean
through the small waves
into the breakers
fell and went over me
a blue-green comber curled and
mouthful of salt and sand
Adam's arm around me in a strong grip
over my shoulder, across, under my other arm
he was swimming
and I with him
automatically moving my legs in a scissors kick
swimming
forever
into timeless darkness

Surrounded
by flashing silvery bodies
tossed up into the air
caught
held between the sleekness of two dolphins
holding me but not hurting
holding and swimming
and then leaping with me up into the air
Basil and Norberta leaping into joy
with me between them
and before us and behind us and beside us

the others of the pod flashing and leaping

and I was being passed from pair to pair

And I knew they were trying to bring me out of the darkness and into the light, but the darkness remained because the light was too heavy to bear

Then I sensed a withdrawing

the pod moving away from me

not out to sea, but away, swimming backward and looking at me, so that I was in the center of a circle

but I was not alone

Norberta was with me

Suddenly she rose so that her flipper was raised, and then she brought it down, wham, on my backside

Ouch!

I submerged, down into the strange green darkness of sea, shot through with ribbons of gold

gulping sea water

choking

rising, sputtering, up into the air

into the blazing blue of sky

and Njord was there, nudging me, and laughing as I choked and spat out salt water, coughing and heaving

And the light no longer bore down on me

but was light

and Njord nudged and poked and made laugh noises

and I grabbed his fin and he soared into the air.

And I played with Njord.

The pod began to sing, the same alien alleluias I had heard first from Basil, then from Norberta and Njord, and the sound wove into the sunlight and into the sparkles of the tiny wavelets and into the darkest depths of the sea.

One last alleluia and they were gone, leaving Basil and Norberta to watch Njord and me play.

And then they were gone, too, flashing out to sea, their great resilient pewter bodies spraying off dazzles of light, pure and endless light.

I watched them until they disappeared into the horizon.

Then I turned and swam into shore.

Adam was at the beach ahead of me, standing on his head.

I body-surfed in, stood up, shaking water, and splashed in to meet him.

He flipped over onto his feet and I looked at him wonderingly. "I called you—"

"And I came," he said.

I moved toward him and we were both caught and lifted in the light, and I felt his arms around me and he held me close.

About the Author

MADELEINE L'ENGLE is the author of many acclaimed and popular books for children and adults, including novels, collections of essays, plays, and poetry. She is perhaps best known for *A Wrinkle in Time*, which won a Newbery Medal. *A Ring of Endless Light*, featuring Vicky Austin, was named a Newbery Honor Book. Other books in the Austin series are *Meet the Austins, The Moon by Night, The Young Unicorns*, and *Troubling a Star*. Adam Eddington, a character in *A Ring of Endless Light*, also appears in *The Arm of the Starfish* and *Troubling a Star.*

Madeleine L'Engle lives and works in New York City.